PURRFECT BOUQUET

THE MYSTERIES OF MAX 56

NIC SAINT

PURRFECT BOUQUET

The Mysteries of Max 56

Copyright © 2022 by Nic Saint

All rights reserved. No part of this book may be reproduced in any form by any electronic or mechanical means including photocopying, recording, or information storage and retrieval without permission in writing from the author.

This is a work of fiction. Names, characters, places, brands, media, and incidents are either the product of the author's imagination or are used fictitiously. The author acknowledges the trademarked status and trademark owners of various products referenced in this work of fiction, which have been used without permission. The publication/use of these trademarks is not authorized, associated with, or sponsored by the trademark owners.

Edited by Chereese Graves

www.nicsaint.com

Give feedback on the book at: info@nicsaint.com

facebook.com/nicsaintauthor
@nicsaintauthor

First Edition

Printed in the U.S.A

PURRFECT BOUQUET

Hair of the Cat That Bit You

As so often happens, I was faced with several problems at once. It required multitasking and I have to admit I'm not an ace in that department. First Odelia received an urgent request from a young woman who was the victim of a vicious slander campaign aimed at destroying her professional reputation. As she started looking into this, things became more complicated when a murder was committed in connection with a local winery. Suddenly it was all paws on deck to find the killer.

Meanwhile Marge felt that her husband and mother had started drinking too much, and imposed a ban on alcohol and sent both Tex and Gran to AA meetings in town. On top of this, Shanille had suddenly vanished without a trace, causing Harriet to take over cat choir, which ended up creating its own problems. Suffice it to say I had my paws full once again. Lucky for me I had a capable assistant in Dooley.

CHAPTER 1

Cat choir is one of those laid-back affairs I very much look forward to each and every day. In fact if it weren't for cat choir, I don't know if my life would be half as enjoyable as it is now. Now don't be fooled by the addition of the word 'choir' in cat choir. I know it looks like a choir when a bunch of cats get together to mewl and meow and generally make a huge caterwauling nuisance of themselves, but in actual fact the singing is a mere excuse for us to socialize and shoot the breeze.

And so it was that the sun had finally set on a glorious day, and that our humans were getting ready to go to bed. Teeth were being brushed, the closing credits on movies and TV shows were rolling, curtains were being pulled, and amid all this hubbub and activity, cats were using the opportunity to gobble up those final pieces of kibble, emptying those bowls before leaving the house and making their trek to the local park. Some of them made a detour, to chase some critter or sharpen those claws on some nearby tree, but in due course Hampton Cove's cat population made its way en masse to the place to be: cat choir.

For as long as I remember, Shanille has led cat choir and has done an excellent job at it, too. Shanille is Father Reilly's cat, you see, and since St. John's Church boasts a long choral tradition, she must have gotten the idea from the great man himself. And very creative she is, too. Always has some new songs she wants us to try out, some new ideas she's come up with. In fact it isn't too much to say that Shanille lives and breathes cat choir. In other words: she is cat choir personified.

Which is why it came as something of a shock to us when we arrived at the park and discovered that Shanille wasn't amongst those present at all!

We rehearse in the park's playground, you see. During the daytime the place is filled with the sounds of frolicking kids having fun, but at night it's our turn, much to the neighbors' chagrin, I might add. Oddly enough the same category of people who hate kids also seem to hate cats, but still prefer living in houses overlooking playgrounds and places where kids and cats like to gather. I guess they must be closet masochists, but don't quote me on that since I'm not a licensed shrink.

As I looked around now, I saw that the jungle gym was there, and so was the seesaw, the swing and the merry-go-round, but of our illustrious and indefatigable conductor there was not a single trace—Shanille was late!

"Where is Shanille, Max?" asked Dooley, who'd also become aware of the marked absence of one usually so undeniably and emphatically present.

"I have no idea," I admitted.

"Maybe she's been delayed," Brutus suggested.

"Or maybe she's sick," Harriet said, a touch of hope in her voice.

Harriet and Shanille's relationship may best be described as fraught with a certain measure of rivalry. They both consider themselves Hampton Cove's First Feline Females or FFF's, and as we all know you can't have two FFF's, the same way you only have one BFF. Their former enmity has morphed into a tenuous truce, especially since they both have important roles to play that they've claimed for their own: Shanille as cat choir's fearless leader and grande dame and Harriet as its lead soprano, also known as its prima donna.

I guess you could argue that you can't have two divas in the same ensemble, but so far Shanille and Harriet have managed to make it work. In a sense.

"I bet she'll show up soon," I said, trying to take the optimistic view.

"And I'll bet she's home being sick as a dog," said Harriet with relish.

"Why do they always say 'sick as a dog,' Max?" asked Dooley. "Why not sick as a cat, or sick as a rabbit? Is it because dogs are more often sick than we are?"

"I'm not sure," I said. The matter wasn't my top priority at that moment. Locating Shanille was. For a choir without a conductor isn't much of a choir at all.

"If she doesn't show up soon, we won't have a choir tonight!" said Brutus.

"She'll show up," I said. "She has to." In all the time I'd known her, Shanille had never missed a rehearsal even once.

"Do you think we can be sick as dogs?" asked Dooley, who liked to march to the beat of his own drum. "Cats aren't dogs. So we can't be sick like dogs, can we?"

"No, I guess we can't," I said.

"We can be 'sick as a cat,'" he continued. "But not 'sick as a dog' or 'sick as a rabbit,' or even 'sick as a mouse.' It just stands to reason, doesn't it?"

"It does," I said, though I was starting to find this conversation a little trying.

"Oh, there she is," said Brutus, as a feline female hove into view.

"That's not Shanille," said Harriet. "That's Samantha."

"Oh, right."

And so the long wait began. I'm not sure if you know this, but not all cats possess the virtue of patience. Harriet, for one, most definitely does not, and neither does Brutus. Dooley, because he often inhabits an alternate universe, is better equipped to deal with these matters. As for myself, I find that it helps if you think of something else entirely. And so I started to imagine what I would find in my food bowl when we got home that night. Odelia likes to change things up, you see. She knows that always eating the same thing gets tedious after a while.

"Look, it's Kingman," said Brutus, causing me to emerge from that perennial discussion about whether I like chicken best or turkey.

Kingman now came waddling up to us, looking distinctly distraught.

"The worst thing happened!" he cried even before he reached us.

"What's wrong?" asked Dooley immediately. "Has the world ended?!"

"No, the world hasn't ended," said Kingman, breathing stertorously as he plunked himself down. "But it wouldn't surprise me if it does. Shanille is gone!"

"Gone? What do you mean, gone?" I asked.

"I dropped by the church earlier, so we could walk here together, as we often do, and she wasn't there!"

I relaxed. This wasn't as bad as I thought. "That doesn't mean she's gone, Kingman. That means she's gone out somewhere."

"But Shanille never goes out! Where would she even go?!"

He was right, of course. Cats rarely go places. We're your

essential homebodies, never happier than adhering to our fixed routines and enjoying the creature comforts of our own wonderful little homes.

"Maybe Father Reilly decided to take a vacation?" I ventured.

The large cat gave me a look of exasperation. "Father Reilly never goes on vacation! His parishioners need him! Just like cat choir needs Shanille!"

"Maybe they've been abducted by aliens," Dooley suggested. "Or maybe Father Reilly has gone to Rome. Don't priests go to Rome to be with the Pope?"

"They do," Kingman confirmed, "but at least she could have told me!"

"Could be that Shanille had an accident," said Harriet with a light shrug.

"I say we organize a search party," said Brutus. "Save Shanille!"

"I'm sure she'll be here any moment," I said, trying to inject some reason into the conversation, which was getting a little out of hand, I felt.

More cats had turned up, and the sound of nervous conversation filled the air. The distinct lack of conductor hadn't escaped anyone's attention, and cats being cats, all possible explanations were being entertained. Shanille had joined a cult and moved to India. Or Shanille had been abducted and was being held for ransom by a gang of catnappers. Though the most original theory was that she had been snapped up by Hollywood, and had moved to LA to star in a movie about her life.

"As if," Harriet scoffed when this possibility was suggested to her. "Shanille's life isn't interesting enough to be turned into a movie." She cleared her throat and raised her voice. "Listen up, you guys! Unfortunately Shanille won't be joining us tonight. So as her second-in-command I'm going to take over. If you could please all take your positions, we'll start with some warm-up exercises for the voice!"

These warm-up exercises apparently consisted of using the full range of our vocal cords and projecting as loudly as possible and as far as possible. The upshot was that within five minutes windows on all sides of the park were being opened, angry heads were being thrust out, and voices were raised in anger, with a few of those hanging from their windows even throwing the odd shoe in our direction.

Personally I wouldn't have minded being pelted in the lower back with a nice sneaker—an Air Jordan, for instance, or an Allen Edmonds. I could even go for a soft Yeezy. But instead I got an old army boot for my trouble. It was big and bulky—not to mention smelly—and not a nice way to start the evening!

Around me, more footwear started raining down, causing cat choir to cut its session short for once. And so Harriet's vocal warm-up exercises, which had sounded like such a good idea, turned out not to be such a good idea after all. And when a police siren sounded in the distance, drawing closer, we decided to skedaddle.

"I hope Shanille is all right," said Dooley as we made a run for it.

"I'm sure she is," I said, as I dodged a pair of Chuck Taylors.

This unexpected hailstorm of shoes didn't bode well for the future, though.

"This is an outrage," Harriet gasped as she barely escaped an incoming Mary Jane. "We should file a complaint against these people! For assault and battery!"

"I'm not sure throwing a shoe at a cat is in the penal code," I said.

"Well, it should be! If they can't guarantee our safety, at

the very least they should give us our own rehearsal space. A nice big conference hall, for instance."

Somehow I doubted whether the powers that be could be enticed to give the cats of Hampton Cove access to a conference hall. Then again, I wouldn't want to spend all my nights indoors. Part of why I like cat choir so much is that it takes place in the great outdoors.

"Maybe we should move to the woods," Brutus suggested as he ducked an Ugg. "Plenty of space out there, and no annoying neighbors to give us any grief."

"I don't like the woods," Dooley intimated with a shiver. "They're dark and creepy and full of animals!"

"You're an animal, Dooley," Brutus reminded him. "We're all animals."

"Yeah, but the animals that live in the woods are wild animals!"

He had a point, of course. After millennia of sharing humans' homes I guess we have become domesticated to some extent. Being released into the wild would come as a big shock to most of the members of cat choir. Having to fend for ourselves, and forage for food and such. "Dooley is right," I said therefore. "The woods are no place for a couple of nice, civilized cats like us. The woods are dangerous, and full of wild creatures who wouldn't take kindly to our presence."

You'll be gratified to know that we finally made it out of the park alive, though it was a narrow escape. And as we wended our way home, Dooley reminded us of more pressing matters than escaping these shoe-throwing anti-cat zealots.

"We have to find Shanille," he said. "She could be in big trouble."

CHAPTER 2

Marge Poole was surprised to find that she was the first one out of bed that morning. When she arrived in the kitchen and didn't find her mom sipping from a cup of coffee, she glanced through the window, but instead of the usual sight of Vesta pottering about in the backyard, busy with her trowel and her flowerbeds, the old lady wasn't anywhere to be seen. Usually an early riser, Marge's mom wasn't in the living room either, nor had she taken the car and gone for a drive.

Figuring she'd probably gone for a stroll, Marge went about her business of getting ready for her day. And she'd already prepared breakfast and put a wash on when she wandered into the bedroom and saw that her hubby was still sound asleep, which was not his habit.

"Rise and shine, sleepyhead," she called out therefore.

Tex mumbled something, then turned and went straight back to sleep.

Walking into her mother's bedroom to put the laundry away, she discovered to her surprise that her mother was still in bed! Now that was odd—very odd!

"Ma, time to get up," she said, as she opened the curtains with a vigorous movement and stood staring out through the window for a moment, as one does.

Behind her, nothing stirred, and when she glanced over, she saw that her mother hadn't moved an inch. She was sleeping on her back, her mouth half open.

A sudden fear gripped Marge, and she crossed the distance to the bed in two seconds, then stared down hard at the gray-haired old lady. But her chest was still rhythmically rising and falling, and soft snores emanated from her lips, so Marge relaxed, stilling her wildly beating heart and telling herself not to be silly. Her mother might not be as young as she liked to think, but she wasn't that old either!

It was ten minutes later when she was taking an empty bottle into the garage and opening the appropriate receptacle so she could deposit it amongst its discarded colleagues when she saw no less than three wine bottles in the bin.

She blinked. Now where had those come from? She wasn't a big drinker, and as far as she knew, neither was Tex. Though it was true that lately he'd started drinking more. An aperitif before dinner, some wine with his meal, and sometimes when they were watching TV he'd have another. But that still didn't explain these empty bottles, so the only person who could have put them there was her mother. Which might go a long way to explaining why she was still in bed instead of getting up at the crack of dawn as she usually did.

Three bottles—but she couldn't possibly have drunk all three of them last night, could she?

Marge thought hard. When was the last time she had looked into this bin? Must have been a couple of days ago—a week at the most. Still, three bottles in perhaps just as many days? That was one bottle of wine per evening!

Time to have a little talk with her mother about her drinking habits!

※

As Dooley and I accompanied our human to work—work for Odelia, that is, nap time for us—my mind was still busy trying to come up with a reason for Shanille's absence last night. There could be a perfectly simple explanation, of course. In fact this idea of Father Reilly having gone on holiday and deciding to take his cat along was the most probable one. You see, Father Reilly, against the strictures of his church, had consorted with his housekeeper Marigold—if consort is the word I want—and from this illicit union in due course offspring had sprung.

The good priest, now having a little flock of his own to care for, had decided not so long ago to be a man of the cloth no more, and to leave his bigger flock of parishioners to some as yet unknown successor. All this so he could make an honest woman out of Marigold. And what do humans do when they have a wife and kids? They go on holiday. And if they're halfway decent humans beings, like Father Reilly most certainly is, they take their pets along with them.

So that's what must have happened. And in spite of Kingman's protestations that Shanille would have told him if such was the case, perhaps Shanille hadn't known herself that these plans were being made. Unlike Odelia some pet parents don't bother consulting their pets when they make their holiday plans, you see. One moment you're happily dozing in your favorite spot, and the next you're being shoved into a pet carrier and taken along on some long-haul holiday!

But even as we settled down in our corner of the office, ready to while away the morning by taking a nice long nap, I wondered if we shouldn't be out there looking for our friend.

This holiday thing was all well and good, but cats being cats, someone would have seen them leave on this much-coveted outing. So shouldn't we at least ask around? Put our minds at ease? But then I decided that Shanille wouldn't want that. She wouldn't want her friends getting all worked up and roaming the streets trying to find her.

"I think Shanille must have found herself a different choir," said Dooley, whose mind had been working along more or less the same lines as mine, but had clearly arrived at a different conclusion. "Remember how she told us two nights ago that we didn't have what it took? That we were a bunch of amateurs and why was she wasting her great talent on the likes of us?"

I frowned at my friend. "I'd totally forgotten about that," I admitted.

"She even said that by rights she should have been snapped up by now by some enterprising impresario to conduct an internationally-renowned choir."

"It's true," I said. "She even said she might look for one herself." Immediately my mood lightened to a not inconsiderable degree. "Yes, that must be it. She must have gone to look for some prestigious choir to conduct. Some famous outfit."

Something along the lines of the Cornell University Choir. Or the Tabernacle Choir at Temple Square. These were the kinds of choirs Shanille often referred to, claiming they were the absolute tippity top, and something for us to aspire to, before throwing up her paws in despair when we actually started singing.

"Oh, well," said Dooley. "Harriet will have to fill in for now, won't she?"

My mood dropped again, and I rubbed the painful spot in my rear where that big boot had connected. "If Harriet becomes the new conductor of cat choir we're going to have to get Odelia to buy us a suit of armor," I grumbled. "To protect us from the shoes these darn neighbors will be throwing at us."

"We could always skip the vocal warm-up," Dooley suggested.

And I'm sure a lot more could have been said on the topic, but at that moment a couple walked into the office, and asked if they could have a word with our human. So we pricked up our ears, and switched to listening mode.

"Sure," said Odelia pleasantly, and offered the couple a seat. "What can I do for you?"

They were both fairly young. Early to mid-twenties at the most. And they were a handsome couple, the woman fair-haired and blue-eyed, and the man dark-haired and brown-eyed. They looked athletic and were dressed in casual clothes: jeans and sweaters.

"We have a problem," the man said. "And we've been told that you might be able to help us."

He spoke with a faint accent which, if I wasn't mistaken, could have been French.

"Maybe we should introduce ourselves first," said the woman. "My name is Stephanie Felfan—though everyone calls me Steph. And this is my husband Jeff Felfan."

"Odelia Kingsley," said Odelia. "But I'm guessing you already knew that."

"The thing is," said Steph, "that I'm in something of a pickle. You see, I'm a fashion designer, or at least that's what I want to be. It's what I studied. And recently a job became available at one of the country's hottest new fashion labels, WelBeQ, which is located in LA. So I sent in my resume and as you can imagine I was over the moon when they offered me the position. Assistant to the head designer at WelBeQ. So a week passes, and we're already making all the necessary arrangements, when suddenly I get an email that they've changed their mind, and that they're going in a different direction. I ask them what happened, but total radio silence. They won't respond to my emails, when I try to call them I can't get anyone on the phone. Complete blackout. So I'm shocked, right? Of course I am."

"What is a welbeck, Max?" asked Dooley, interrupting Steph's story.

"A famous fashion brand," I said.

"I've never heard of it."

"Me neither," I said.

At the sound of our voices, Steph smiled and glanced in our direction. "Oh, will you look at those two cuties! Are they yours?"

"They are," said Odelia. "The big one is Max, and the smaller one is Dooley."

"They're absolutely adorable," said Steph. "Aren't they adorable, Jeff?"

"Very adorable," said Jeff, and pronounced adorable the way the French do.

"My husband is French," Steph explained. "We met in Paris, when I studied at the fashion academy there."

"Oh, so you're also a fashion designer?" asked Odelia.

"Oh, no," said Steph with a laugh.

"I'm a banker," said Jeff. "Not one ounce of designer blood."

"We like to joke that he'll bankroll me so I can start my own label."

"But I'm not a very good banker, I'm afraid," said Jeff. "I'm a poor banker. I don't have the money to bankroll Steph's career. But maybe one day."

"Jeff works for the Capital First Bank in Manhattan," Steph explained.

"As a lowly employee," said Jeff. "Not the bank's manager, unfortunately."

As it transpired, the couple had met in Paris, but had soon moved to New York, where Jeff found a well-paying job with the main branch of Capital First Bank. But even though they lived in the fashion capital of the country, Steph's dream was to move back to France and work for one of the big labels in Paris.

"But you're not originally from Paris, are you?" asked Odelia.

"Oh, no. My parents live in Hampton Cove," said Steph. "Ian and Raimunda Stewart? They run the Stewart Winery, one of the biggest on Long Island."

"Oh, right!" said Odelia. "Of course. I did a piece on your family's winery once."

"I know," said Steph with a smile. "My mom framed it and put it on the wall of her office. She does the winery's PR, while my dad runs the company, along with my brother Kevin."

"But you're not bitten by the wine bug?"

"Absolutely not. I don't know why, but I always wanted to be a designer. And lucky for me Mom and Dad have supported me from the start to follow my own heart and carve my own path, and not feel obligated to follow in their footsteps."

"Okay, and so now you want to move to LA and start to work for WelBeQ and for some reason they first hired you, then changed their mind," said Odelia.

"That's right. And the worst part was that they wouldn't tell me why. So I finally decided to drop it, figuring maybe it just wasn't for me. And then yesterday, out of the blue, I get a call from someone who works in the HR department at WelBeQ. It wasn't an official call, and she wouldn't give me her name, but she read my emails, and said she was under strict instructions from the legal department not to respond. But she must have felt sorry for me, which is why she called."

She took a deep breath. "Turns out someone launched a smear campaign against me."

"Someone did what?" asked Odelia, her astonishment obvious.

"A smear campaign. In the final round, there were only two candidates left for the job: me and a guy called Edmundo Crowley. And so when they selected me, someone sent them a bunch of pictures of me, passed out drunk on the couch, Zoe on the floor next to me."

"Zoe?"

"Our baby girl," said Steph. "She'll be nine months next week." A brief smile flitted across her face. "For the record, I never, ever passed out drunk—ever. These pictures are obviously doctored. They were sent from an anonymous email account, and the story they were trying to convey was that I'm an unfit mother, an alcoholic, that I was a troublemaker, and probably a drug addict."

"Did she send you the email?"

"She did. It's disgusting—and completely fake, of course. But from their point of view I can understand why they decided to go with the other candidate."

"Who sent the email? Any idea?"

"I have a pretty good idea who sent it," said Steph, her expression hardening.

"Crowley," said Jeff. "He is the candidate Steph was competing against."

"He's the one who got the job when they ditched me," Steph clarified. "And I'm pretty sure he's the one who launched this campaign against me to damage my reputation. I mean, who else can it be?"

"Did the person who called you tell you this?" asked Odelia.

"I asked her, and she said she couldn't be one hundred

percent sure, but she thought it must be Crowley. At least that's the consensus among her colleagues."

"There must be something you can do. Did you sign a contract?"

"Verbal agreement only. I was going to sign the contract on my first day."

"I see," said Odelia thoughtfully. "So what—"

"I want you to look into this email business. Find out who's behind it. And if it is Crowley I want to expose him, and file a complaint against him. And then I will go to WelBeQ and tell them what's going on."

"You still want to work for them?"

"Of course! This is my dream job. WelBeQ may not be one of the major fashion houses, but they have a great reputation as an innovative brand. They just might be the next Fenty. You know, Rihanna's brand? And if I can get in from the start, it's going to do wonders for my career. So yeah, I still want to work for them. And I want to prove that they picked the wrong candidate."

"It's not right that this Crowley got in by slandering Steph's reputation," said Jeff. "And if WelBeQ thinks she's an unreliable person, they might spread the word and talk to other companies, and very soon she will become unhirable."

"Which is why I want you to find out if it's really Edmundo Crowley who's behind this," said Steph. "To prove it somehow, so I can do something about it."

CHAPTER 3

"It's a nasty business, Max," said Dooley. "Slandering the reputation of a nice girl like Steph. Who would do such a thing? It's not okay."

I smiled. "You're absolutely right, Dooley. It's not okay."

"And all this just to get a job. There should be a law against that kind of thing."

"I'm sure there is. But first we need to figure out who's behind this campaign."

A day had passed since Steph and Jeff had paid us a visit in the office, and now we were in the car with Odelia, cruising along the Long Island Expressway and making great progress. Odelia's old pickup was being overtaken by bigger, faster, newer cars, but she didn't mind. As long as it got us from point A—Hampton Cove—to point B—the residence of Edmundo Crowley—that was all that mattered.

The moment Steph and Jeff Felfan had left the office, Odelia had consulted with her editor Dan Goory. The white-bearded newspaperman had given his wholehearted approval to do what lay in our power to help the Felfans. They both sniffed a great story, and if it tied in with the Stewart Winery, that was even better. They might be able to launch a series of articles about the incident.

Odelia had phoned Mr. Crowley, and the man had agreed to do an interview. In fact it wasn't too much to say he was flattered when a reporter called him and complimented him on his achievements as a budding designer. A little flattery never hurts when talking to ambitious people like Steph's alleged nemesis.

"Are you sure you shouldn't have asked Chase to come along?" asked Dooley. "Just in case this Mr. Crowley proves to be a dangerous individual, I mean?"

"I doubt that he's dangerous," said Odelia. "He's a fashion designer, not an ax murderer."

"One doesn't exclude the other," Dooley insisted. "But just so you know: Max and I have your back, Odelia. The moment the man turns homicidal, we'll pounce."

"Good to know," said Odelia with a smile.

I have to say I admired her courage. It's not always easy to go and talk to complete strangers. You never know what you'll find. Like Dooley said, maybe reporters should travel in pairs, just like police officers, just in case.

Edmundo Crowley lived in Brooklyn, though if Steph was to be believed, not for very much longer. In fact we probably caught him just in time, as he was moving to LA soon, to start work for WelBeQ. A quick perusal of the man's apartment, once we got there, bore out my theory: suitcases were on his bedroom floor, his cupboards looked as if they'd been ransacked, clothes strewn about indiscriminately, and generally the place looked as if a minor tornado had recently landed there and done some serious damage.

"Moving, Mr. Crowley?" asked Odelia, showing what a keen reporter's eye she had. She was sitting in front of the young man, tablet in hand, ready to write down the pearls of wisdom that were about to fall from the designer's lips.

Contrary to the state of his lodgings, the designer himself looked more like an accountant than a hot young artiste. Perhaps for this special occasion, he was dressed in an off-white shirt and tie and perfectly pressed and creased black pants, and even his shoes looked polished. He wore designer glasses and his hair was neatly coiffed.

"Yes, I'm sorry about the mess," he said, taking a seat. "I'm starting a new job soon, so I've been packing."

"A new job. Isn't that exciting?"

"Yeah, I was accepted at WelBeQ," said Edmundo with not a little bit of pride. "They're one of the hottest new brands on the market, but I'm sure you know all about that, being a fashion reporter and all."

Odelia smiled a sweet smile. "About that, I was contacted recently by Stephanie Felfan. I don't know if you've heard of her?"

The transformation was remarkable. The kind demeanor was instantly replaced by a cagey expression. "Stephanie Felfan?" he asked with a touch of suspicion.

"Yes, she was also in the running for the job at WelBeQ, same as you. She was even accepted and was offered the position. But then suddenly she got a message that there had been a mistake, and that she wasn't moving to LA after all."

"I see," said the young man, as he pushed his glasses up his nose. "I'm afraid I've never heard of this person. Stephanie Felfan, did you say?"

"That's right. So Stephanie did a little digging, and turns out that you took the job that was initially promised to her. And what's more, the reason WelBeQ decided to go in a different direction is because some very damaging information about Stephanie found its way into their mailbox."

The man frowned in confusion. "Is that so?"

"It is. And what's more, she seems to think that one of the other candidates may have launched a smear campaign against her, trying to remove her from the equation. And so obviously this has her wondering who this person might be."

"Of course," said Edmundo, nodding. "If something like that happened to me, I'd also want to know who was behind it." He shrugged. "It's all news to me, I'm afraid, Mrs. Kingsley. No one at WelBeQ told me anything about the other candidates. I never even met the people at WelBeQ face to face, since everything was done over Zoom. So I'm afraid I can't help you." The frown returned. "So… if I understand you correctly, you're here on behalf of this… Stephanie Felfan?"

"Yes, I am," said Odelia. "Steph had her hopes set on this job, you see, and when it fell through, she was devastated."

"Oh, but I understand," said Edmundo, nodding. "It's a great opportunity."

"So… you're saying you don't know anything about this smear campaign?"

"That's correct," Edmundo confirmed. "I don't know anything about it. They kept us totally in the dark about the other candidates or even if there were other candidates. I assumed there were, of course, since the opportunity was so great, but as I said, I never met any of them and didn't even know their names."

"I understand," said Odelia thoughtfully.

I had the impression that the designer was a little disappointed that the reporter hadn't come to ask him about his stellar career as a promising young talent. But if he was, he was exceedingly decent about it. "It must have come as a great shock to your friend that she wasn't hired by WelBeQ," he said kindly. "And if I were in her shoes, I'd probably want to know what happened, too."

"It was her dream job," said Odelia simply.

"As it is for me," said Edmundo.

CHAPTER 4

The moment Edmundo realized no more questions about his person were forthcoming, and no extensive article would be written about his career, the interview quickly came to an end. He more or less ushered us out, claiming he had a lot more packing to do, and that was that.

The moment we were back in the car, Odelia turned to us. "So what do you think? Was he lying, or was he telling the truth?"

"I thought he seemed pretty sincere," I said.

"He's a great designer," said Dooley. "His clothes were very nice."

"I don't think he made those clothes himself, Dooley," I said.

"He didn't? But I thought he was a fashion designer?"

"Not all fashion designers design their own clothes."

"Okay, so what do I tell Steph?" asked Odelia, getting the conversation back on track. "She really thought Edmundo was the guy trying to destroy her reputation."

"It's possible that he's a very good liar," I said. "But if it's true that WelBeQ didn't supply information about the other candidates, I don't see how Edmundo could have known that he was competing against Stephanie. Or that she was the candidate he had to beat if he were to succeed in landing the job."

"No, that kind of information must have come from WelBeQ," said Odelia. She turned and started up the car. "Let's give Steph the bad news," she said, and soon we were mobile again, this time navigating Brooklyn's notoriously busy streets.

"There's a lot more traffic here than in Hampton Cove, isn't there, Max?" said Dooley.

"That's because New York is a much bigger place," I said. "More people means more traffic and busier streets."

"I don't think I'd want to live here. Too busy. And they don't even have a nice park where we can meet our friends."

"I'm sure New York has plenty of parks," I said with a smile. "And in fact it's not really one big city, but a collection of smaller boroughs. Like Brooklyn is one borough, and Manhattan, where Jeff works, is a different one. And in each borough you have neighborhoods, which are also very different."

"Almost like a lot of small cities in one big city."

Fortunately for us, Steph and Jeff also lived in Brooklyn, and when we arrived on their doorstep, they were clearly happy to see us. Or at least Steph was. Her husband was at work, so it was just her.

"So how did it go?" she asked the moment we entered the modest apartment. It had a homely feel, and was very airy and bright, but also very, very small, at least by our standards. But then we're used to living in a house, of course, with plenty of space. The same space in the big city clearly comes at a premium.

"I'm afraid I didn't get very far with Mr. Crowley," said Odelia, opting for the direct approach. "He claims he had no information on the other candidates, so he wouldn't have been in a position to launch a smear campaign against them. He'd never even heard your name, so he couldn't possibly have tried to slander you."

"He's lying," said Steph immediately. "He must have known."

"If he did, he must have received the information from someone at WelBeQ," said Odelia. "Which means you have an enemy in the HR department, Steph."

"I thought as much," said the young woman. "Clearly they wanted Crowley to get the job, and when it looked as if I was going to come out on top, they started this campaign against me." Thought wrinkles appeared on her brow. "It must be someone who's not very high up. Not a person in a position to decide which candidate is chosen. Someone who's friends with Crowley. Or maybe a relative."

"Can't you ask your contact at WelBeQ? Maybe they know something?"

"I've tried, but the person who called me said she's already stuck her neck out by telling me what she knew, and if she starts digging even deeper she might get in trouble herself." She heaved a sigh. "Looks like it's a dead end, isn't it?"

"Not necessarily," said Odelia. "You could always file an official complaint with the police. They did send these fake pictures of you, slandering your reputation."

Steph waved the suggestion away. "I had another job offer last night. Junior designer at a reputable fashion house in Paris. Jeff is ecstatic, of course, since it would mean we could move back to Paris and be closer to his family again. And for me it would be a great opportunity as well. Maybe not my dream job, like the one at WelBeQ, but definitely something I think I will love."

"Hey, but that's great," said Odelia.

"It is. And something else has happened. Jeff's godmother died last night. Thing is that she made a will leaving her entire estate to Jeff. She didn't have kids of her own and loved Jeff. It includes an apartment and a sizable sum of money."

"How old was Jeff's godmother?"

"Ninety-six. She was in a bad way for a while now. We paid her a visit when we were in Paris. She was a very lively and funny lady. Crazy about dogs. Her apartment was crawling with them. I think she had about a dozen. She was a patron at one of the big dog shelters in Paris, and couldn't resist to adopt one each time she visited." She smiled at the memory. "I'll miss her. She was a real pistol."

"So that means you'll have a job in Paris and maybe an apartment," said Odelia, summing things up. "And what about Jeff? Does he have a job lined up?"

"Jeff can't wait to go back. If my dream was to move to LA, his dream is Paris. And as far as jobs is concerned, he has his pick. His dad is well-connected."

"What does he do, your father-in-law?"

"He's a politician. Could very well be the next mayor of Paris. He was a candidate in the last election and lost, but this time he's expected to win."

"Looks like WelBeQ is in Steph's rearview mirror already," said Dooley.

"Yeah, I don't think she's going to shed any tears about what happened," I said.

And a good thing, too. There didn't seem to be a lot she could do about the smear campaign. Unless she was willing to file an official complaint. But she seemed reluctant to go down that route, and I could understand why. It can be a hassle.

"I just want to leave the whole mess behind me," Steph said now, confirming our estimation of the situation. "And if

I'm absolutely honest I don't think I even want to work for WelBeQ anymore, after the way they treated me. At the very least they could have talked to me before believing these filthy stories. But instead they took them at face value and didn't even offer me a chance to defend myself."

"Yeah, their HR department has a lot to answer for," Odelia agreed.

"In normal circumstances a person is innocent until proven guilty, but at WelBeQ that doesn't seem to be the case." She shrugged. "We talked about it last night, Jeff and I, after the Paris offer came in, and we decided to accept and move on."

"So no more WelBeQ?"

"No more WelBeQ."

CHAPTER 5

Our mission at an end, we returned to Hampton Cove forthwith, to devote ourselves to that other, perhaps more compelling mystery: the disappearance of Shanille!

Last night we had all gathered in the park again for cat choir, but for the second night in a row, of our noble conductor there was no trace. This time Harriet hadn't offered to lead the choir, and since no singing had taken place, no barrage of shoes had landed on our collective heads either. The neighbors were clearly happy that Shanille had downed tools, but we most definitely were not!

"Finally!" said Harriet when Dooley and I walked in through the pet flap and into our cozy little home. "I thought you'd never get here."

"Just a minor mission that took us all the way to New York City," I said. "But everything has been arranged to Odelia's client's satisfaction, and so we're back."

"A fashion designer was being slandered by another fashion designer," Dooley explained, even though Harriet hadn't asked, "and so we paid a visit to the second fashion designer, who claimed he didn't even know the first fashion designer, so how could he be slandering her? It made a lot of sense to me, and now Steph—that's the first fashion designer—is moving to Paris with her family."

"Dooley, read my lips," said Harriet. "I don't care!"

Dooley, who'd been intently staring at Harriet's lips, frowned. "I don't understand. How can I read your lips? There's nothing written there."

"It's just an expression," I said. "I think what Harriet means to say is that we've got more important things to worry about than this fashion designer business."

"Exactly!" Harriet said. "We need to find Shanille. Otherwise cat choir will go out of business and then where does that leave us? In big doo-doo!"

Dooley frowned even deeper. Between the 'read my lips' statement and this reference to excrement it was obvious he had a hard time keeping track of the conversation.

"I thought you were going to take over from Shanille?" Brutus asked.

"I wanted to, but you saw what happened. Those annoying neighbors sabotaged my first rehearsal. I don't know what it is about me that they don't like, but it's obvious that they've taken a vote and decided to start a boycott against my person." She shook her head in distinct dismay. "They don't appreciate talent, that's what it is. Cultural barbarians, every single one of them."

"They do wear nice shoes," said Dooley.

At this reminder of the shoe incident, I automatically rubbed my bum. Tough to be an artist when you're being pelted in the rear end with solid objects!

And so the meeting ended and we moved along, in search of Shanille. Harriet may initially have been pleased to know that her big competitor was out of the picture, but somehow she'd had a change of heart. And I could understand why, of course. When you're locked into this kind of intense rivalry, and suddenly the second party abruptly calls it quits, it leaves one reeling. Out of balance, if you see what I mean. And this must be what happened to Harriet. One moment she was happily fighting tooth and claw with the feisty choir conductor, and the next her opponent was gone—and so was a pleasant and entertaining pastime. A pastime that gave meaning to her existence, and had become part of her day-to-day life.

Harriet needed to find Shanille so she could be herself again.

We moved through the pet flap in single file, and soon found ourselves amid the hustle and bustle of our small town.

"It's a lot more peaceful here than in New York, isn't it, Max?" said Dooley, and he emitted a little sigh of satisfaction. "And so much nicer, too."

"It is," I said. The big city is fine and good, but nothing beats being home.

Our first destination, as chosen by Harriet, was St. John's Church, heart of Father Reilly's parish, and also home to the good priest and Shanille. We arrived there in due course, and found to our surprise that the great oak doors of the church were closed, and a notice had been pinned on them.

'Closed until further notice,' the note read.

"Closed?" asked Harriet. "How can a church be closed? Aren't they always supposed to be open?"

She had a point, of course. Historically churches have always been havens where people could find refuge and spiritual succor. And as far as I knew, St. John's Church ascribed to this great tradition by never closing its doors.

Until now.

"If the church is closed, Shanille can't be here," said

Brutus, pointing out an obvious truth. "Which means she's probably somewhere else."

"Father Reilly and Shanille don't actually live in the church," I felt compelled to point out. "A church is not a home, Brutus. At least not in the more mundane sense of the word."

"So where do they live?" asked the big black cat.

"Next door," I said, pointing to the rectory which was located next to the church. It was a modest house, but fulfilled Father Reilly's needs adequately.

"Does Marigold also live there?" asked Dooley, referring to Father Reilly's housekeeper-slash-girlfriend. "And her daughter Angel?"

"I don't think so," I said. At least Marigold didn't use to live at the rectory. Maybe she had changed her mind and had moved in with her future husband.

"It's odd that in some religions priests or pastors are allowed to marry and in others not," said Dooley. "Who makes up these rules anyway?"

"The people who start these religions?" I ventured.

"Can anyone start a religion?"

"I guess so," I said.

"So maybe we should start a religion?"

This had Harriet and Brutus in stitches. "Start our own religion?" said Brutus when he was finally able to speak again. "And who would be the leader? You?"

"I don't see why not," said Dooley with a shrug. "If anyone can start a religion, why not we? And if anyone can lead a religion, why not me?"

"And what would you call your church, Father Dooley?" asked Harriet, wiping a tear from her eyes.

"The Church of Dooley," said Dooley decidedly. "And I would accept anyone, not just cats. Dogs can be members, too, and even humans. I'm fair-minded."

"And what are you going to preach?" asked Brutus. "What are your teachings?"

This had Dooley stumped for a moment, but he soon rallied. "Peace and good will," he said decidedly. "And kibble for all."

"Now that's a church I wouldn't mind joining," said Brutus with a grin.

"Look, you guys," said Harriet, as she pointed to the front door of the rectory. "Another note."

She was right. On the door of the rectory a note had been pinned, just like at the church. This one read, 'No deliveries until further notice.'

"I don't like this," said Harriet. "Looks like they've left town or something."

"See?" I said. "I told you they're on holiday."

"No way," said Harriet. "Not without telling us first."

It was all very odd, of course. And not a little bit worrying.

"That note doesn't mean they're not home, though, does it?" said Brutus. "It just means Father Reilly doesn't want anything delivered. So maybe he's home, but he's in bed with the flu or something. And Shanille won't leave his side."

"You know, Brutus," I said. "You may well be right."

"Of course I'm right," said the cat. "I'm always right."

That wasn't perhaps the case, but it was true that Shanille was exactly the kind of cat who wouldn't leave her human's side when he was in bed with some illness. She was like a Good Samaritan in that sense. Always ready to lend a helping paw.

"Let's see if we can't get in through the back door," I suggested.

And so we circled the rectory, in search of some means of entry. But when we arrived at the back, the place was as locked down as the front, with even the blinds having been pulled, and the windows closed shut. There wasn't even a convenient basement window we could use to get in.

And we were ready to give up when I saw movement from the corner of my eye. And when I glanced over, I saw Gran exiting the church, carrying two bottles of wine in her hands!

CHAPTER 6

"Gran, do you know where Father Reilly is?" asked Harriet.

"Or Shanille?" I added.

Gran, who seemed taken aback by the sight of the four of us, was curt in her response. "I have no idea," she snapped. "I'm not my brother's keeper, you know."

"Gran!" Dooley cried. "I didn't know Father Reilly was your brother!"

"He isn't. Now leave me alone," said the old lady, and tried to make herself scarce. But it's not so easy to get rid of four cats who've made up their minds to find a person.

"Are they in the church?" Harriet insisted. "Cause if they are, you have to let us in. Shanille hasn't shown up for choir practice two nights in a row, and if she thinks she can get away with this kind of irresponsible behavior she's got another thing coming."

"They're not in there," said Gran, as she tried to get past us.

"So what were you doing in the church?" I asked. "And how did you get in?"

"Francis gave me a key. Now can you please leave me alone, you busybodies?"

"Why are you carrying two bottles of wine, Gran?" asked Dooley, who had only now recovered from the shock of discovering that Gran might be Father Reilly's sister. "And why are you holding them behind your back?"

"She thinks we can't see them," Harriet clarified.

"Oh, for crying out loud!" said Gran, clearly annoyed by this third degree. "Did anyone ever tell you that you're far too nosy for your own good? Now clear off!"

But instead, it was she who cleared off, hurrying away, still clutching those bottles as if they were her lifeline to a better future. A future in which cats weren't so nosy.

"What is Gran doing with those bottles?" asked Dooley. "And why was she sneaking in and out of the church? And why aren't we supposed to know what she's up to? And where are Father Reilly and Shanille!"

"Wherever they are, it's not here," said Harriet.

That much was obvious, and Gran's peculiar behavior had made the priest and his cat's sudden disappearance only more puzzling.

"I think we should tell Odelia," said Harriet. "So she can tell her uncle, so he can start a search." Her eyes went wide. "You guys, Shanille could be lying dead in a ditch somewhere as we speak, and so could Father Reilly!"

Even though only two nights ago the prospect of her frenemy lying in a ditch somewhere had seemed like a pleasing prospect to the white Persian, the passage of time had clearly made her change her mind about that.

"The police aren't interested in missing pets," said Brutus.

"But they are interested in missing humans," said Harriet. "And wherever Father Reilly is, we're likely to find Shanille, since she wouldn't leave his side."

"He could have lost his mind," said Dooley. "I saw a documentary a couple of weeks ago about a man who lost his marbles and wandered off into the woods. He was accompanied by his dog at the time. A nice Labrador retriever named Sue."

"So what happened?" asked Harriet. "Did they find them?"

"They did, three years later. There wasn't much left of him, though, except a gnawed-off skeleton and some remnants of his clothes."

"And Sue?"

"According to the policeman they interviewed it was Sue who'd done the gnawing, actually," said Dooley. "When her owner got lost in those woods, and eventually died of exposure, she had no alternative but to do a little snacking, especially since she was still tied to him with a leash." When we all stared at him, he smiled. "There's some good news, though. Eventually Sue managed to chew through the leash and was found living with a nearby farmer, who said she was a fine dog."

"She ate her human!" Brutus cried. "Not what I would call a fine dog!"

"She had no other choice," Dooley pointed out. "It's a dog-eat-dog world out there, Brutus. Or in this case, a dog-eat-person world, I guess."

"Okay," I said, and shivered slightly at the images his story had conjured up. "Thank you for that, Dooley."

"So you see? If Father Reilly really has lost his mind, and ends up dying from exposure, Shanille can simply eat him and be fine. For a vegetarian like me this would be a big no-no, of course, but Shanille isn't a vegetarian, so she'll be okay."

"Father Reilly won't be okay," said Harriet. "In fact he'll be dead."

"Let's not get ahead of ourselves here," I said. "He's not dead yet."

"He could be dead," said Brutus, striking the gloomy note. "Dead in a ditch."

"Then we better find him before Shanille eats him," said Harriet.

"Shanille won't have to eat him," I pointed out. "Since Shanille isn't a dog, she's not tied to her dead human with a leash."

Another strong point in favor of getting a cat and not a dog: at least when you die from exposure a cat won't eat you, and a dog would.

"I say we tell Odelia," said Harriet. "And let the police find them."

"And I say we do it ourselves," said Brutus. "You know what the police are like. They'll tell us we have to wait forty-eight hours, and even then they'll say Father Reilly isn't a missing person since he left of his own accord, as evidenced by the notes he pinned up on the church and rectory doors." He shook his head sadly. "I'm afraid that if we want to find our friend, we're on our own here, you guys."

And he might have had a point. It did look as if Father Reilly hadn't gone missing, but had simply left. But why? And where? The police would simply figure this was his own personal business—nothing to do with us. And so they wouldn't touch the case. And all the while cat choir would have to go without its conductor.

"I agree with Brutus," I said therefore. "If we want to find Shanille, we'll have to find her ourselves."

"Where do we start?" asked Harriet simply.

And that, of course, was where things got complicated. Where do you start looking for a missing person? Or cat? Or cat and person? The police have all kinds of resources at their disposal. They can look at a person's bank account, to see if any cash withdrawals have been made. Or they can check a person's phone records to see if he made any calls.

Or they can organize a house-to-house inquiry, to see if anyone saw anything. They could talk to friends and relatives. Plenty of possibilities that weren't available to four cats with limited resources.

But what we did have was resolve. A firm determination to find our friend. Preferably before she started snacking on the dead corpse of her human!

CHAPTER 7

Steph Felfan was nursing her baby when her phone chimed. Expecting it to be her husband, she immediately picked up. But instead of Jeff's pleasant voice, the tones reaching her ear were of a much harsher variety. They sounded French, and were distinctly clipped and to the point.

"Stephanie Felfan? My name is Julie Clairmont and I'm calling from the HR department at Sofie Fashion. I'm sorry to inform you that the job offer has been rescinded, Mrs. Felfan, so you no longer will be working for us."

"Wait, what?" she said, stunned at this piece of news. "Is this a joke?"

"No joke," said the woman. "And can I just say that we're all shocked that a mother would do such a thing?"

"Thing? What thing?"

"Oh, you know," said the woman coldly.

"No, I don't, actually," said Steph.

"Drunk, passed out on the couch, your baby on the floor playing with a dirty diaper. I'm a mother myself, Mrs. Felfan, and frankly I was shocked. If it were up to me I would report your appalling behavior to social services in your country. Please turn your life around, I implore you. If not for you, at least for your baby."

"But—"

"Good day, Mrs. Felfan."

And then she hung up.

Steph sat staring at her phone. It was the WelBeQ scenario all over again, wasn't it? Somehow the same pictures and the same story had found their way into the Sofie Fashion's HR department's mailbox, and had made them change their mind about offering her the job. She wanted to yell at them that it was all lies, but knew they wouldn't believe her. Somehow pictures spoke louder than words—at least her words—even when those pictures had been doctored.

And she was still feeling dazed when a key clicked in the front door lock and her husband walked in. When he found her looking like death warmed over, he immediately crossed the floor to where she was still clutching her phone.

"Honey, what's wrong?" he asked as he sat down next to her and took her hand in his. "You're completely pale. Is it Zoe?"

"No, Zoe is fine," she assured him. "It's the Paris job. It's gone." And as she explained what just happened, a cloud seemed to pass over his face.

"I have some bad news also," he said. "You remember I told you about my godmother Evelyne de Taché?"

"Of course. What happened?"

"They read her will, and it turns out she donated her apartment and all of her possessions to the dog shelter she's been a patron of for all these many years."

"But I don't understand. I thought you were the sole beneficiary of her will?"

He shook his head sadly. "Not anymore. She made a new

will the day before she died, leaving everything to the shelter."

"But why?"

"I don't know. But I bet my parents do. Is it all right if I call them?"

She nodded distractedly. What was happening? It seemed like good opportunities left and right were vanishing into thin air. Was it a hate campaign against them? Or simply coincidence that Jeff's godmother had a change of heart?

Her husband had taken out his phone and held it up in front of them while it connected. Moments later his parents appeared, both looking pleased to see them. David Felfan, who was in his early fifties, looked like an older version of his son, and Pauline Felfan was a distinguished-looking lady in her mid-forties. Ever since David, who had run a successful law practice in Paris before launching himself in local politics, had expressed his ambition to become the next mayor of Paris, his wife had supported him unstintingly, hosting dinner parties, organizing fundraisers and building the kind of network one needs for such an endeavor.

David had said many times that without Pauline's support he would never have been able to get this far. With the election less than a year away, he was the frontrunner in the upcoming campaign, with many predicting he might even be the next president. After all Jacques Chirac had been mayor of Paris before he became president of the country.

"Tell us about Evelyne," said Jeff. "What happened, exactly?"

"Well, I talked to the notary responsible for the new will," said David. "And he told me that the day before she died, he received an urgent message to come to her apartment. She was very weak, and very ill, but she was adamant that she wanted to have a new will made up. Her doctor was there, and he said she was of sound mind and body, and is prepared to testify to this under oath if necessary. But the notary said he didn't need her doctor's reassurances. He could see that even though Evelyne's health might be failing, her mind was still sharp as a tack."

"So why did she change her will?"

"It turns out she heard some very worrying things about you," said David.

"Me?"

"Steph, actually." David seemed embarrassed having to say this. "I'm simply repeating what the notary told me. Evelyne said that information had been brought to her attention that Stephanie is an unfit mother, a raging alcoholic and drug addict who neglects her daughter and is a danger to herself and others."

Steph gasped in shock, even as Jeff took her hand and squeezed it in support. "I don't understand," said Steph. "She said those things about me? Jeff's godmother?"

"She did, actually," said David. "And when I asked where she had heard these preposterous things, the notary said a letter had arrived containing several very disturbing photographs. I took the liberty of taking a picture," he said, and suddenly the screen changed and a picture from the same collection Steph had seen before, when sent to her by the HR person from WelBeQ, came into view. It depicted her passed out on the couch, an empty bottle of vodka in her hand, drool dripping from the corner of her mouth, and Zoe alone on the floor, playing with a dirty diaper.

She closed her eyes in horror. "This is just..."

"These are doctored," Jeff explained. "You understand that these have been doctored, right? They took these pictures and put Steph and Zoe's faces on them."

"Of course we understand, Jeff," said Pauline, once David had switched the image back to the live footage from the parental pair. "You don't have to tell us. We know Steph isn't anything like the person in those pictures. And she would never neglect Zoe like that. But the damage is done, I'm afraid. The apartment is gone."

"At least she donated it to a good cause," said Steph quietly.

This was a nightmare. First WelBeQ, then Sofie Fashion, and now this. Someone was out to get her. Out to destroy her utterly and completely.

"I think I know who's behind this," she said. "And I'm going to prove it."

"There is one glimmer of hope," said Pauline. "Your father and I have been discussing things, and we think we might be in the position to offer you an alternative for Evelyne's apartment. It won't be as nice, of course, since Evelyne's apartment is located in the fourth arrondissement, one of the best neighborhoods in Paris, but we may have a surprise for you."

The screen changed once again, and a picture of a great-looking apartment building appeared. It was built in the typical Haussmannian style, with the cream-colored facade and the mansard roof with the dormer windows. Next came a series of pictures of the interior of a spacious apartment that looked simply wonderful. It was sparsely decorated, presumably by the real estate agent, but looked like an absolute dream in comparison with their cramped Brooklyn flat.

"What's this?" asked Jeff, after exchanging a look of surprise with Steph.

David and Pauline returned, all smiles this time. "It's yours if you want," said Pauline. "We closed escrow last week, and were going to put it on the rental market. But now that the opportunity to live in Evelyne's apartment has fallen through, we thought you should have it."

Steph and Jeff's faces must have revealed their shock, for David and Pauline laughed. *"Maman! Papa!"* said Jeff. "Are you serious?"

"Of course," said David. "I never joke about real estate. And if you don't want it, it's still a sound investment for us, so no harm done."

"You have got to be kidding," said Steph.

"No, we're not," said Pauline. "You deserve it, after all your hard work. Jeff told us about the job you've just landed with Sofie Fashion, and David is already pulling some strings to land Jeff a job at a very prestigious bank in the eighth arrondissement, so Paris awaits. And frankly we can't wait for you to arrive, so we can finally see our granddaughter again. Because Skype is very nice, but it's simply not the same as being in the same room." She must have noticed something in Steph's expression, though, for her face fell. "What is it? Something I said?"

"The job at Sofie Fashion fell through," said Steph. "They received the same terrible pictures WelBeQ received, and also Evelyne."

"Someone is out to get Steph," said Jeff. "Sabotage her career."

"Not just my career—my entire life," said Steph.

"Have you talked to the police yet?" asked David.

"We talked to a reporter who works with the police," said Jeff. "Odelia Kingsley. We've heard good things about her, and she gets results."

"She also told us to go to the police, though," said Steph. "To file an official complaint with the NYPD."

"Well, you should," said Pauline. "You can't allow this to go on. Who knows what this person is going to do next? Post these pictures on the internet? Destroy your reputation for good? Once these things are out there, they take on a life of their own, Stephanie, darling. And before you know it, the story goes viral and your life is ruined. So you have to stop this before it's too late."

"You're right," said Steph. "I should have gone to the

police sooner."

"Go now. Don't wait another minute. File this complaint today," David advised.

"I will. I'll go right now, and tell them the whole story. Can you send me the pictures? I'm going to show them to the police. They need to stop this person."

"Of course. I'm sending them now," said David. "And the letter as well. I took a picture of the envelope, too. Maybe the postage stamp will tell them something."

"I wonder where they got Evelyne's address," said Jeff. "Or how they even knew she was bequeathing her apartment to me. These people, whoever they are, seem to know an awful lot about us, don't they?"

"Did you post about Evelyne on Facebook, maybe?" asked Pauline.

Jeff thought for a moment. "I don't think so. I did mention it to a colleague, but I don't see how she would... I mean, why would she even..."

"Just talk to the police," David stressed again. "They'll figure it out. It's their job."

And so it was decided. Steph would go to the police and get this terrible business with the slanderous letters and emails stopped once and for all.

"Where is Zoe?" asked Pauline, a constant refrain whenever Jeff's parents called in. "How is she doing?" And when Jeff pointed the phone to their little girl, the oohs and aahs were something to behold. "She's getting so big!"

"You have to come to Paris," said David. "I'm sure that once you have this slander business sorted out Sofie Fashion will apologize and offer you a job. And if not them, there's hundreds of other places that will be glad to have you."

"Thanks, David," said Steph. The support of her in-laws meant a great deal to her. They'd been on her side from the start, never wavering in their opinion that she was the victim in all of this, and whatever was being said about her was nothing but a bunch of malicious lies. "And we'd love to move to Paris. Wouldn't we, honey?"

"We'll discuss it tonight," Jeff said diplomatically. But she could see from the sparkle in his eyes that as far as he was concerned, the decision had already been made. He'd always wanted to return to Paris, and so had she, actually. So maybe the fact that the contract at WelBeQ had fallen through was a blessing in disguise. Otherwise they would have spent the next couple of years out in LA, and perhaps wouldn't even have liked it all that much.

And Jeff had given up so much for her already, moving to New York, and prepared to move to LA. So maybe it was finally time to return to his hometown.

After cooing and fussing over Zoe for a few minutes, the call ended, and they both sat there for a moment, before asking, simultaneously, "What do you think?"

Jeff's grin spread from ear to ear. It was obvious what he thought.

"Let's do it," she said finally. "Let's go back to Paris."

"Only if you want to," said Jeff cautiously.

She smiled and wrapped her arms around her husband. "I want to. In fact I can't wait."

"Then let's do it," he said, and planted a sweet kiss on her lips.

CHAPTER 8

When Tex arrived home from a long day at the doctor's office, he liked to unwind by enjoying a nice cooling aperitif before dinner. Campari, soda and plenty of ice were all it took for him to relax. Then during dinner he drank a glass of wine, and when stretched out in front of the television at night, his arm around his wife, another one or two before going to bed. It was a habit he'd gradually gotten into, and even though from time to time Marge frowned when he topped up his glass during dinner, generally she was fine with it. Even though she didn't drink a lot herself, or only on special occasions, she didn't mind when he did.

But today, when he opened the fridge to take out the Campari, preparatory to mixing his drink, he discovered to his surprise that it was no longer there. Which made him wonder if he'd drunk the last of it yesterday? He didn't think so. In fact he'd only cracked open a new bottle yesterday. Or was it the day before?

He turned to his wife, who was busy tending to her

containers filled with herbs, located on the kitchen windowsill. "Have you seen that bottle of Campari? I could have sworn it was still almost full." When Marge didn't respond, he repeated, "My bottle of Campari, honey? Have you seen it?"

Suddenly she turned on him. "I poured it down the sink," she said, and gave him a slightly challenging look that told him something was going on, even though he had no idea what. "Along with all of your other bottles. And Vesta's, too."

He blinked in confusion. "But... but... but..."

"You have a problem, Tex," said Marge decidedly. "And if you can't see that, you're even further gone than I thought."

"A problem? What problem?"

"A problem with alcohol!"

He stared at his wife of twenty-five years. "I don't have a problem with alcohol."

"Oh, honey," said Marge as she shook her head in dismay. "You need help."

"What help? What are you talking about?"

"You're an alcoholic, Tex. And the sooner you realize this the better."

"An alcoholic! Me!"

"Yes, you."

"I'm not an alcoholic. I can stop whenever I want."

"No, you can't. I found three bottles in the recycle bin yesterday morning, and another two this morning. That means that between you and my mother, you managed to drink two bottles last night."

"I didn't drink two bottles," he said. "I can't drink two bottles. Two bottles, that's... two liters, right? I didn't drink two liters of alcohol. Two glasses, maybe."

But Marge was implacable. "Two bottles, Tex. Two whole bottles."

He was shaking his head, but could already see the way the wind was blowing. "I'll stop," he announced. "Not one more drop of alcohol. Just to prove to you I don't have a problem. I don't!" he cried when she didn't look convinced.

But instead of arguing with him, Marge handed him a flyer instead.

"What's this?" he asked as he frowned at the thing. "Alcoholics Anon— Honey!"

"You're going," she said, planting her hands on her hips. And from the set look on her face he knew he wasn't going to win this battle. So he didn't even try.

"Yes, honey," he said meekly.

"There's a meeting tonight, at the community center."

"Tonight! But…" There was that look again. "Yes, honey."

"No more aperitif before dinner."

"No, honey."

"No more wine during dinner."

"Of course, honey."

"And no more wine when we're watching TV."

He sighed. "Yes, honey. No more wine."

She offered him a very frosty smile. "Good."

Then she turned on her heel and left the kitchen.

৯

It wasn't a happy Tex who showed up at the AA meeting that night. More a reluctant participant in the revels, if revels were to be had, which was unlikely. He would have argued that a man of his standing in the community could hardly be expected to get up in front of a crowd of people and announce that he was an alcoholic. It might damage his reputation. What patient in their right mind would visit a doctor who was a known drunk? A man who might be expected to perform the kind of minor surgery all family doctors perform with trembling hands?

But he knew that resistance was futile, and even though he was dragging his feet, he knew that attend he must. He did tell himself he wouldn't get up at any point during the proceedings, and no words would escape his lips. He would sit at the back and make himself as invisible as possible. And if anyone asked, he'd tell them he was simply there as an observer. In his capacity as a medical professional, just in case someone collapsed and needed medical attention.

And so he snuck into the hall, glanced around, and quickly took a seat. He would have preferred to be in the last row, but the last three rows were filled already when he got there. But at least he wasn't in the front. To his surprise all the chairs were occupied, and the meeting enjoyed the benefit of a full house. In front, a woman was standing, who introduced herself as Betsy Brogue. She was the chairperson, and in a few words described the AA program for the benefit of the newcomers.

And as he listened carefully, he didn't notice how a person slid in next to him. Only when a sharp prod in the ribs caused him to look up, did he see who his neighbor was.

"Vesta!" he loud-whispered. "What are you doing here!"

"I could ask you the same thing!" she loud-whispered back.

"If you want to say something, I suggest you do it in front of the group," Betsy called out.

But both Tex and his mother-in-law quickly shook their heads, their faces having turned a light crimson when all those present turned to look at them. They shrunk in their seats and would have preferred, if possible, to have disappeared.

Fortunately no one called on them to testify or stand in

front of the group, and they both kept their mouths shut, and sat in uncomfortable silence throughout Betsy's introduction of the first speaker, in whom Tex recognized a former patient of his, and then a second and third speaker, both current patients.

This was a nightmare, he thought, as he was sweating profusely. Not only wasn't he an alcoholic, and so completely out of place, but with Vesta present, he could be sure that pretty soon the whole town would know about his attendance, Vesta being an inveterate blabbermouth of the worst kind.

Finally the meeting ended, but as he decided to slip out quietly and unobserved, he was stopped by the chairperson herself. "First-timers?" she asked, addressing both himself and Vesta. "I think you'll find that things are going to be a lot easier if you don't have to face this problem alone," she explained. "Which is why we have something called the sponsor system. Now I know that typically a sponsor is someone who's been dry for a while, but unfortunately we've been seeing so many newcomers that frankly we've run out of available sponsors. So I'm going to take a gamble here and I'm going to put the two of you together."

"Wait, what?!" Tex cried.

"You have got to be kidding me," Vesta growled.

"Just bear with me," said Betsy implacably. "I know this might seem a little unusual, but I can assure you the system works. So whenever you find yourself in trouble…"

"Tex," said Tex with some reluctance.

"You simply call on…"

"Vesta," said Vesta with even more reluctance.

"Vesta here. And vice versa. You'll see that between meetings the support you get from your sponsor will prove invaluable."

"Oh, I'll bet it will," said Vesta, looking distinctly unhappy.

Not as unhappy as Tex, though. "The thing is," he said, "that we're actually related, Vesta and me. She's my mother-in-law, you see, and I'm her son-in-law."

"That usually goes together," said Betsy.

"No, but you see, I'm a doctor, and so…"

But Betsy merely smiled. "Well, I hope to see you folks soon, and I look forward to hearing your personal stories." She then placed a flyer in both their hands and tapped it smartly. "And don't forget about the twelve steps, you two!"

They left the conference room, with Tex feeling as if he'd been hit on the head with a mallet. When he looked up, he found Vesta staring at him intently.

"That's another fine mess you got us into, Tex," she said with vehemence.

"Me! I didn't get us in this mess. You did. By putting two bottles in the recycle bin last night. Marge found them, you see, and she blames me."

"She blames me, too," said Vesta unhappily. "And so she removed every last bottle from the house. Can you believe she even raided my room? I actually caught her looking under the mattress."

"And did she find anything?"

"My bottle of Pinot Noir. I told her it was meant as a present for her, and what was she doing in my room, but she wasn't having any of it. Said I was an alcoholic, and if I hoped to keep living under her roof I was going to have to start going to these AA meetings." She shook her head. "I ask you: *her* roof. It's not *her* roof. It's our roof, all three of us. And the cats, of course," she added.

"I'm not an alcoholic either," said Tex. But when his mother-in-law gave a snort of derision, he cried, "Well, I'm not!"

"That's what they all say. Those two bottles in the bin? I

didn't put them there. And I didn't put those three bottles in there two days ago either. Guess who did?"

"I have no idea," he said stiffly. "I certainly never drank two bottles of wine in one evening."

"And I certainly never did anything as dumb as putting the evidence of my drinking in the recycle bin, where I'm sure my wife would find them the next morning." She shook her head. "For a clever guy you're not so clever, are you?"

"I did not put those bottles in the bin. And I did not drink them."

"It didn't help, of course," said Vesta, ignoring him, "that I arrived home with another two bottles of altar wine from Francis Reilly's stock." When Tex gasped in shock, she shrugged. "He told me that when I found myself in need of a pick-me-up I should come to the church and help myself. Even gave me the church keys."

"He meant a spiritual pick-me-up! Not for you to raid the church wine cellar!"

"I had to, all right? Marge has told Wilbur not to sell me any more alcohol, and I didn't feel like going to the mall, where I'm sure Marge also has her spies."

"Marge has spies at the mall?" asked Tex, marveling at this strange new world that was opening up before him.

"Marge has her spies everywhere," Vesta assured him. "She's a librarian, you know," she added, as if that explained everything.

"Look, this buddy system—"

"Sponsor system."

"Whatever. It's not going to work."

"What do you mean?"

"You and me? We can't be buddies."

"Sponsors."

"Whatever! I won't do it."

"Well, you have to. If Marge finds out that you're refusing to play by the rules, there will be hell to pay, sonny boy."

"You mean…"

Vesta wiggled her eyebrows meaningfully. "Ever heard of a sex strike?"

God. This was just getting worse and worse and worse!

CHAPTER 9

Steph and Jeff were on their way to Hampton Cove when it happened. They'd been discussing Steph's visit to the police station that morning, and how unhelpful and discouraging the police officer had been, when suddenly a car cut in front of them, and Jeff was forced to perform a dangerous maneuver by jerking his wheel to the right and almost hitting the guardrail. Lucky for them he managed to get the car under control and bring it to a full stop on the shoulder.

They were both panting and staring at each other in wide-eyed shock, then immediately Steph turned round to see if Zoe was all right.

But the little girl was still strapped safely in her car seat, and was babbling happily and trying to catch a fly that had somehow managed to enter the car.

"That maniac!" Jeff cried. "He could have killed us!"

Steph's heart was beating a mile a minute, and she said a quick prayer of gratitude for her husband's lightning-fast reflexes and excellent driving skills.

"But I've got him," said Jeff as he tapped the rearview

mirror where his dashcam was mounted. "He won't get away with this." And then he released a stream of vituperative in his native tongue that sounded very colorful indeed!

"Jeff, the baby," she said.

"Oops."

"God. It's been an eventful couple of days, hasn't it?"

"Let's hope things settle down now," said Jeff as he eased the car on the road again. "Maybe we can use our time at the winery to come up with a plan."

"What plan?"

"About the future? About my parents' offer?"

She smiled. "I thought we already decided that?"

"I guess I wanted to double-check," he said. Clearly he couldn't believe his luck.

"I could see your eyes light up and I knew you were going to say yes."

"I want to say yes," said Jeff. "Of course I want to say yes. But there's two of us in this marriage, and we have Zoe to think about also. We have to decide what's best for her as well."

"We're already raising her to be bilingual, and I'm sure Paris has great nurseries and great schools. And of course some of the best fashion houses."

"Not to mention some of the best banks," said Jeff with a smile.

"So I say we take a chance on Paris." Just like she had taken a chance on Jeff when he proposed to her, not coincidentally in a Paris restaurant on the banks of the Seine. It was, after all, where it had all begun for them, and it just felt right to go back there now, and build a new life for them.

"Your parents won't like it," Jeff said. "They want you here, close to them."

"I know," she said. She had always known this was going to be the difficulty when she married a Frenchman: if they lived in the States, his parents would be unhappy, and if they lived in France, her parents would. At the end of the day, they had to figure out what would make them happy. Where their future lay.

"It's not forever, though, is it?" he said. "Maybe we live in Paris for a few years, and then we move here again. Let's see where life takes us, mh?"

She dug her fingers through his curly dark hair. "You're so wise."

"Ha!" he said with a grin. "My hair isn't white enough to be wise."

"It might be white one day, like your dad's hair. But for now I'll settle for a wise man with gorgeous dark hair."

"My dad's hair has been white for a long time. It started turning grey when he was only thirty-five. So let's hope he won't go bald soon, because that would mean I'll be a bald wise man."

"I don't mind," she said. Though she had to admit she loved that he had a full head of hair she could slide her fingers through.

They arrived at the winery just in time for lunch, and as they drove along the long drive, past the wine fields her parents took such pride in and which had proved such a blessing both in terms of the financial reward but also the prestige and standing in the local community that success invariably brings.

They parked in the circular drive in front of the main house, and were warmly welcomed by Steph's parents Ian and Raimunda, and her brother Kevin. And as Raimunda fussed over Zoe, every inch the proud and doting grandmother, Steph wondered when she'd break the news to them of their imminent departure to Europe. She hoped they wouldn't be too heartbroken. Not so much over the absence of their daughter—they'd had to live with her absence since she left for college seven years ago—but their granddaughter, who they absolutely adored.

But when the time came to tell them about their plans, their reaction was more measured than she would have expected.

"If you think Paris is the best for you, then Paris it is," said her dad.

They were out on the patio, enjoying a meal as a family, just like they had done almost every weekend since Steph and Jeff had settled in New York.

"We can Skype," said her mom as she took a sip from her glass of wine—home brew, of course. "I mean, in this day and age distance doesn't matter anymore, does it? You can be on the other side of the world and still feel as if you're in the same room. Like we did when you were in Paris last time, remember? When you were in your kitchen trying to roast a duck and asked me how to go about it?"

Steph smiled at the memory. Mom was right. Distance had become relative. You could talk to the person, and sit down for dinner together while you were talking. And it was true: it was almost as if you were in the same room—though not really. And she could tell that even though Mom was putting on a brave face, she was going to miss her daughter something fierce, and her granddaughter even more.

CHAPTER 10

After lunch, Steph decided to go for a stroll. She had a lot on her mind, and needed time to process what had happened. In the space of just a few days her world had been turned upside down several times, and she felt as if she'd been through the wars. First they were going to move to LA, then that all fell apart, then she discovered someone had launched a slander campaign against her. Then the Paris job had popped up, then the offer had been rescinded again. And of course that whole business with Jeff's godmother had been the clincher. She still couldn't believe that the sweet old lady was gone. But more importantly that she had died believing that her treasured godson had married a woman who had proved an unfit mother and a drug and alcohol addict to boot. Such a tragedy. If only Evelyne had talked to Jeff. He could have told her it was all a web of lies.

She hoped the police would identify the person who was behind this attempt to destroy her future prospects. It must be someone with an intimate knowledge of her, though of course they could have found out a lot through her social media. Perhaps she should take Jeff's advice, and stop posting so much on Facebook. They'd both taken the decision when Zoe was born never to post her pictures anywhere or on any platform. You never knew who might see them—the world was full of weirdos, as the events of these last couple of days had amply shown.

At least there was the amazingly generous offer from David and Pauline now. They'd actually bought them an apartment in Paris. It must have cost a fortune, and she felt she hadn't properly thanked them. But then her mind had been a whirlwind of conflicting thoughts lately, as she had experienced a welter of emotions. So much so that she needed time to unwind, and what better place than the winery where she had spent such a happy time growing up?

She idly wandered through the fields, where the grapes were proudly growing on the vines. The sun was giving of its best, covering the world in a warm glow. And as she walked along, she felt her mood lift and her mind become more tranquil. Or at least as tranquil as could be expected under the circumstances.

"Steph!" suddenly a voice rang out behind her. "Hey, Steph!"

She immediately recognized the voice as belonging to Robbie Scunner. She turned and waved at the young man, who was the same age she was.

"Hey, Robbie," she said, happy to see him.

Robbie was the son of the winery foreman Larry Scunner, and her childhood sweetheart. They'd dated off and on for a couple of years when they were both in their teens, but nothing had ever come of it. She'd always considered Robbie more a dear friend than a boyfriend, and once she turned eighteen and left for fashion design school in Paris—her greatest wish come true—Robbie had disappeared from her orbit. And then when she met Jeff and eventually got married, Robbie had been relegated to a treasured but distant past. She still saw him when she visited her parents, of course, and she still appreciated his company, but no powerful emotions were involved—at least from her side. Robbie had seemed more reluctant to let go of the notion that they were meant to be together.

"Back so soon?" asked Robbie when he finally caught up with her. He was dressed in his customary attire of sturdy boots, jeans and a lumberjack shirt. Put a Stetson on his head and he would have the cowboy look down pat.

"I've come to say goodbye," said Steph as she shielded her eyes from the sun.

"I thought you weren't leaving for LA for another couple of weeks?"

"The LA thing fell through," she said, but didn't elaborate. "We're off to Paris instead."

His handsome face was marred by a sudden frown. "Paris again, huh?"

"Yeah, Paris again," she said. "So what's happening here?"

"Nothing much. Same old, same old," he said. She could have been mistaken but he suddenly seemed a little sullen. Probably the fact that she was leaving. She often had the impression he took it as a personal affront that she had left the winery to spread her wings elsewhere. In that sense he was of the same view as her parents, who would have loved nothing more than for her to become active in the family business. Running the winery together with her brother Kevin.

But the wine business didn't interest her. It never had. Fashion did. Even as a little girl she loved dressing up, and even though that's probably something a lot of girls have in common, and eventually grow out of, with her it had stuck.

"So how long will you be gone for this time?" he asked as he stared into the middle distance, refusing to meet her gaze.

The conversation had quickly turned awkward, the way it often did between them.

"I don't know, Robbie. It depends."

"I see. Well, I guess it's goodbye, then." He gave a curt nod and walked off.

"Robbie—don't be like that," she said at his retreating back. But she could see from the stiff way he moved that he was going to prove implacable again.

She sighed. Just what she needed. A quarrel with her longtime friend.

She had spoken too soon anyway. They probably weren't going to leave for Paris for another couple of weeks. Jeff's mom had told them that the Paris flat had to be completely remodeled, since the couple who sold it to them had lived there for more than fifty years, and were now moving into a retirement home. Pauline said the electricity and plumbing needed to be brought up to code so it could meet modern standards before Jeff and Steph could move in, and she wanted to put in a new kitchen and bathroom as well, which might take a couple of weeks.

And anyway Jeff would need to give notice at Capital First, which would also not happen overnight.

So she didn't know why she'd told Robbie this was goodbye. Maybe because she knew how he would react, and she wanted to get the awkwardness out of the way.

But as she resumed her stroll, Robbie and his hangups soon vanished from her mind, and she enjoyed the peace and quiet of the vineyard, which stretched around her for what seemed like miles in every direction. She'd miss this place. She'd miss the vastness of it—the tranquility. But that couldn't be helped. She would never have been happy if she stuck around—that much she knew. And now that new adventures awaited in the City of Light, her heart was at peace with her decision.

That night Steph was sound asleep in her old bedroom—though it didn't look anything like her old bedroom anymore since at some point her parents had decided to redecorate—when the sound of a crash awoke her.

She sat up with a jerk. Next to her, Jeff barely stirred.

For a moment she wondered if she was dreaming, but then decided that she had indeed heard a loud crash and the sound of broken glass. Almost as if a window had been smashed.

Unable to sleep unless she knew what was going on, she slipped from underneath the covers and moments later was in the corridor, listening intently. And there it was: another loud crash! This time it came from the end of the corridor, where a window looked out across the drive.

She hurried in the direction of the sound, and as she did, a door opened to her left, and her dad appeared.

"What's going on?" he asked, tying the sash of his velvet dressing gown.

"Someone is throwing rocks through the windows," she said.

"Christ," said her dad, and together they made for the window.

It was as she had surmised: two panes in the multi-pane window had been destroyed, rocks lying on the carpet amongst the shards of glass.

"Careful," said her dad as she bent down. "Don't cut yourself." Then he uttered a loud curse, and when she looked where he was pointing, she saw a person running away from the house. It was too dark to see who it was, but she could have sworn it was a man from the way he was moving.

"We have to call the police," she said immediately.

"Don't worry, I will," her dad assured her.

Behind them, soft steps alerted her of the presence of her mom, who was coming up the stairs.

"What's going on?" she asked. "What are you two doing up?"

To Steph's surprise, her mom was fully dressed. "Where did you come from?" she asked.

"I couldn't sleep so I went for a walk," said her mother, who shared a meaningful look with her husband before becoming aware of the broken glass. "Oh, my God, what happened!"

"Someone threw a couple of rocks through the window, that's what happened," said Steph's dad angrily. "We saw him running off just now."

"Yeah, Mom, you probably just missed him," said Steph.

"Oh, will you look at my nice table," said Mom, pointing to the pretty piecrust table which had been positioned in front of the window but was now covered in glass. One of the rocks must have hit it, for it had fallen over, taking down the ponytail palm which it had supported. "That used to belong to my aunt Mabel."

"No letter," said Steph's dad, who'd crouched down to examine the rocks.

"It's only in the movies that they wrap a letter around a rock and throw it through the window, Dad," said Steph. "And you better don't touch anything. The police will want to look for fingerprints on those rocks."

"Fat chance they'll find anything," Dad grumbled.

Suddenly Steph became aware that her brother was missing.

"Where's Kevin?"

"Sound asleep, probably," said Mom. "You know your brother. You can fire off a cannon next to him and he still won't wake up."

A door opened at the end of the corridor and a male figure stumbled out, looking sleepy and bleary-eyed. It was Jeff. "What's going on?" he asked, stifling a yawn.

"Someone is throwing rocks through the windows now," said Steph.

"Oh, no," he said as he joined them to assess the damage. "And here I thought you didn't have criminals in Hampton Cove."

"Well, you better think again," said Dad grimly. "And the worst criminal of all is that bastard Beniamino Kosinski!" And he actually shook his fist as he said this.

CHAPTER 11

Once again Odelia had been called upon to assist Stephanie Felfan in a matter of grave concern. This time a stone or stones had been thrown through a window of her family's residence where she was staying. And since her dad had called 911, we showed up on the Stewart family doorstep bright and early, this time accompanied by Chase, in his capacity as an officer of the law.

When we arrived, remnants of the incident were partially scattered across the drive, and when we followed Steph up the stairs to the third floor, more glass could be seen, and also the two stones or rocks that had caused all the damage.

"Why do people throw stones at other people's windows, Max?" asked Dooley, as we both studied the scene with some astonishment. Mostly Chase deals with murder and all manner of mayhem, but a knocked-out window was definitely a first.

"I'm not sure," I said. "To make a point, maybe?"

"What point could that be?"

And there he had me. What point could this nocturnal intruder possibly have wanted to make? He hadn't even left a note to state the reasoning behind his initiative, or made a phone call claiming responsibility, like terrorists do.

No, to be absolutely honest this stone business was as much a mystery to me as it obviously was to our humans.

Chase stood scratching his scalp, and Odelia stood looking dumbfounded.

"Oh, and one other thing," said Steph. "Jeff and I were almost driven off the road yesterday. I didn't tell my parents, since I don't want to alarm them, but Jeff got the license plate off the dashcam." And as she supplied the details to Chase, who gratefully jotted them down, she said, "My dad seems to think it's the Kosinskis, but I don't know. I've known them for years, and even though they're not exactly great neighbors, I don't think they'd do a thing like this. And besides, why would they? They have no reason to."

"Who are these Kosinskis?" asked Odelia.

"Beniamino Kosinski. He's the owner of the Kosinski Winery, along with his son Dominic. They're our closest neighbors, and also our competitors. Dad and Beniamino have never gotten along, but I doubt he'd start throwing stones through our windows. But I just thought I'd mention it, since Dad seems to feel very strongly about this."

"Beniamino Kosinski," said Odelia as she wrote this down on her tablet. "And son Dominic. Competing winery."

"There's some discussion as to who was here first," Steph explained. "The Stewarts or the Kosinskis. Both wineries were founded in the seventies, though neither can claim to have been the first on Long Island. The Hargraves founded that one, in 1973." And as she gave us a brief history of Hamptons wine, Chase called in the license plate number. When he received a reply, he was frowning.

"Guess who owns the car that almost drove you off the road yesterday," he said as he joined us again. "Edmundo Crowley."

Steph was obviously dumbfounded. "I knew it," she said finally, when she had recovered from the shock. "I knew he was behind this business with the slander. Both at WelBeQ and Sofie Fashion."

"Sofie Fashion?" asked Odelia.

"Oh, I haven't told you this yet, but there has been a new development," said Steph. "Or developments, plural. And I'm sure Crowley is behind both of them." And she proceeded to tell us about her latest job offer that hadn't gone through. All because someone had sent those same photographs to Sofie Fashion, a Paris fashion house that had offered Steph a job. And as if that wasn't bad enough, the same person had convinced Jeff's godmother that Steph was some kind of addict. As a consequence, the woman had drawn up a new will, cutting out her godson. And to add insult to injury, she had bequeathed her vast fortune to a dog shelter!

"A dog shelter," said Dooley, as appalled as I was. "Who in their right mind gives all of their money to a shelter for dogs? The woman must have been crazy."

"I'm sure she had her reasons," I said, not wanting to get sidetracked here. Though I have to say I agreed wholeheartedly with my friend.

"Now if she would have given her money to a cat shelter, that would be fine," Dooley continued. "But a dog shelter, Max! A shelter for dogs!"

"I know what a dog shelter is, Dooley," I said. "And truth be told, there must be a lot of dogs in Paris who could use the benefit of a shelter." As we all know, cats are perfectly capable of taking care of themselves, but the same cannot be said about dogs, who always seem to need a human to take care of them. "So we shouldn't judge Jeff's godmother too harshly," I finished my assertions.

"I guess you're right," said my friend. "Dogs need shelters.

Cats don't. So maybe this woman, even if she wasn't right in the head, did the right thing."

Not according to Jeff, though. That stalwart young man had joined us, and when he heard that the same person was responsible for almost driving them off the road, and also thwarting his wife's chances at landing her dream job, he uttered a few choice curse words. At least I thought that was what they were. I don't speak French, you see, and the young man cursed exclusively in his native tongue. The only thing I understood was the word 'merde,' which means poo.

"What's *espèce de merde?*" asked Dooley, who had been listening attentively.

"I'm not sure about *espèce*, but *merde* means poo," I said. We once spent a couple of days in Paris, and I'd picked up a few words here and there from a nice French cat named Marion.

Odelia must have overheard our conversation, for she smiled and bent down, and whispered into my ear, "*Espèce* means piece."

"So basically he's calling Edmundo a piece of poo?" asked Dooley.

"Something like that," I said. Obviously Jeff was very upset. And when he showed us the footage from his dashcam, I can't say I blamed him. This Edmundo character could have killed them. Talk about road rage.

"He's a very angry young man," said Odelia, and that was putting it mildly.

"We'll go and have a chat with him," Chase assured the young couple.

"Please do," said Steph. "I filed a complaint with the NYPD, just like you said, but I don't think they took me seriously. They didn't seem to think it was important enough for them to bother with."

"I know some people in the department," said Chase, who

had been an NYPD cop himself before moving to Hampton Cove. "I'll talk to the person in charge of the investigation and see if I can't get them to speed things up a little."

"Thanks," said Steph gratefully. "I just want this to stop, you know."

"Of course. This kind of behavior simply cannot be tolerated."

Two more men had joined us. Steph introduced them as Larry and Robbie Scunner, father and son. Larry was the foreman at the winery, and basically in charge of the practical ins and outs of running the place, alongside Ian Stewart. And Robbie pretty much handled any job that needed doing. Larry had been in the Stewarts' employ since the late nineties, and had even worked for Steph's grandfather for a while, back when he was in charge of the place.

"Bad business," said Larry, shaking his head. He was a rugged-looking man, and like his son dressed in jeans and a check shirt. His skin was the consistency of leather, and even though he wore a baseball cap, clearly he hadn't been adhering to the generally accepted advice to liberally use sunscreen when out and about, and to stay out of the sun and seek shade when your shadow is shorter than you.

His son Robbie was also very tan, and from the occasional glances he stole at Steph, I had the impression his concern was mainly centered around her.

"Do you think Beniamino could be behind this?" asked Steph. "It's just that my dad seems to think so."

"I doubt it," said Larry. "We may not always see eye to eye, but there's never been any violence. And Ben has absolutely no reason to resort to violence now. No, whatever this is, I'm sure it's got nothing to do with the Kosinskis."

"Is it true you were almost driven off the road yesterday?" asked Robbie now.

Steph nodded.

"Why didn't you tell me?" said Robbie, who suddenly seemed worked up for some reason. "Your dad tells me you could have been killed!"

"Dad told you that? But I haven't said anything. I didn't want him and Mom to worry."

"I told them," said Jeff. "After the incident with the window, I thought they should know. I also told them about the slander campaign and everything."

Steph clearly didn't agree with her husband in this matter, for she shook her head. Maybe she had a point. No reason to get her parents all worked up.

Suddenly Robbie Scunner turned on Steph's husband. "This is your fault," he said, stabbing the Frenchman in the chest with his finger. "It's your responsibility to take care of Stephanie, and clearly you're not up to the job, buddy!"

"Say that again and I will beat you!" said Jeff, balling his fists.

"Bring it on!" Robbie said, and the two men started pushing and shoving each other in some kind of weird tussle. The air was suddenly filled with testosterone, and at any moment they could start slugging it out like two schoolyard scrappers.

"Stop it, you two!" said Steph as she tried to come between the men. But before she could, Chase had stepped forward, and so had Larry. And while Larry held his son back, Chase provided the same service to Jeff. At this point Jeff was talking about *merde* again, and coincidentally or not Robbie used the exact same expression but in English. Clearly these men did not like each other very much.

"Walk away, son," said Larry in a deep, booming voice. "Now!"

"If something happens to her, it's on your head!" Robbie yelled, and then followed his dad's advice and did indeed walk away.

"Now they were both talking about pieces of *merde*, Max," said Dooley.

"Well observed, Dooley," I said. "It appears to be a popular expression on both sides of the Atlantic."

"What's wrong with you!" Steph cried. She had turned to her husband, and was clearly unhappy with the way he had reacted to the situation.

"He insulted me!" said the young man.

"So? That doesn't mean you have to respond in kind."

"Oh, whatever," said Jeff with a throwaway gesture, and also walked off.

"What's the deal with those two?" asked Chase.

Larry sighed, expressing a father's frustration. "Robbie worries about Steph's wellbeing, and when something like this happens, he feels Jeff isn't doing a good enough job at protecting her."

"It wasn't Jeff's fault that this maniac tried to drive us off the road," said Steph. "And in fact he probably saved our lives." She was darting a concerned look in the direction her husband had stalked off. "I better go and talk to him," she said finally, and followed the young man to wherever he'd gone.

"The thing is," said Larry, "and I don't think I'm betraying any confidences here, that Robbie and Steph used to be an item. This was a long time ago, and it ended when Steph went off to Paris for her fashion school. Then she met Jeff and they moved in together in Jeff's flat in Paris, and a year later they got married. Big wedding here at the winery. And Robbie—well, I guess he took it pretty hard."

"He's still in love with Steph," said Odelia.

"Yeah, I guess he is. He'll never admit it, though. Every time I try to talk about it, he shuts me down. But I think he feels that Steph was the one for him, and for a long time it looked as if they'd end up together. So the fact that she went and married Jeff must have stung. See, the thing is that my wife handled this kind of stuff a lot better than I ever could. Wendy died ten years ago, and we both took it hard. Robbie is a great kid, but he doesn't exactly wear his heart on his sleeve. And neither do I. His mom, she could get him to open up. But I never could."

We watched through the window as Robbie furiously walked away, crunching gravel underfoot. His dad sighed. His heart was clearly bleeding for his son.

CHAPTER 12

It didn't take long for Chase to find out where Edmundo Crowley could be found. As it happens the aspiring fashion designer was staying at the Star Hotel, which is located in the heart of Hampton Cove. He admitted as much to Chase, when he called him on the number Odelia had for him. And so the detecting duo decided to pay a visit to the young man, accompanied by yours truly and Dooley.

When Chase knocked on the door of his hotel room, it was opened by a very nervous-looking Edmundo. He was also a lot paler than the last time we saw him in his Brooklyn apartment. "Hello, officer," he said. "Mrs. Kingsley." He gave Dooley and me a sort of blank look, but awarded us no greeting, kindly or otherwise. Instead he turned around, expecting us to follow him into the room.

"You probably know why we're here," said Chase.

"Actually I don't," said Edmundo as he stood around awkwardly. It's never enjoyable when the police come knocking on your door, and since they don't teach the social niceties to be observed in such a contingency at school, it's always interesting to see how different people react in quite different ways.

Edmundo clearly didn't know what to do with himself. He folded his arms across his chest first, then clasped them behind his back, and finally decided to take a seat at a table near the window, offering the accompanying chairs to his present company.

And while Odelia accepted the offered seat, Chase remained standing, and towering over the distinctly ill-at-ease designer.

"Yesterday at eleven hundred hours you very nearly caused a collision on I-495 through the negligent operation of your vehicle," Chase began, switching to the lingo of his trade. "thereby endangering the safety of a fellow driver. This is called reckless driving and is illegal, Mr. Crowley."

"But I didn't—I never—I mean I wasn't…"

"You were filmed by the dashcam of the driver who was a victim of your illegal maneuver, Mr. Crowley. Your license plate is KDP-2022?"

"Y-yes, it is," said Crowley, breaking out into a sweat.

"Can I ask what you are doing in Hampton Cove, sir?"

"I-I'm here as a tourist. Just-just for the beach."

"Is that so?" said Chase, directing a stern look at the man, who was wilting before our eyes.

"S-swimming," he stammered weakly. "I like swimming."

"Isn't it so that for whatever reason you have decided to start a personal vendetta against Stephanie Felfan and her husband Jeff? A personal vendetta that has resulted in a campaign of slanderous photographs and messages sent to Mrs. Felfan's potential employers, dissuading them from offering her employment? And isn't it so, Mr. Crowley," said Chase, raising his voice when Crowley tried to voice a meek protest, "that destroying Mrs. Felfan's career opportunities wasn't enough for you, so you decided to follow her to

Hampton Cove and try to drive the car she was traveling in off the road? And I put it to you, sir!" Chase said, his voice reverberating through the room like a carnival barker. "That last night at oh two hundred hours you threw no less than two rocks through a window at the Stewart residence, where Mrs. Felfan and her family are currently staying!"

"I didn't throw no stones!" said the man, who looked more miserable than ever. Guilt was clearly written across his features, and denial was futile, but he wasn't giving up without a fight. "Okay, so I may have cut off her car, but I didn't even know she was in it—you have to believe me. Just my rotten luck, I guess. And I definitely did not throw any stones or send any photographs or messages. I already told Mrs. Kingsley I had nothing to do with any of that. I wouldn't even know how to doctor pictures. And besides, why would I? I'm not that kind of guy—you have to believe me. I'm simply not!"

"All right, all right, settle down," said Chase, holding out a big slab of a hand.

"Chase would have made a great traffic cop," said Dooley admiringly. "With big strong hands like that he could stop any car or truck dead in its tracks."

He was certainly stopping Edmundo dead in his tracks, for the young man swallowed whatever else he had planned to say and closed his mouth. He was staring up at the burly cop with a scared look, as if afraid he was going to hit him.

"Look, you just can't go around driving like a maniac, son," said Chase, switching gears and adopting a more fatherly tone. "Or throwing stones through people's windows, just because they applied for the same job you did."

"But I didn't, I swear!" the man bleated weakly.

"So you're actually going to sit there and tell me that you coming to Hampton Cove, of all places, is just a coincidence?"

"It is, I'm telling you!"

"You're a lousy liar, Crowley," Chase grunted.

"But I'm telling you the truth," he said softly. He had sort of collapsed in on himself, and was sitting slumped in his chair, a miserable pile of human being.

"You're lucky no one got hurt this time," Chase grumbled. And he proceeded to give the designer a lecture on respect for other people's property and the proper way to behave in traffic.

"Is he going to arrest him?" asked Dooley.

"I doubt it," I said. "No one actually got hurt in that driving incident, and there's no evidence linking him to the broken window, so that's going to be hard to prove. And as far as the smear campaign against Steph is concerned, that incident is being handled by the NYPD as a separate investigation."

"It's possible he's telling the truth. A lot of people come to Hampton Cove just to enjoy some fun time at the beach. And he did say how much he likes to swim."

"It's too much of a coincidence," I said, shaking my head. "The same person who competed with Steph for that job ends up in the same place at the same time, and even manages to cut her off while traveling in the same direction? He's up to something, that's for sure." But whatever Edmundo had in mind for whatever reason would hopefully end now. Chase's little speech would go a long way toward accomplishing that. And if the aspiring designer knew what was good for him, he'd stop now.

Though it would have been good to know what had possessed the guy to do a thing like that. One thing was for sure: it wasn't because he liked swimming.

CHAPTER 13

While Chase returned to the office to type up his report, and Odelia returned to her office to type up her article, Dooley and I decided to pay a visit to Kingman. We hadn't forgotten about the equally important task we'd taken upon ourselves of trying to locate Shanille, and I thought that maybe Kingman would know more. The big cat proudly carries the proverbial badge of best-informed feline in Hampton Cove, and now was his chance to prove it.

Unfortunately when we arrived, it soon became clear that he had no idea about our missing conductor's whereabouts either.

"It's a mystery, fellas!" he cried, throwing up his paws in despair.

Harriet and Brutus had also had the same idea I'd had, and so the five of us organized an impromptu brainstorming session, trying to come up with some kind of plan. It's always important to have a plan, you see, before you go off on some mission. James Bond always has a plan before he tries to save the world from yet another bomb-building evil genius located in some weirdly remote spot on the globe. But at least James gets his plans from his superiors, who are identified not by their names but by a letter. Like M. Or Q. Or maybe even Z.

"Okay, I suggest we start by interviewing anyone who could have seen Shanille before she disappeared," said Harriet, quickly taking control of the meeting.

"But humans can't understand us," Dooley pointed out. "So we can't talk to them."

"Who said anything about talking to humans? We're going to talk to pets, Dooley. Because wherever humans are, there will always be pets—and plenty of them, too. So all we need to do is talk to all the pets who live in the neighborhood. Someone is bound to have seen something. A car drive off with Father Reilly behind the wheel. Or a camper van parked in front of the rectory. Anything."

"So you agree with me that Father Reilly is on vacation and took Shanille along?" I asked.

"At this point it's my main line of inquiry," Harriet confirmed. "The other possibility is simply too horrendous to even contemplate."

"Alien abduction?" Dooley ventured.

"Mischief," Harriet countered.

"What do you mean?"

"Do I have to spell it out to you?"

"Yes, please," he said happily.

Harriet rolled her eyes, but then Brutus beat her to the punch. "What Harriet means is that something could have happened to Father Reilly. Something bad."

"Like bad breath?" asked Dooley. "Or maybe he ate a bad apple?"

"No, Dooley," said Brutus, adopting a grave tone. "More like a bad person did something bad to him."

They were right. It was a possibility I didn't like to entertain. Nevertheless, it was feasible, of course, that some gangster or gangsters had gained access to the rectory and had abducted the priest and his cat for monetary gain. Or they could still be in there, victims of what is generally referred to as a home invasion. But then a thought occurred to me. "Why would anyone target a priest?" I asked. "I mean, Father Reilly isn't a bank manager, or the CEO of a Fortune 500 company. He's not rich, and he doesn't have rich relatives willing to pay through the nose."

"You don't know that, Max," said Harriet. "Father Reilly may be a dark horse."

"He doesn't look like a horse," said Dooley. "Though he does make a sound like a horse sometimes, when someone tells him a funny joke."

Father Reilly did have a very pronounced laugh, but that still didn't make him a horse. But I saw what Harriet meant. "You mean he might have some money tucked away somewhere."

"Money or valuables," said Harriet. "And these crooks could have found out and decided to hold him for ransom until he agrees to hand over his fortune."

"I don't think Father Reilly is rich," said Kingman, adding his two cents to the discussion. "If he were, he wouldn't be a small-town priest. He'd be a bishop by now, or a cardinal, or even the Pope. He wouldn't stick around here."

"He would, because he's an honorable man," Harriet argued. "The way I see it," she said, and got that faraway look in her eyes she often gets when she's about to tell a long story, "is that Francis Reilly comes from a long line of very rich men."

"Why not women?" asked Dooley. "Women can be rich."

"Shush, Dooley," said Harriet. "I'm talking."

That, she most certainly was.

"So he comes from a long line of European princes—the Reilly's. Or maybe a long line of Irish noblemen. At any rate, his family is rich beyond measure. But young Francis understands that money isn't everything, and so he tells his mommy and daddy that he wants to be a priest. And even though they had hoped for him to become the next Bill Gates or the next Jeff Bezos, they support the path he's chosen."

"I didn't know Bill Gates and Jeff Bezos were Irish?" said Dooley.

"Dooley, shush. So Mommy and Daddy Reilly give young Francis their blessing, but the moment he starts priest school—"

"I think you'll find it's called a seminary," I interjected, risking Harriet's ire for interrupting her story.

"Fine. Seminary. Whatever," she said with the sigh of a much-put-upon cat. "So Francis Reilly goes to the seminary when the news arrives that his parents have both passed away."

"Poor Father Reilly!" Dooley cried.

"No, rich Father Reilly, for he inherits the entire family fortune. So now he's rich, but he's also a priest. So what does he do?"

"He gives all his money to the dog shelter," said Dooley.

"What?! Are you nuts? Who in their right mind gives money to a dog shelter!"

"Our thoughts exactly," I said with satisfaction.

"No, he keeps the money for a rainy day, because he knows that one day he will be a priest no more. One day he'll reach the ripe old age of sixty-five and need his nice little nest egg to retire on. So he invests his money in a balanced investment portfolio consisting of US Treasury bonds and a high-yield savings account and goes about his priestly business… until the bad men come knocking!"

Her story had us all on the tips of our toes. Though I saw one minor flaw. "Priests don't actually retire at sixty-five," I said. "At least not like the rest of us."

"Cats don't retire either, Max," said Kingman with a grin.

"So when do priests retire?" asked Harriet with a frown.

"It depends on the diocese," I said.

"The dio-what?"

"It's the district a priest is assigned to. Some retire at seventy, others at seventy-five. Like I said, it all depends on the diocese."

"Seventy-five!" Dooley said. "That's a long time to wait for retirement."

"That's it then!" Harriet cried. "Father Reilly must have been tired of waiting for his retirement, so he's gone in search of a better diocese!"

"You're forgetting that Father Reilly was going to leave the church so he could marry Marigold," I said. "In which case he doesn't have to change dioceses."

"Okay, so maybe he took Marigold to Florida for a vacation," said Harriet with a shrug. "And Shanille tagged along, wanting to work on her tan."

"Of course she did," Kingman scoffed. "Because Shanille is the kind of cat who likes to work on her tan!"

"Fine. If you have a better idea of what happened, let's hear it," said Harriet.

But Kingman didn't have a better idea, and neither did any of us.

"So all in favor of doing things my way?" said Harriet.

And since we all know that Harriet always gets her way, we dutifully stuck our paws in the air. Looked like the house-to-house canvass was on. Or rather: the pet-to-pet canvass.

CHAPTER 14

Tex was staring before him with what are often termed unseeing eyes. He was between patients at the moment, and suddenly found himself in want of a pick-me-up. His last patient had been Ida Baumgartner, and the woman had given him a lot of grief by demanding that he visit her at home from now on, insisting that she was a sick woman—too sick to make the trip to the office for her appointments. He couldn't very well point out she wasn't really all that sick—and that there were actual sick people who needed his advice a lot more than she did.

He was feeling sandbagged, which was the customary sensation associated with a visit from that formidable woman. Which is why he was in need of a pick-me-up.

Absentmindedly he opened the bottom drawer of his desk, and reached for the hip flask he kept there for emergencies—and Ida's visits. And he'd just unscrewed the cap and put the little metal bottle to his lips when suddenly the door of the office flew open and Vesta burst in.

"Don't do it!" she cried, and before he could stop her, had slapped the flask from his grasp, causing it to describe a perfect arc across the office, bounce off the examination table and hit the wall with a dull thwack, causing alcohol to spill all over the floor.

"What did you do that for!" he said, appalled by this spillage of perfectly good whiskey. Immediately the smell filled his nostrils, and he sniffed with relish.

"Don't worry, buddy," said Vesta, patting his shoulder. "I've got your back."

Belatedly he remembered Vesta was his sponsor now, and he was hers. He closed his eyes. "Oh, God."

"I know, I know. It's tough, but we have to power through, Tex. I've been reading up on this twelve-step business and the first few weeks are the hardest. After that it's going to be a breeze. So you just hang in there, you hear me?" She eyed him keenly. "Speaking of the twelve steps, I've got one for you. I once destroyed all of your underwear. There, I've said it. Now it's your turn."

"What are you talking about?!" he said, feeling the strain more keenly by the second.

"Step eight! I made a list of all the people I've harmed, and I'm willing to make amends to them. So this is me making amends to you."

"I see. But what does my underwear have to do with the twelve steps, pray tell?"

"You're going to laugh," she said, and produced a sort of high-pitched giggle, "but I once read that some men have trouble conceiving because their underwear is too tight. Squeezes the male undercarriage and… well, you know more about the human anatomy than me. Cuts off the blood supply or the oxygen to the male machinery or whatever. So when you and Marge had been married a year, and still no baby, I figured you were strapping your stuff in too tight, and so one morning I snuck into your bedroom and removed all of your underwear and destroyed it. I figured I'd get you to go commando, like the Scots, at least until you got yourself a new set. And I was right! One month later Marge gave me the good news." She winked at him. "Listen to your dear old mom, buddy. She knows."

He would have reminded her that she was not his mom, but there was no point. And besides, he was experiencing a spell of weakness. Vesta must have noticed, too, for she studied him closely, then said, "You're showing all the symptoms of alcohol withdrawal, Tex. You need to talk to people. Open up."

"I don't think…"

But before he could stop her, she was hugging him to her chest, and patting his hair. "There, there," she murmured soothingly. "Vesta's here. Everything's fine."

"Oh, sweet Jesus," he muttered brokenly.

༄

Steph was rocking Zoe on her lap, and singing softly. The baby had just been fed, and was ready for beddy-bye. They were on the patio, enjoying some quiet time. Her mom and dad were off doing whatever they did for the winery, and so was her brother. And Jeff was upstairs getting ready to go out. He came out of the house now, looking very smart in a polo shirt and fashionable white jeans. With his sunglasses and a light pink pastel sweater draped across his shoulders he could have walked straight out of a Ralph Lauren commercial.

"Are you sure you want to do this?" she asked.

"Of course. It's going to be a chance to meet outside work, in a casual setting."

Jeff was meeting a work colleague with whom he'd never seen eye to eye from day one. Clive Balcerak came from a long line of bankers, and for some reason that Jeff had never been able to understand, had taken an instant dislike to Jeff from the moment the latter had joined the team. Somehow he felt threatened by Jeff, seeing in him a competitor and not a colleague. It had resulted in some petty sniping, some undermining of Jeff's authority, accusing him of all kinds of things and generally making an absolute nuisance of himself.

And now all of a sudden, and quite out of the blue, Clive had sent him a message and suggested they meet in town. It so happened that Clive's family owned a house in Hampton Cove, and he must have heard that Jeff's in-laws owned the well-known Stewart Winery.

"I think he wants to call a truce," said Jeff as he kissed his wife gently on the lips. "He must have finally seen the error of his ways."

"Or maybe someone at the bank told him this nonsense has to stop."

"Yeah, that's also a possibility," Jeff admitted.

After enduring Clive's pestering for a year, Jeff had finally mentioned his annoyance with the man's behavior during his quarterly performance review. Chances were that Jeff's boss had talked to Clive, and told him enough was enough. And so now Clive was ready to offer his colleague an olive branch.

"I think it'll be great for both of us," said Jeff. "Especially with me leaving soon, it will be nice to depart as friends, and not this weird enmity that has sprung up."

"You're right," said Steph. "Of course you're right. But if he starts accusing you of all kinds of stuff, make sure you record the conversation, you hear?"

"I will," said Jeff as he pressed a kiss to Zoe's little head. "See you later."

And as she watched him leave, suddenly she got a strange sort of premonition. For a moment she wondered if she shouldn't tell him not to go. But then she dismissed the thought. She was just being silly. This business with the road rage and the broken window was threatening to make her paranoid. And she couldn't have that. She wouldn't allow this man Crowley to affect her like that. It would mean he had won, and she wasn't going to let the little creep do that to her.

CHAPTER 15

*I*t was late afternoon when the call came. Steph had just been updating her resume and looking at the website of one of the big Paris fashion houses for job openings, when her phone chimed. As she glanced at the display, she saw that Odelia Kingsley was trying to reach her. Having grown fond of the soft-spoken and kind-hearted reporter, she picked up with a pleasant, "Hey, Odelia. What's up?"

But as she listened, terror gripped her heart. "It's Jeff. Something has happened."

"What?" she said, her voice sounding strained to her own ears. And even before Odelia spoke the words, she knew what she was going to say. "I'm afraid he's dead."

૭૭

*D*ooley and I had planned to accompany Harriet and Brutus on their house-to-house in search of clues to what had happened to Shanille, but as we got ready to move out, Odelia's car suddenly swerved and came screeching to a halt right in front of the General Store. She opened the passenger door and yelled, "Max and Dooley! Get in the car now!"

So of course we did as we were told.

"I hope we're not in any trouble," said Dooley nervously. "Did you raid the fridge, Max?"

"No, I did not," I said. "And I resent the accusation, Dooley."

"Oh, but I didn't mean it like that," said my friend. "It's just that you get hungry, and when your bowl is empty, and so are all the other bowls, you get cranky. It's because you have low blood sugar, Max. And when you have low blood sugar you need to eat at regular intervals otherwise you get cranky. Like you are right now."

"I'm not cranky!" I said, though of course then I understood that I actually was cranky. I guess I'm not used to being kidnapped by my own human in broad daylight! But then she proceeded to explain what was actually going on.

"There's been a murder," she said curtly. "It's Jeff Felfan."

"Steph's Jeff?" said Dooley. "Oh, no!"

"Oh, yes. And what's even worse—"

"How can anything be worse than murder!" Dooley cried.

"He was found next to a prostitute, who's also been murdered."

"A prostitute? Jeff?" I said with a frown. "That doesn't sound like him."

"No, it doesn't, does it?" said Odelia. "Which is why I didn't tell Steph when I called her just now." She shook her head. "I liked Jeff, I really did. Steph is going to be devastated."

We rode on in silence, though I could tell that Dooley was bursting at the seams to talk. Finally he couldn't hold it in anymore. "But Jeff was so nice!"

"Nice people get murdered, too, Dooley," said Odelia as she gripped the wheel a little tighter. "Unfortunately."

"It must be Edmundo. First he tried to drive Jeff's car off the road, then he threw those rocks through the window, and now he's gone and murdered the poor man!"

"Let's just wait and see what actually happened before we jump to any conclusions," I suggested.

The flat where Jeff's body had been discovered was located near the canal lock on McMillan Street. It wasn't a pleasant neighborhood, but not all that unpleasant either, since Hampton Cove doesn't really have bad neighborhoods. Not anymore, that is.

The street had been temporarily cordoned off, and plenty of police officers were present, talking to neighbors and doing a house-to-house, just like the one Harriet and Brutus were presently engaged in.

Abe Cornwall's car stood parked in front of the building, and when we arrived on the third floor, the coroner was already busy examining the body. Or bodies.

Chase was also there, having arrived before we did.

"So what do we have, Abe?" he asked, nodding a greeting at his wife and her feline escort.

"Both dead," said the coroner matter-of-factly. "Both shot at close range. Possibly with the gun over there."

He was pointing to the gun that was in the hand of a woman of slim build, who was dressed in a red dress that was far too revealing for a casual afternoon meeting. It looked more like the kind of dress one would wear to a party. Next to her on the bed, Jeff was lying, the two side by side as if they were peacefully sleeping.

"Murder-suicide?" asked Chase.

"Possibly," Abe said. "We'll have to check to see if they both died from shots fired from the same gun—ballistics will tell us—but the scenario is a possibility."

"They met up for an afternoon tryst, she shot him, then she shot herself," said Chase. He shook his head. "Sad business. And both still so young."

Abe cut him a curious glance. "You're becoming lyrical in your old age, detective. Maybe you should write poetry. Something to fill your evenings."

"Thanks for the suggestion, Abe, but I think I'll pass," said Chase dryly.

"Who found her?" asked Odelia.

"In the kitchen," said Abe, and jerked his thumb in that direction.

When we followed the coroner's instructions, we found a blond-haired woman being kept company by a police officer. The woman answered to the name Hailey Harper, and was the roommate of the female victim, who was called Cipriana Cilke. And as far as the officer Odelia and Chase talked to knew, Hailey was also in the same profession, and had shared the flat with her.

Chase and Odelia took a seat at the kitchen table. Obviously Hailey Harper was greatly distressed by the news of her friend's death, and so Odelia asked if it was all right if they asked her a couple of questions. The woman blew her nose and nodded. Her face was red and puffy and her eyes even redder and puffier. Her blond hair was almost white, and I had the impression it wasn't her natural color since her eyebrows were a velvety black.

"I don't understand," said Miss Harper. "She said she had a client, but I know most of her clients and I've never seen this person before. He must have been new."

"You don't think Cipriana knew Jeff Felfan?" asked Chase.

"Is that his name? No, I'm sure I've never seen him and neither had Cipriana. She was my best friend. We had no secrets from each other. I knew all of her clients and she knew all of mine."

"You work alone here?" asked Odelia. "I mean you don't have a, um…"

"Pimp? No, we work without a pimp," said Hailey. She shook her head. "I don't understand. She was fine when I left her."

"When did you leave?"

"Quarter to two. Cipriana's client was arriving at three so I had time to do some shopping and get back here before he arrived. But when I got back…" She welled up. "I found her… like that!"

"Did you know if Cipriana owned a gun?" asked Chase. He held out a plastic evidence bag containing the gun in question. "This gun, to be precise?"

Hailey stared at the gun. "Is that what he used to…"

"Actually we think it was the other way around," said Chase. "She shot Mr. Felfan first before she turned the gun on herself."

But Hailey shook her head adamantly. "Never! She would never do that. She was happy. She was going to leave the business and have a baby."

"She was pregnant?"

"No, but she had a boyfriend, and she wanted to start a family with him."

"Who is he, this boyfriend?" asked Chase, and wrote down the name she gave him, and the address. "So the gun? Was it hers?"

"No way. Cipriana didn't own a gun. She hated guns, and so do I."

"You're sure? Maybe she got it to protect herself against difficult clients?"

"Absolutely not. It's the whole reason we decided to share this flat, and why we never left the other person alone with a client. I mean, not that we were in the room with them, but we made sure we were in the same apartment, just in case."

"So no gun," said Chase, processing this information. "And you're sure Cipriana had never seen Jeff Felfan before."

"Absolutely. I would know if she had. Like I said, we shared everything and kept no secrets from each other." She broke down at this point, and wailed, "What am I going to do now that she's gone!"

It didn't seem advisable to go on, and so Chase ended the interview, with the caveat that he might need to speak to Hailey again at a later stage.

"Odd, isn't it, Max?" said Dooley. "This Cipriana woman had never met Jeff before in her life, and yet she shot him and then killed herself. Now why would she go and do a thing like that?"

"Unless she didn't," I said thoughtfully. "And in actual fact someone else killed them both and then staged the scene to make it look like a murder-suicide."

"Steph isn't going to be happy when she discovers that her husband was seeing a prostitute," said Dooley. "Unless they had an arrangement, of course."

I smiled at my friend. "What do you know about marital arrangements, Dooley?"

"It was all over General Hospital last week. Doctor Jake was caught having an affair with one of the nurses, only his wife knew all about it, and was having an affair with the plumber. Turns out that's the kind of arrangement they had to keep things interesting." He frowned. "Though Gran said only trouble could come from this, and she was right. In the next episode Doctor Jake's wife said she wanted a divorce on the grounds of extreme cruelty and inhuman treatment. Turns out Doctor Jake's nurse was his wife's younger sister, and she didn't like that."

"No, I can see how that would break the terms of the arrangement," I said. It gave me pause, though. If Dooley was right, and the Felfans had an arrangement whereby they could cheat, perhaps Jeff's visit to a prostitute was a common thing in their marriage. We would have to speak to Steph, of course, and I could already foresee that the conversation would be fraught with a touch of awkwardness.

CHAPTER 16

Steph had arrived at the scene, and one look at her was enough to tell us she was heartbroken by the news. So even though they might have had an arrangement, clearly it didn't include one of the spouses being shot to death by their casual partner.

Odelia and Chase talked to Steph in the flat's living room, which was located at the front of the building, and looked out across the street. It was modestly appointed, with plenty of IKEA furniture in bright and pleasant colors, and I could tell that Hailey and Cipriana had enjoyed each other's company from the framed pictures of the two of them together, mugging for the camera and goofing around.

"Is that her?" asked a teary-eyed Steph, studying one of the pictures.

"No, that's the roommate," said Odelia. She pointed to a picture that showed Cipriana, her glorious red hair aflame by the rays of a setting sun, her freckled face smiling as she held a small puppy in her arms.

I looked around for a sign of the puppy, but saw nor

smelled a canine presence anywhere. Too bad. If a dog had been there, he might have proved a good witness.

"I don't understand," said Steph. "He said he was meeting a work colleague. So how did he end up here?"

"Who was the work colleague?" asked Chase dutifully.

"Um, Clive Balcerak. He works in the same department, but never got on with Jeff. So when he sent a message saying he happened to be in town, and asked to meet for a chat, Jeff thought it was a great idea."

"Where was Jeff supposed to meet Clive?"

"I have no idea. You can check his phone." She paced up and down the room. "So you're telling me this woman shot Jeff and then she shot herself? But why?"

"There's no easy way for me to say this, Steph," said Odelia, "so I'm just going to come out and say it. Cipriana Cilke was a prostitute. She and Hailey both. This flat is where they invited men—paying customers. And the room where Jeff and Cipriana were found was the room where she did her... well, her business."

Steph blinked as she processed this information. "Oh, wow," she said quietly. "I did not see that coming." But then she frowned. "Wait—are you telling me Jeff was here to have sex with this woman? No way, Odelia. Absolutely no way. Don't you think I'd know if my husband was having sex with another woman? I would."

"She wasn't Jeff's girlfriend, Steph. She was a woman men paid to have sex with."

"Still..." She bit her lower lip as she thought about this. But then shook her head. "Uh-uh. No. Just no. Jeff would never do something like that. He wasn't the kind of man who visits prostitutes. And besides, he was meeting Clive Balcerak."

"It's possible that Jeff used his colleague as an excuse to come here?"

Steph hesitated, then said in a small voice, "You know what? I don't know. I mean, I don't think he would do a thing like that, but I just don't know. It's true that these last couple of months have been difficult for us. I mean..." She made a tentative motion with her hand as she bit back tears. "Ever since Zoe was born... Well, you know how it is. Nothing much was happening in the bedroom department. So maybe Jeff was unhappy about that. And maybe he had certain... needs that weren't being met. Needs that I couldn't meet. I mean, men are different than women. Some men see sex as sport. Like going to the gym."

"Yes, I know," said Odelia quietly.

"But Jeff wasn't like that. He simply wasn't. He was a gentle, beautiful soul. The most wonderful man I ever met. And he was the father of our beautiful little girl. Who will have to grow up without a father now, all because of this..." She gestured to the picture of the red-haired prostitute. "Why? Why did she have to do this?"

"We don't know," said Odelia. "But I promise you we will find out."

"Was she depressed or something? Was she having mental issues?"

"It's too soon to tell. But the moment we know more, we'll tell you."

"Please do. Cause I'm having a really hard time understanding why this happened, you know. It's all so... random. So senseless."

There was nothing they could say to that, so neither spoke.

"Odelia should ask Steph about the arrangement," said Dooley.

Odelia must have heard, for she cleared her throat. "You and Jeff, you didn't happen to have some kind of arrangement, did you?" she asked. "I mean, some couples do, you know."

"An open marriage, you mean? No, we most certainly did not have an open marriage. Unless Jeff had decided he wanted one and failed to inform me. But then that wouldn't exactly constitute an open marriage now would it? That would simply be called cheating." She looked away for a moment. "Can I see him?"

"I don't think that's a good idea," said Odelia, alarmed.

"But I want to. I want to see him. I want to say goodbye to my husband."

"Not right now," said Chase. "The crime scene people are busy collecting evidence and trying to find out what happened, exactly. But you will be able to see him soon, I promise."

That seemed to satisfy her, for she nodded. But then before we knew what was happening, suddenly she was off in the direction of the bedroom. And before anyone could stop her, she was standing on the threshold, staring at the ghastly scene. Abe Cornwall looked up with a touch of annoyance. He hated to be disturbed when he was working. But he must have sensed that Steph wasn't a cop, for he said kindly, "Let's get you out of here, shall we, sweetheart?"

And quite willingly Steph allowed Odelia to take her by the arm, and lead her from the room. She held on for another minute or so, then broke down in loud sobs and wails.

"I don't think they had an arrangement," said Dooley softly.

CHAPTER 17

For a moment there Harriet had felt out of her depth. Max and Dooley had been scooped up so suddenly and irrevocably by Odelia that it almost felt like an abduction! Clearly their services were needed elsewhere, and now it was up to her and her alone to find Shanille and save the conductor from an uncertain fate.

"Why is it that Odelia always takes Max and Dooley along on her investigations and not us?" Brutus grumbled, not for the first time.

"She takes Max along because she seems to think he's some kind of prodigy," said Harriet. "Which means Odelia must be dumber than she looks, cause the real prodigy is you, my sweet. You're the real brains in this outfit, and if Odelia can't see that, then it's her loss."

Slightly mollified by this vote of confidence from his mate, Brutus said, "And what about Dooley? Why does he get to go on these investigations with Max?"

"Because Max and Dooley are attached at the hip," Harriet said blankly. "Where one goes, the other goes. It's always been like that." She shook her head in bewilderment. "You would think they came from the same litter, but they didn't."

"It may have something to do with the fact that Dooley helps Max think. At least that's what he told me once. And also, Dooley's mind comes up with the most surprising associations, and sometimes, quite by accident, one of those might trigger a thought process and lead Max to come up with a vital clue."

"Whatever," said Harriet, who had long ago decided not to bother too much with the family's favorite pastime, which seemed to be solving murders. An icky hobby as far as she was concerned, and nothing a lady like herself should get involved with.

"So where do we start?"

"We start by interrogating Shanille's neighbors," said Harriet. "Like we agreed."

Her beloved didn't seem very keen on the prospect of talking to all of Shanille's neighbors. And he probably had a point. It's hard work having to talk to a bunch of pets that more often than not are scattered across a sprawling maze of houses and alleyways. Like looking for a needle in a haystack, if that haystack consisted of hundreds, perhaps even thousands of cats and dogs, each with their own hangups and quirks, and not always all that keen on helping out a fellow pet.

"Let's go," she said, before she lost her resolve. "We have a job to do."

"Maybe we should wait for Max and Dooley to return?" Brutus suggested. But when Harriet gave him a censorious look that left no room for doubt as to what she thought of that suggestion, he quickly shut up.

"Whatever Max can do, we can do better," she said. "You are a proud and capable feline, Brutus. Where is the time that you were going to take Hampton Cove by storm? Challenge

Max and beat him at his own game?" It wasn't that long ago that Brutus had arrived in town, full of piss and vinegar and strutting his stuff like nobody's business. He was a cat's cat. A real he-cat in every sense of the word, which was the reason she had fallen for him hard.

"I know," said Brutus. "Somewhere along the line I seem to have lost my self-confidence. Or maybe I've become complacent. I don't know what it is."

"You've settled down, that's what. Like all men who settle down you've lost your edge, Brutus. And don't get me wrong, that's not necessarily a bad thing. All bad boys lose their wildness at some point, and for good reason. Imagine being a bad boy all your life, picking fights and busting heads wherever you go." She directed a tender smile at her beloved. "But it wouldn't hurt if you showed some of that old fighting spirit from time to time, sugar plum. Especially when we need to find a dear, dear friend like Shanille, and help her in her hour of need."

Her little pep talk seemed to have a profound effect on the butch black cat, for he puffed out his chest, and some of that old defiance returned to his features.

"We're going to show Max that we're the best detectives in town," he said.

"Now you're talking," she said with satisfaction. "Let's move out, detective!"

And so move out they did.

As expected, the expedition proved a tough slog. They talked to cats, dogs, parrots and even pet turtles resting in their tanks on the windowsill, taking in some of that nice sunshine that is all the rage in the summer. But what they didn't find was a clue that would lead to the unraveling of the baffling mystery of cat choir's missing conductor. Until finally a sleepy-looking canine who lived across the street from the rectory provided a glimmer of hope.

"Oh, sure I saw them," said the raggedy old dog. His eyes were droopy, and so Harriet wasn't sure if she could rely on this witness to have seen what he said he saw. "They loaded up the car and took off. Must be… four or five days ago now?"

"They packed up the car and left?" asked Harriet, excitement making her voice squeaky. "Where did they go? Did they pack a lot? Who was in the car? Tell us!"

"Hey, slow down, little lady," said the dog, whose name was Bruce. "They didn't pack an awful lot, just one suitcase as far as I could tell. That and a couple of cardboard boxes. And it was just Father Reilly behind the wheel, not his lady. Oh, and Shanille, of course. She was also traveling in the car with her human."

"So Marigold wasn't in the car?"

"No, she left last week. In her own car. Slammed the door on her way out, too." He smiled at the recollection. "You should have seen Father Reilly's face when she walked out. He didn't look happy, I can tell you that. Was frowning and wringing his hands and pleading with her not to go. But she wasn't having it. She just got in that car with that daughter of hers and that was that. Haven't seen them since."

Harriet exchanged a look of excitement with Brutus. Now this was the goods. This was the stuff. And they didn't even need Max to get them this vital clue!

"Thank you so much, Bruce," said Harriet.

"Yeah, thanks, Bruce," said Brutus. "You've been a great help, buddy."

"You're welcome, Brutus." The old dog smiled, revealing yellowed teeth. A dollop of drool dripped from his lip and splashed on the sidewalk where he was lying. It seemed to be his favorite spot to see the world go by and do some people-watching—one of the daily highlights in any pet's life.

"Funny your name should be Brutus and mine is Bruce. Almost as if we're brothers from another mother."

"Put it there, pal," said Brutus, and held up his paw. Bruce obliged by bumping his own paw against the black cat's, and Harriet could see that a bond for life had been established. So important if you were going to be a pet detective.

"Good job, sweetie," she said as they went on their way.

"Yeah, Bruce provided us with some very important information," said Brutus.

"Okay, so now we know that Marigold and Father Reilly had some kind of fight, and Marigold left with her daughter last week. And four or five days ago Father Reilly also left, in his own car, and with only Shanille as company."

"Looks like Father Reilly was in a serious hurry," said Brutus, nodding. "Which is probably the reason Shanille didn't tell anyone where she was going. She simply didn't have the time." He gave Harriet an expectant look. "So now what?"

"Now…" She hesitated. Bruce had told them the direction the car had traveled in, but that didn't tell them where Father Reilly had gone off to. For all they knew he could be in Florida right now, or lying on a beach in the South of France. "Now at least we know that Shanille is all right. If she was seen leaving in the car with Father Reilly a couple of days ago, chances are that she wasn't abducted by aliens, or killed by home invaders. So that's all good news—very good news."

But frankly where did that leave them? Exactly nowhere.

And she was thinking hard when Brutus spoke those fateful words: "Maybe we should ask Max what to do next."

"Absolutely not! We're going to solve this mystery ourselves, Brutus."

"Yes, of course. We don't need Max."

"That's right. We don't need Max!"

Still. She had no idea what to do. Which is when she

spotted a familiar figure slinking along the street in her customary graceful pantherine way.

"Clarice!" she called out. "Hey, Clarice!"

The feral cat slowly turned, eyed them with a touch of menace in her gaze, then, when she had ascertained that she had been hailed not by a foe but by a friend, she turned and came ambling in their direction. Her expression hadn't changed, and it was hard to make out what she was thinking at that moment. Was she happy to see them? Annoyed? With Clarice one simply never knew!

"Harriet, Brutus," she said once she had reached them. "What are you doing here?"

"We're looking for Shanille, actually," said Harriet. "She hasn't turned up for cat choir a couple of nights in a row, and we're starting to get worried about her."

"She left," said Clarice as her slitted eyes took in her surroundings, flitting here and there and missing nothing. "Left with that human of hers. Father Reilly. Left in his car never to return, I imagine."

"Never to return!" said Brutus. "But why?"

"Yeah, we figured they'd gone on holiday," said Harriet.

Clarice produced a sound that reminded Harriet of Odelia's car starting. It sounded halfway between a raspy cough and a metallic rattle. It took her a while to realize Clarice was laughing. "Nice holiday," said the battle-scarred street cat. "Shacked up in the middle of the woods with no one but each other for company? Not my idea of a holiday, I can tell you that!"

"Father Reilly is in the woods?"

"Yeah, in one of those derelict shacks out there. I bumped into him last night, doing his business against a tree, the filthy animal. And I can tell you he didn't look like a happy camper!"

"But... but why? What is he doing out there? I don't understand."

"He didn't tell me why, and frankly I don't care. Humans are a weird and dangerous species, so the moment I clocked him I took a big detour. By the same token he would have caught me and strung me up and roasted me over a slow fire." She raised her upper lip in an expression of contempt. "Humans. Give me a break."

"Oh, dear," said Harriet. "Poor Shanille. Having to sleep rough like that."

Clarice directed a look of such venom in her direction she involuntarily took a step back. "Rough! You don't know what rough means, princess! They've got a roof over their heads, don't they? They've got food and plenty of it, don't they? Well then. Spoiled brats, the lot of them."

Harriet wasn't sure if Clarice was referring to the human race in general, or Father Reilly in particular, but she decided not to ask. Clearly she wasn't in a good mood. "Did you see Shanille at all? Is she all right out there?" she asked instead.

But Clarice must have lost interest in the conversation, for she darted a suspicious glance at the sky, then mumbled, "Might have rain later. And lots of it." And then, without another word, or even a glance back, she simply walked away.

"Someone should teach that cat some manners," said Harriet once Clarice was safely out of earshot.

"I like her," said Brutus, much to Harriet's surprise. "She's feisty, isn't she?"

That, she most certainly was. And at least she'd given them the missing clue: Father Reilly, for whatever reason, was living in some derelict shack in the woods!

CHAPTER 18

Dooley and I had been granted the rare privilege of being present in a meeting that took place in Uncle Alec's office. Odelia's police chief uncle liked to organize these meetings to get an update on the ongoing investigation, and give his own input when appropriate. Odelia was present, and so was Chase of course, and Dooley and myself, but only after we had promised to be quiet and not interfere.

"So let's hear it, people," said the voluminous chief of police as he sat forward in his chair, his beefy arms on his desk blotter. "Tell me what's going on here."

In a few words Chase told his boss about the murder-suicide of Cipriana Cilke and Jeff Felfan. "Though there is some doubt about the murder-suicide theory," he said now. "The toxicology report for Cipriana shows a high level of GBH in her blood, and it's more than likely she wasn't conscious when she was shot. Also there was no gunpowder residue on her hands, so she couldn't have fired the shot. And what's more, analysis of the gun and the bullets provided a hit in the database with a gun used in a gangland killing in New York a couple of months ago."

"Organized crime?" asked the Chief as he listened intently. "What is a local prostitute doing with a gun like that?"

"Most likely it wasn't her gun," said Odelia, picking up the tale. "One of the neighbors saw a man entering Cipriana's apartment shortly before two. We showed her a picture of Jeff but she said it was a different man."

"Description?"

"Male. Tall."

"Very helpful," the Chief growled.

"Well, it is helpful," said Chase. "Since we now have a better picture of what happened. Hailey Harper, that's Cipriana's roommate, left the flat at a quarter to two to do some shopping. She said a client was arriving at three, and she was planning to be back before then, since the two girls always made sure they were both in the flat when a client stopped by. So a couple of minutes after she left, this tall man must have arrived and drugged Cipriana with the GBH, which was administered with coffee, according to Cipriana's stomach contents, then waited for Jeff to arrive. At which point he must have forced him at gunpoint to lie down on the bed and then proceeded to shoot and kill him, before shooting Cipriana with the same gun, and arranging the bodies to make it look like a murder-suicide scenario. At least that's the theory we're working from now."

"So who was the intended victim?" asked Uncle Alec. "Cipriana or Jeff?"

Chase glanced at Odelia, who said, "We think that Jeff was lured there under false pretenses. His wife says he was meeting a work colleague in town. One Clive Balcerak. But we called Mr. Balcerak and he claims he never sent that message. And the address in the message was Cipriana's, so Jeff must have thought he was meeting his colleague, when in actual fact he was meeting Cipriana."

"Who was already unconscious at this point," said Uncle Alec, nodding.

"Exactly. So the person who let him in was most likely his killer."

The Chief looked thoughtful. "So you're saying Jeff Felfan was the intended victim? And not Cipriana?"

"As far as Hailey knows Cipriana didn't have any enemies. The girls were self-employed and didn't have a pimp, and they never got in trouble with anyone."

"A disgruntled client?"

"Hailey says not," said Chase. "Jeff, on the other hand, was almost killed yesterday, when his car was forced off the road in an aggressive maneuver by Edmundo Crowley. We talked to Mr. Crowley and he claims it was just a coincidence that he would have been involved in the incident. But Crowley and Jeff's wife have a history." He explained how Crowley and Steph had been in competition for the same job, until a campaign of slanderous emails and pictures had made Crowley come out on top, with Steph's reputation in tatters.

"Edmundo Crowley is not a mobster, though, is he?" asked the Chief.

"No, but he could have bought the gun on the black market. Or the internet. It's not that hard, Chief, to acquire an illegal gun. You just have to know where to look. And if he was behind that smear campaign, he knows his way around a computer."

"Okay, fine. You better have another chat with this Crowley fellow. Though there's a big difference between organizing a smear campaign to get rid of the competition, and actually going out and murdering a person. And besides," he added with a frown, "if Crowley was targeting Steph, why kill her husband?"

"To further destroy her life?" Odelia suggested.

"But why? He got the job, didn't he? Why go on? What does he have against the Felfans anyway?"

"That's what we're hoping to find out," said Chase as he got up.

❧

"We should have asked Clarice whereabouts in the woods Father Reilly was holed up," said Brutus. They'd been searching the woods for going on two hours now, and still nothing. His paws were hurting, and if the rumbling sensation in his stomach was any indication, he was starving, too.

"It's very hard to give exact directions in a place this vast," said Harriet. "It's not like 'Go left by the big tree, then take a right at the smaller tree,' is it now?"

"No, I guess not," he said, carefully eyeing a suspicious-looking branch. "Is that a snake? Cause if it's a snake, we better don't go near it."

"I think it's a branch, Brutus," said Harriet. "Now don't be a baby and let's keep going. We're intrepid detectives, remember? And when has a little snake ever stopped you from getting where you wanted to go?"

"It's not a little snake, it's a pretty big one," he muttered darkly. This whole 'Let's find Shanille and save her from a perilous fate' gag had sounded like a good idea at the time. If he'd known it would include having to talk to dozens of pets and having to traipse through miles of woods he would never have agreed to join the search. And besides, why was it so important they found the missing pair anyway? Clearly they had left under their own steam, and of their own volition. No crime had been committed. Nobody was dying or in danger. So why bother?

"Poor Shanille," said Harriet. "Being reduced to living in a filthy old shack like some beggar. And to think she's such a cultured creature. And now this."

"I'll bet she's fine," said Brutus. "I'll bet she's having the time of her life."

"No, she is not," said Harriet sharply. "I can feel it in my bones. She's not fine."

They'd reached another clearing—the hundred-and-sixtieth already—and once again there was no sign of any shack, derelict or otherwise. They'd come across two shacks already. One was the famous one owned by Hetta Fried, where celebrity authors came to pen their latest bestsellers in absolute peace and quiet. The other was a less luxurious dwelling, where only a few months ago a couple had been found who had also gone missing.

But unfortunately neither of these had produced a priest and his cat. The first had been occupied by John Grisham, who hadn't looked too well pleased when two cats came trudging up and destroyed his concentration. And the second was now home to a couple of boars, who shared not even a fleeting resemblance to Father Reilly and Shanille, unfortunately.

"We should have asked Clarice to show us the way," Brutus grumbled.

"Did she look like she would have said yes? You know what she's like. Clarice does what Clarice wants—nothing more, nothing less. And clearly she was not in the mood to play tour guide for a pair of clueless cats."

"We are clueless, aren't we, snookums?" said Brutus.

"Pretty clueless, yes," Harriet admitted with a smile. "But what we lack in skill we make up for in determination and perseverance, don't we, sparky star?"

He didn't know about that. He was feeling pretty low on perseverance right now. And he was just about to suggest they abandon their mission and leave it to the professionals

—the police, in other words, or Odelia and Chase—when another clearing loomed in the distance, beyond a cluster of bramble bushes. And in the middle of the clearing, a shack. And on top of that shack, a chimney. And from that chimney smoke was crinkling skyward!

"Stud muffin!" said Harriet. "I think this is it!"

"I think you just might be right, sugar lips!"

They hurried in the direction of the clearing, and the moment they clapped eyes on that shack, Brutus knew they'd hit the jackpot—finally! For there, sitting on the windowsill, cool as dammit, was Shanille!

"Shanille!" Harriet cried. "Shanille, it's us!"

"It's us, Shanille!" Brutus echoed.

Shanille looked up, and a tired smile spread across her features. "Oh, hey, you guys. What brings you out here?"

"We've been looking for you everywhere!" said Harriet. "How are you?"

"As well as can be expected," said Shanille, which didn't sound very fine.

"What are you doing here?" asked Brutus. "And why did you leave without telling anyone?"

"Cat choir hasn't been the same without you," said Harriet. "I've tried to take over, but it hasn't been easy." She wisely neglected to recount the shoe incident.

"It's Father Reilly," said Shanille. "He hasn't been feeling well."

"Cancer, is it?" asked Brutus. "Hasn't got much longer to live?"

"No, not cancer. Though at this rate I don't think he'll survive."

This caused Harriet and Brutus to exchange a worried glance.

"Just take a look in there," said Shanille, when pressed.

And so they both joined the slim gray cat on the

windowsill and glanced into the shack. The sight that met their eyes was shocking, to say the least: there he lay on a cot, an empty bottle in his hand, and several more bottles on the floor next to him, passed out and looking like death warmed over. His hair was matted to his skull, his skin was mottled, and he was in his underwear, a dirty undershirt and even dirtier underpants that had once been white but were now gray and soiled.

"What happened to him!" Harriet cried.

"Marigold left, and took their daughter," said Shanille. "So he packed a suitcase, took the car, and drove us out here, where he's been steadily drinking ever since."

"Some people say that alcohol is food," said Brutus carefully.

"Only drunks say that," Shanille scoffed. "No, I'm afraid he'll be a goner soon. If he keeps drinking like this he won't last another month."

Brutus's eyes traveled across the plank floor to several cardboard boxes in the corner of the small space. "Is that…"

"Wine, yes," Shanille confirmed, who'd followed Brutus's gaze. "He packed up all the sacramental wine he could find and said he's going to drink it all."

"We saw Gran steal two bottles from the church," said Harriet.

"Must have been a couple of bottles Francis forgot to pack," said Shanille.

"But Shanille, we can't let this happen!" said Harriet. "We can't just sit back and let the man drink himself to death! It's too terrible to contemplate!"

"What can we do? Ever since Marigold left he hasn't been himself."

"Why did she leave?" asked Brutus.

"Because she was tired of waiting for Francis to leave the priesthood and make an honest woman out of her, of course.

He promised her he was going to marry her months and months ago, but he kept postponing. Said he felt bad about abandoning his parishioners. About leaving the church. The man has never been anything but a priest, and frankly I think he was afraid of falling into a dark hole when he left his post. So he kept dithering and finally Marigold had enough and took off."

"Where is she now?"

"Canada. Her parents live in Toronto, so she and Angel are staying with them for now. Until Marigold can find a job and rent an apartment. She said she wants to start a new life. Without Francis."

"Poor Francis," said Brutus.

"Poor Marigold!" said Harriet. "Imagine having to wait years and years for a wedding proposal, and then when finally one comes along, nothing happens!"

"Francis did talk to the bishop," said Shanille, "and explained the situation. So the bishop said he should simply live together with Marigold, but be discreet about it. That way he could remain a priest, and be with Marigold at the same time. But Marigold didn't see it that way. She didn't want to be Francis's guilty secret. If they were going to be together, it had to be official, not in secret."

"The bishop probably didn't want to lose a good priest like Francis," said Brutus. "Which is why he came up with this compromise. Marigold should have said yes, then everybody would have been happy." When both Shanille and Harriet stared at him with daggers firing from their eyes, he said, "What?"

"Are you crazy?" said Shanille. "Marigold has been in this situation for years! She felt she deserved better than being tucked away in some corner of Francis's life. Like a leper. And she's right."

"I guess so," said Brutus dubiously. He stared at the priest, who was passed out, and thought he was taking the whole thing very hard indeed. But then who could blame him? If Harriet walked out on him he would also take it hard. Though he probably wouldn't go to a shack in the woods with a car full of altar wine.

"Okay, so here's what we'll do," said Harriet. "We can't leave him like this. So we talk to a good friend of his and she'll get him out of this terrible situation."

Shanille eyed her with suspicion. "What friend?"

"Why, Gran, of course!"

CHAPTER 19

Once again our humans had decided to call on Mr. Crowley, hoping to confront him with the new suspicions that they were about to level against that uber-ambitious young designer. When we arrived at the hotel, the receptionist kindly informed us that their esteemed guest was still on the premises as far as they could tell. At least he hadn't checked out yet.

But when we arrived on the third floor, and made our way to his room, persistent knocking didn't yield any meaningful result. Hollering, "Police, Mr. Crowley—open up!" didn't affect a lot of movement either. And so finally a maid was called in, who kindly opened the door for us with her passkey.

A very curious sight played out in front of us: as we entered, we had a perfect view of a man's underpants, as he tried to scrabble through the window. The underpants didn't give us a lot of clues as to the man's identity, other than that he was probably male, and that he favored red polka dots on his undergarments.

He was also wearing red socks, but no shoes. And when

finally Chase grabbed a firm hold of one leg, and Odelia of the other, and pulled, there was a sort of rending sound, and a loud whine as if from a caged animal, and Edmundo Crowley fell back into the room, his face red and angry, and his mood below zero.

"This is police harassment!" he cried as he put on a show of umbrage. "I will bring charges against you people, just you wait and see! You can't do this!"

"Where were you going in such a hurry, Mr. Crowley?" asked Chase, who wasn't the least bit impressed by the man's diatribe. "And in your underwear, no less."

"I don't see how that's any of your business, but if you must know I was trying to get some fresh air. But since this darned window is blocked, the only way I could get out was by squeezing myself through it. Stupid thing."

"I realize that Brooklynites have a special way of doing things," said Chase, "but this is the first time I've ever seen a man trying to take in fresh air by wedging himself in like this."

"Looks to me like he was trying to escape," said Odelia.

"Now why would he do that?" asked Chase.

"Because he's guilty, no doubt."

"Guilty of what, I wonder?"

"Oh, cut the theatrics, will you?" said the man. "What do you want?"

"We wanted to ask you about your whereabouts this afternoon, Mr. Crowley. Let's say between two and three?"

"What do you mean?"

Chase sighed. "It's a simple question. Where were you between two and three?"

"Why?"

"Indulge us, please."

"If you must know, I was here, working on my next collection."

"Can anyone vouch for you?"

"Well... no, actually. Why? What's going on?"

"Two people were murdered," said Odelia. "And one of them is Jeff Felfan, Stephanie Felfan's husband."

To his credit, the man blanched when the news hit him. "M-m-murdered?"

"Yes, Mr. Crowley. The man you tried to drive off the road yesterday was murdered. Do you own a gun?"

"A g-g-gun?"

"Yes, a gun."

"N-n-no, of course not. Why would I need a gun?"

"So if we were to arrest you and get a warrant to search your computer, we wouldn't find a search history indicating that you were in the market for a gun?"

"No! Look, I can see how this looks. And I admit that I was a little out of order yesterday, with that road incident. But I wouldn't *murder* the man. I didn't even know him!"

"So now you do admit that you deliberately tried to drive Jeff Felfan's car off the road yesterday," said Chase.

"Well... yes, okay. So I was upset, all right? And a little worked up. But that stupid woman sent the NYPD to my apartment! They asked me all kinds of questions and made me look like a criminal! They even had a warrant to search my computer, and my phone, and they said that if they found anything to tie me to this harassment campaign they'd bring charges against me and I'd go to prison!"

"It wasn't a harassment campaign," said Odelia. "Though with the road incident and those rocks thrown through the window last night it's certainly starting to look like one."

"Did you throw those rocks, Mr. Crowley?" asked Chase. He was leaning into the man, and seeing as he was still only dressed in his underwear Crowley didn't look very confident right now. In fact he looked downright intimidated.

"Y-y-yes?" he said weakly.

"So not only do you admit using your car as a weapon, but also throwing rocks through the window of the house where Stephanie Felfan was staying?"

"Yes, all right. I threw those rocks. It's just that... That NYPD officer who paid me a visit? She also talked to the folks at WelBeQ. Asked them to hand over the emails and the photographs they received. So WelBeQ called me and said that in light of recent developments they were going in a different direction and were no longer interested in engaging my services." At the recollection of that phone call some of his old belligerence returned to the fore. "So Stephanie Felfan managed to ruin everything! By filing that complaint —that *unfounded* complaint—she lost me a unique opportunity. An opportunity that would have changed my life!"

"So you tried to drive her off the road, then broke that window, and this afternoon you lured her husband Jeff to a flat in town and killed him," said Chase.

"What?! No! Of course not!"

"But you were angry, Mr. Crowley. Very angry with Stephanie Felfan. So angry you followed her all the way out here to Hampton Cove. So angry you acquired an illegal gun and killed the man you knew she loved more than anyone in the world. You could have killed her, of course, but you wanted to make her suffer. You wanted her to feel your pain. Like she made you suffer when she lost you that job—a job that meant everything to you. Isn't that what happened, Mr. Crowley?!"

He was face to face now with the aspiring designer, and Crowley stared into the man's eyes, transfixed, and said, "Yes..." But then he seemed to realize what he was saying and quickly amended his response. "No! Of course not!"

"You killed Jeff Felfan and Cipriana Cilke. Cipriana was a prostitute, and you wanted to make it look as if Jeff Felfan had acquired her services, then was shot by her, at which point you made it look as if she shot herself."

"I didn't do that," said Crowley, shaking his head. Sweat was beading on his brow, and I had the impression he had soiled himself during the interrogation. "The car and the window—yes. But I didn't kill anyone. I'm not a murderer."

But Chase wasn't placated. He clapped a heavy hand on the man's shoulder and said, "Edmundo Crowley, I'm arresting you for the murder of Jeff Felfan and Cipriana Cilke."

CHAPTER 20

Unfortunately for Chase, Crowley wouldn't admit to murder, no matter how hard he leaned on the man. His phone and laptop were seized—yet again, for the NYPD had apparently done the same thing—but revealed nothing incriminating. His search history, his call and message history—nothing to indicate he bought that gun, much less had sent a message to Jeff arranging that fateful meeting.

"I'm going to keep him overnight," said Chase as he conferred with his boss. We were in the little room next to the interview room, with a clear view of the suspect as he sat at the table, his head in his hands. "Let him think about what he did. Maybe tomorrow he'll be more amenable to assist us in our inquiries."

"I don't think he did it, babe," said Odelia. "Just look at him. Does he look like a killer? I don't think so. He was upset about losing the job, of course. And so he reacted out of spite. But this double murder is an entirely different thing. It's calculated and planned. Not something you do on the spur of the moment just because you're angry that someone made you lose your dream job."

"That doesn't mean anything. He hasn't admitted to the smear campaign either, so we know he's lying about that as well."

"I still think we're wasting our time here," said Odelia.

"Okay, so let him sweat for a while," the Chief suggested. "And in the meantime I want you back at the Stewart Winery to talk to the family. See if you can't dig a little deeper. Maybe the Felfans have other enemies besides Mr. Crowley here. Though I have to admit he looks like the perfect suspect to me."

"He did it, Chief, I can feel it in my bones," said Chase.

"Which isn't to say we shouldn't keep an open mind," Uncle Alec added. "So talk to Stephanie Felfan again, and her parents. Talk to her husband's folks. See what else you can dig up. It's only going to make your case stronger, buddy," he said when Chase made to interrupt.

"Fine," the detective finally said. "We'll look at other suspects. But I'm willing to bet good money that Crowley is our guy."

"Betting during office hours is strictly prohibited," the Chief warned. "And now go. Find me some more suspects—this one isn't going anywhere, I promise you."

&.

When Vesta laid eyes on her old friend Francis Reilly she was shocked. The man looked terrible. In fact she had never seen him like this before. The priest was always neatly attired, cleanly shaven, perfectly coiffed, and soft-spoken. Now he looked as if he'd been through a bacchanal of Romanesque proportions.

"What do you want!" he slurred when she managed to wake him up. "Leave me alone, woman!"

"I will not leave you alone, Francis," said Vesta with determination.

Her friend Scarlett, whom she had brought along, and also Tex, who was there as much in his capacity as a doctor but also as a personal friend of the priest, were both equally shocked and appalled.

"He's in a terrible state," said Scarlett, who had wrinkled her nose in abhorrence at the smell of drink and lack of hygiene. "He's not dying, is he?"

"No, he's not," said Tex. "He's drunk, that's what he is."

"So we need to sober him up," said Vesta. "And get rid of that stuff over there." She was pointing to the bottles of sacramental wine. It broke her heart to say it but she was compelled to by the circumstances. "Better get rid of them. You better do it, Tex. I can't."

"I'll do it," said Scarlett.

"No!" said Vesta, who knew how much her friend loved a good glass of wine. "Maybe just leave them. Some bum who visits these woods might get lucky and find them."

"We can't leave them here!" said Scarlett. "That's some perfectly fine wine!"

"You're on the wagon, remember?" said Vesta.

After she and Tex had gone dry, she had convinced Scarlett to do the same. Her friend had always been a social drinker. A drink for every occasion. But lately she was also drinking when she wasn't visiting people or going out. Once Vesta had even found her passed out on the couch, an empty bottle of Prosecco on the floor. So it was high time that she joined the AA—in fact the whole town should probably join that fine organization. But perhaps that was too ambitious. For now she would suffice with her closest friends and relatives. Like Francis Reilly.

"And you're saying he's been like this since Marigold left?" asked Tex.

"Yeah, he was dragging his feet on the marriage business, so she left him."

"That's a little harsh, isn't it?" said Scarlett who was making sure she didn't touch anything located in the shack, and clearly couldn't wait to get out of there.

"Harsh or not, the man took it badly, and it's up to us to be there for him."

"Maybe we can ask Marigold to come back?" Scarlett suggested. "The moment she hears about what happened, she might have a change of heart."

"I doubt it. Now let's get Francis out of here, shall we?"

"I'm not touching that," said Scarlett with a look of distaste. "He smells."

"So take a bath when we're done. I'm sure you've touched men in far worse conditions."

Scarlett shot her an indignant look but finally relented. "Fine. But I'm not going in the shower with him. You'll have to do that."

"I'm not going in the shower with him!"

They both looked to Tex, who sputtered, "*I'm* not taking a shower with him!"

"Why not? You're the doctor," said Vesta with perfect logic. "*And* you're a man."

And so it was decided. And as they took Francis under the armpits—which were pretty ripe, Vesta had to admit—they managed to get the priest out of the shack and into the car, which they'd driven along the old dirt road that led deep into the woods.

When Harriet and Brutus had told them what had happened, it hadn't taken Vesta long to take decisive action. Now that she was following the twelve-step program, she felt as if she had finally found her true purpose in life: helping people, even if they didn't necessarily want to be helped. Like Francis. But it was for his own good. So she'd assembled her troops: Tex and Scarlett, and here they were, executing her plan. First they were going to clean him up, then they were going to put some fresh clothes on the man, and finally they were going to keep an eye on him, making sure he ate his three square meals a day, and no alcohol!

And so they took the ailing man of the cloth home. Tex removed those clothes, such as they were, and somehow managed to get the man into the shower. It wasn't easy, for Francis Reilly was a big man, and wasn't very helpful. In fact once the water hit him he struggled and yelled like a cat being given a bath. Tex was soaking wet, the bathroom was soaking wet, in fact everything was wet, but luckily so was the priest, who at this point looked a little more alert than before.

"Tex?" he muttered, as if he'd seen the Holy Ghost. "Is that you?"

"It is. Now let's get you into some fresh clothes and into bed," Tex said.

"Bed? But I don't want to go to bed."

"Well, you're gonna, whether you like it or not. You're not well, Francis."

"Oh, all right," said the man, possibly realizing that resistance was futile.

And it was with a renewed appreciation for the hard work nurses did, that Tex dressed the man, and then tucked him into bed to sleep off his five-day bender.

Feeling that his work was done, Tex removed himself from the scene. At this point he could have used a nice pick-me-up, but instead he opted for some dry and clean clothes for himself and a swig from the Coca-Cola bottle in the fridge.

In the bedroom, the sleeping priest was being watched

over by two women. They were satisfied that they'd done all they could—or at least Tex had. "A fine job well done!" said Vesta when the mission was accomplished. "Now all we have to do is keep an eye on him."

"I'll do it," said Scarlett. "The poor man. Being left by his wife."

"Marigold wasn't his wife," Vesta pointed out. "That was exactly the problem."

"Well, anyway. He's still handsome for his age," said Scarlett, who had warmed to the man now that he was clean and sober. "Though he could use a haircut." She sighed. "All he needs is a good woman to look after him."

"Scarlett," said Vesta warningly.

"What? I'm just saying. Sometimes all a man needs is the love and support of a good woman. It just might be the making of him."

"Please tell me you're not envisioning yourself in that role? Just keep an eye on him. And when he starts thrashing about or demanding a drink, be tough and say no. Can you do that? Can you say no to a man?"

Scarlett's face flushed with indignation. "Of course I can say no to a man. Who do you think I am?"

"Well, mind that you do. We're all relying on you."

And as she left the bedroom, she heard Scarlett mutter, "I can say no to a man. Just you wait and see."

CHAPTER 21

We were back at the winery, for more interviews with more people, trying to shed some light on the life and times of Jeff Felfan.

"So has it been decided that Cipriana wasn't the intended victim?" asked Dooley.

"Yes, I think so," I said.

"So she was murdered just so the killer could make Jeff look bad?"

"It certainly looks that way," I agreed.

"Poor woman. At least whoever did this could have showed her the common courtesy of murdering her for who she was, not for the purpose she could fulfill."

I eyed my friend keenly. "That was a very insightful thing to say, Dooley."

"I can be insightful."

"I know you can."

Odelia and Chase were talking to Steph once more, out on the patio, where she was sipping from what looked like a cup of tea. The housekeeper now brought out a tray with more cups and saucers, and a big pot of tea for the visitors.

There were also cookies on the tray, but as far as I could tell no kibble.

"They always forget about us, don't they, Max?" said Dooley sadly.

"Very often," I agreed. Especially the people who didn't have pets themselves, like the Stewarts, forgot that cats have needs—mostly in the food department.

But we could be strong and skip a meal. It was going to be tough, but we could power through, for the sake of bringing the killer of Steph's husband to justice.

"I knew Jeff wouldn't have paid a visit to a prostitute," said Steph after Odelia had finished telling her about the newly acquired insight that Jeff's murder was actually a premeditated affair, and that Cipriana had been drugged before she was shot—and not shot by her own hand either, since she would have been unconscious by then. "So have you talked to Clive Balcerak? He's the one who lured him to that flat."

"We're going to talk to him soon," Chase promised. "How well do you know the man?"

"Not well, I'm afraid. I've never even met him. He worked in the same department as Jeff, but they never got on. Clive had started a couple of months before Jeff, and for some reason felt threatened by him. You see, Clive is a very ambitious man, and wants to make a career at Capital First. And somehow he got it into his head that Jeff was the man to beat. He's extremely competitive."

"Enough to kill your husband, you think?"

"Like I said, I never met the man. But from what Jeff told me he has a ruthless streak. There was an error in the books one day, and Clive was quick to spread the rumor that Jeff was responsible, and was going to get fired soon. That kind of thing. It made it very unpleasant for Jeff to work there. Though he also got a lot of support from some of his other colleagues. And his direct manager wasn't fooled by these rumors. He even reprimanded Clive on one occasion."

"I'll bet he didn't like that."

"No, he didn't. But at least things became better after that."

"Can you think of anyone else who had a grudge against your husband, Steph?" asked Odelia. She had poured some tea from the pot and was sipping from it now, nibbling on a cookie as she did. And ignoring Dooley and me as we both stared at her. I mean, it's pretty tough to have to watch other people eat when you don't have anything to eat yourself! Talk about being selfish!

"No one," said Steph decidedly. "Jeff was such a sweet man. Everybody loved him. His colleagues—except Clive, of course. But also his family, his friends. No one ever had a bad word to say about him. He was so kind and so wonderful." She brought a distraught hand to her face as she remembered her husband, and tears sprung to her eyes afresh. "It's just so hard, you know. I miss him so much..."

"I know you do," said Odelia, who had scooted forward, and was rubbing the woman on the back. "And I'm sorry we have to ask you all these questions."

"No, it's fine. You want to catch the person who did this, and I want to help you in any way I can. Just ask me anything."

"So no enemies that you can think of?" Chase reiterated.

"None. Jeff had no enemies," said Steph. "We're all devastated here. Jeff's parents most of all, of course. They're flying in tomorrow from France. They're going to be a great support to me—and I want to be there for them also."

"We would like to talk to your parents," said Chase. "Are they around?"

"Yeah, they are. I'm not sure about my brother, though. He keeps disappearing on me. Last night with the window being busted he didn't even show up. And this morning I wanted to tell him about what happened with Jeff and I couldn't find him." She shook her head. "This family is falling apart, that's the truth."

"Where is your brother now?" asked Odelia.

"I have no idea. I caught him just before you arrived, and when I asked him where he was this afternoon, he said he went for a drive. He keeps going for drives for some reason. Even when everything is going to hell, he…" She raised her hands and dropped them in her lap in a gesture of desperation. "It's all just so… so utterly and completely…" But words failed to describe how she felt. Which I could certainly understand. And so we left, and went in search of her dad.

§

We found Ian Stewart in his office, where he oversaw the day-to-day business of running a successful winery. Even though I had expected him to be amongst the vines, or stomping grapes in a big vat with his bare feet, he looked more like a banker or a businessman in his clean shirt and tie and sitting behind his desk.

He got up when we entered, and shook Chase and Odelia's hands with a strained grimace. "Terrible business, simply terrible," he said. "We're all devastated here. Especially Steph, of course, who's gone completely to pieces."

The detecting duo took the offered seats in front of the man's desk and Chase asked the inexorable question: "To your knowledge, did your son-in-law have any enemies, sir?"

"Oh, no, absolutely not. The man was loved by everyone he met. He was French, of course," he added, "so if you want to know about his life before he came to America you'll have to talk to his parents—who are flying in tomorrow, by the way."

"Yes, Steph told us," said Odelia. "So you can't think of anyone who might have wanted to harm him?"

"I thought you already had a man in custody?" asked Ian as he leaned back.

"You're well-informed, sir," said Chase.

"I called Chief Lip just now. He told me about this man Crowley. Apparently he's the one who threw a couple of rocks through my window last night. So what makes you think he isn't the one who killed my son-in-law?"

"We're looking at all possible angles, sir. Crowley is one possibility, but there may be others."

"So he hasn't confessed, has he? Too bad. It would be a weight off my daughter's mind if she knew the man responsible for Jeff's murder has been caught."

"So anyone you can think of who might have wanted to harm your son-in-law?" Odelia asked, reiterating her question.

"Well, one name springs to mind, of course. Though not necessarily as someone who would harm Jeff in particular. More the whole family, I guess."

"And what name would that be, sir?" asked Chase.

"Beniamino Kosinski. His family and mine have been at daggers drawn for years. A feud that dates back to the eighties. I actually thought he was the one who busted my window last night, though now it seems I was wrong. But I certainly wouldn't put it past him to kill Jeff. The man is ruthless and will stop at nothing to get back at us."

"Even commit murder?"

"Oh, absolutely. No doubt about it. In fact it surprises me it's taken him so long. He's been hurling threats at us for years, and minor acts of sabotage."

"Sabotage, sir?" asked Odelia.

"Well, he opened the taps of one of the big fermentation tanks once. We lost gallons and gallons that night. Couldn't prove it, of course, but who else would do such a thing? And then there was that infestation of vine weevils, of course."

"Vine weevils?"

"Nasty bugs. Eat away at the vines, severely damaging young vines. One spring morning they were suddenly everywhere. Larry figured the Kosinskis must have brought them in to infect our vines. Lucky for us Larry is a genius, and he managed to get the pests under control before they could do too much damage. That little stunt could have cost us the entire crop that year."

"And you think it was Kosinski?" asked Chase.

"No doubt in my mind that he was behind it. So you see, the man is dangerous."

"There's a big difference between scattering weevils across a couple of vines and murdering two people, though, Mr. Stewart."

"He's escalating, that's what I'm trying to tell you. Every year it gets worse, and if he's not stopped, he might murder us all in our beds one night. Jeff was just a warning, you see. Part of the family but not really. He's telling us that we're next. He'll go after the kids first, then me and my wife. But I'm taking no chances."

"What do you mean?"

"I've taken the necessary precautions. I'm installing an alarm system—something I should have done years ago—and I've told Larry to hire some extra men to stand guard at night. Make sure Kosinski doesn't stand a chance."

The door to the office opened and Steph's mother walked in. "Oh, I hope I'm not interrupting anything?" she said.

"Please join us, darling," said Ian. "I was just telling Detective Kingsley and his wife about Ben Kosinski, and how I'm convinced he's the one who killed Jeff."

"Do you agree with your husband about the role Kosinski

played in the death of your son-in-law, Mrs. Stewart?" asked Chase.

"Oh, absolutely. The Kosinskis are bad news, both Beniamino and his son Dominic. Dirty tricks and sabotage and now murder. Wouldn't surprise me."

"See? I told you," said Ian. "Ask anyone, and they'll tell you."

"The gun that was used to kill Jeff and Miss Cilke... we have reason to believe there is an organized crime connection," said Chase.

Ian turned to his wife with a triumphant expression on his face. "Didn't I tell you? The Kosinskis are in bed with the mafia—I've been saying it for years! They're being bankrolled by the Polish mafia, and have been doing their bidding. Laundering money, possibly drugs—and guns, of course." He nodded seriously. "Look, I'm not saying Beniamino or Dominic personally pulled that trigger. But they know people—mobsters—who'd happily do the job for them. Can't you see? This proves what I've been saying all along: the mafia is trying to take over the Long Island wine industry, and if we let them we'll all perish." He tapped his desk with an insistent finger. "We have to stop them in their tracks, detective. Before it's too late. Or else you'll have a whole spate of killings on your hands soon."

Suddenly we heard a voice behind us, and when we turned around, we saw a young man standing at the door opening. He looked angry, and his eyes were blazing as he took in the scene. He must have been listening for a while, and overheard the conversation, for he now said, "I don't believe this!" And stomped off without another word!

"Kevin!" Mrs. Stewart yelled. "Kevin, come back here!"

"Oh, just leave him be," said Ian. "Can't you see what's going on?"

"What's going on?" asked Chase, who was as bewildered as we were.

"Just family business," said Ian. "You'll have to forgive Kevin. He's young."

"So that was Kevin," said Odelia as she got up and headed to the door. But before she got there, the loud roar of a car engine being turned over sounded. It was so loud it made the windows in the office rattle.

Odelia hurried to the window to look out, and so did Dooley and me. We were just in time to see a bright red Ferrari race off at considerable speed, the tires spitting up gravel as it did.

"And he's off again," said Ian with a touch of exasperation in his voice. "As usual when things get hard." He shook his head in dismay. "I hate to say this, detective, but my son isn't the most mature person in the world. Then again, like I said, he's still young. I'm sure he'll grow out of this phase eventually."

"He's been in this phase for a long time now," said Raimunda, who looked distinctly concerned.

"He'll be fine," Ian said. "He has to get it out of his system, that's all."

He didn't say what exactly his son had to get out of his system, though, and I had the feeling he wasn't going to tell us. He placed both hands flat on his desk, plastered a smile on his face and pushed himself into a standing position. "Now if there's nothing else…"

CHAPTER 22

The Kosinski Winery might be located right next to the Stewart Winery, but that didn't mean we could simply pop over. It took us about half an hour to get to the main entrance to the winery owned by Ian's much-despised neighbor, and when we got there it took a while before we were allowed to enter through the gate. Only when Chase showed his badge did it finally swing open enough for the cop to pass through in his squad car.

"They're not so keen on visitors in this place," said Odelia's husband as he navigated the drive up to the main house. We passed spreading fields of grapevine, which offered an impressive sight I have to say. Now I'm not a grape connoisseur, per se, but I can appreciate how some people are.

"I wonder how they taste," said Dooley.

"Bitter, I'll bet," I said.

"No, sweet," said Odelia. "Grapes are very sweet, with just a touch of bitterness."

"So many grapes," said Dooley. "Who's going to eat them all?"

"They turn them into wine," said Odelia. "Basically they first crush and then press them, squeezing out the juice, to which yeast is then added, to start the fermentation process. The sugar in the grapes turns into alcohol, and eventually the wine is bottled. Some of the best wines in the country are made here."

"Odd," I said. "How humans like to drink wine so much." I once had a lick of the stuff, and have to say I didn't care for the taste at all. Very bitter, I thought.

When we finally arrived at the house, which had been built in the hacienda style, Odelia suddenly called out, "Look, it's Kevin's car!"

And indeed it was. The same red Ferrari we'd seen pulling out of the Stewart driveway now stood parked in the Kosinski driveway. Odd, that.

"Could be the same type of car," said Chase. "I'll bet red Ferraris are popular."

"No, I think it's the same one," said Odelia as Chase parked right next to the expensive sports car. "So what is Kevin doing here?" Then a thought must have occurred to her, for she added, "Let's hope he's not out for revenge!"

Chase directed a look of concern at his wife, and instantly got out of the car and hurried up to the house. And just as he got there, the door opened and a man strode out. He was sporting dark sunglasses and rocking a ponytail, and was dressed in faded jeans and a black leather jacket. He looked more like a rock star than a vintner.

"Did a young man arrive here just now?" asked Chase, gripping the man's outstretched hand and giving it a quick shake. "Kevin Stewart? Only that's his car over there and we have reason to believe he may wish you harm, sir. You are Beniamino Kosinski?"

"That's right," said the winery owner. "But you can call me Ben. And as far as Kevin is concerned, I wouldn't worry too much about him if I were you. He's in and out of this place all the time, and has never caused us any trouble yet."

"He's a regular visitor?" asked Chase.

"That's right. Does that surprise you?"

"Well, his parents seem to think—"

"That I'm the devil in disguise?" The man laughed a hearty laugh. "Still up to his old tricks, is he, Ian? Well, I can promise you I'm not as bad as he makes me out to be. So what can I do for you, Detective Kingsley? I have to say I was surprised when they told me you suddenly showed up here out of the blue. But I'm always willing to help the police with their inquiries, so let's have it, shall we?"

He took us into the house, then out the back onto the patio, where the humans took a seat in wicker chairs around a small table where a couple of wine bottles stood on display.

"Yours?" asked Chase as he picked up one of the bottles.

"Yep. Finest wine in the county. Though Ian might disagree."

"Do you also happen to know Ian's son-in-law, Mr. Kosinski?"

"Ben, please. Yeah, of course. Jeff. Though I've never had the pleasure of actually making his personal acquaintance. But I know of him, absolutely."

"So you never actually met Jeff? Face to face, I mean?"

"Nope. But then the Stewarts and the Kosinskis don't exactly socialize. We keep ourselves to ourselves, and they do the same, and that's the way it's been for as long as I can remember. We did send Steph a present for the wedding and she sent us a very sweet note back, thanking us for our kindness. She's a good kid, Steph. Kevin, too." He frowned and shifted in his seat. "But what's all this about? Did something happen with Steph's husband that I should know about?"

"You haven't heard?" asked Chase. "Jeff was murdered this afternoon, along with one other person."

"Christ," said the vintner, looking instantly distraught. "What happened?"

"That's what we're trying to find out. But Ian tells us that you might be—"

"Involved in that young man's death? God—has he completely lost his mind?"

"He seems to think that you might be out to harm his family," said Odelia.

"I know. He's been spreading rumors about me for years. How I'm a member of the Polish mob, and how I run a drug racket, and launder money through my wine business. I've always let it go, even though by rights I should have pressed charges against the fool for defamation of character. But I didn't want to stir up a hornets' nest, so I just let it slide. But if he's accusing me of murder now, I might want to have a word with the man. And maybe talk to a lawyer this time, cause he's taking things too far."

"Where were you this afternoon between two and three, Mr. Kosinski?" asked Chase.

"I told you to call me Ben," said the man frostily, then glowered at the cop. "Are you calling me a murderer now?"

"Just a routine question, Ben," said Chase smoothly. "So we can eliminate you from our inquiries."

"Well, I was here, of course. At the house. And I've got about a dozen people who can confirm this."

"Looks like you're off the hook then," said Chase with a tight smile.

"Look, this nonsense about the mafia is exactly that: a lot of nonsense. Kosinski may be a Polish name and I may have some Polish blood owing to some great-great-grandfather, but I've got nothing to do with the mafia, Polish or otherwise. I run a respectable business, and if Ian Stewart thinks he can try and destroy my good reputation I'll see him in court. And I mean that. He's gone too far this time. There's only so much I'm prepared to take from that man."

"Is there anyone else you can think of who might want to harm the Stewarts?" asked Odelia. "Or Jeff in particular?"

"Like I said, I didn't know Jeff personally, but what I can tell you is that when Steph got married to the guy there was one person who was extremely unhappy about it. And that person was Robbie Scunner."

"Larry Scunner's son."

Ben nodded. "Steph and Robbie used to date in high school, but when she left for college that ended. Not that it was ever anything serious, mind you. Just a boy and girl affair. At least to Steph it was never serious. But to Robbie it was. That young man suffered when Steph broke it off with him. Sulked for months. His dad even thought he might never recover. See, his mom died when he was a young boy, and so when Steph left, it must have done something to Robbie's psyche. Now I'm not a psychologist, but it doesn't take a genius to see that's one very damaged kid. So it's hardly surprising that he wasn't happy when Steph finally returned from France with Jeff Felfan in tow. Kevin tells me that when Steph and Jeff tied the knot Robbie was dressed in black. And told everyone he was in mourning."

CHAPTER 23

Once outside, and on our way back to the car, we looked around for Kevin, but he proved as elusive now as he was before. His car was gone, and so, presumably, was the man himself.

"Tough guy to pin down," said Chase.

"Yeah, he seems to come and go as he pleases," said Odelia.

In light of what Ben Kosinski had told us about Robbie Scunner, our humans decided to pay another visit to the Stewart Winery for a little chat with the foreman's son. And possibly Kevin Stewart, who kept eluding us somehow.

We found Robbie Scunner in the warehouse where the large stainless steel tanks were housed, which are used to ferment the wine. As we had learned, this was the best way to give white wine its crisp flavor, whereas red wine is fermented in oak barrels, giving them a smoother, creamier flavor, often with notes of vanilla and oak. Not that I cared one bit how wine tasted. To me it was all vinegar, but then I'm just a cat, so what do I know?

Robbie was checking some gauges on the tanks, and

when he saw us looked none too pleased. It immediately made me suspicious of the man. As they say: an innocent person has nothing to fear from a visit by the constabulary, whereas a guilty man might become shifty-eyed and wary, just like Robbie right now.

"Chase Kingsley, Hampton Cove Police Department," said Chase, briefly holding up his badge. "And this is my wife Odelia, civilian consultant. Can we have a quick word, Mr. Scunner?"

"Sure," said Robbie, wiping his hands on a dirty rag. This time he was dressed in clean blue coveralls, and not in his cowboy do. "Is this about Steph's husband?"

"Oh, so you've heard about that, have you?"

"Who hasn't? It's big news around here."

"First off, could you tell us where you were between two and three? Just a routine question. We're asking everyone."

"I was right here," said Robbie, gesturing to the giant metal tanks.

"Can anyone corroborate that, Mr. Scunner?"

"Sure. Ask my dad. He'll tell you."

"That would be Larry Scunner?"

"That's right."

"So how well did you know Mr. Felfan, sir?"

"Not very well. I mean, I've seen him around, of course. But the Felfans spend most of their time in New York, and only come out here for the weekends."

"Only we saw you and Jeff go toe to toe last night, almost coming to blows."

"Yeah, that was unfortunate," said Robbie, scratching his scalp. "I overreacted when I heard that their car had been driven off the road that morning."

"You and Steph used to date, is that correct?"

"Years ago," said Robbie. "We were high school sweethearts, but that didn't last very long."

"Oh? We heard it lasted a couple of years. Until Steph went off to Paris and the relationship ended."

Robbie laughed nervously. "I wouldn't exactly call it a relationship. Just kids fooling around, you know. Nothing serious. Well, you know how it is at that age."

"We have it on good authority you took it very seriously," said Chase, studying the man closely. "And that when Steph broke it off you were heartbroken."

"Who told you that?" said the young man, frowning now. "That just isn't true."

"And when Steph married Jeff you wore black at the wedding, and told anyone who would listen that you were in mourning because Steph had married another man. That you'd always think of her as the one, no matter who she married."

"That was a joke! I figured that's what people were thinking, so I just made a joke. I didn't mean it. And doesn't everyone wear black at a wedding? Well, except the bride of course, who's in white." He tugged at his ear. "Look, I don't know who fed you this garbage, but you've received some bad information, detective. I'm not hung up on Steph. Like I said, there was never anything serious between us, and anyway, that all ended a long time ago. I've moved on, and so has she."

"So you didn't bear a grudge against Jeff Felfan?"

"Of course not! I wished them well. I wished *him* well."

"One more question, Mr. Scunner. Do you own a firearm?"

"No, I don't. Why would I need a firearm?"

"Where can we find your father?"

"He's inspecting the vines," said Robbie, pointing in the general direction of the wine fields.

"Thank you, sir," said Chase, and that was that.

. . .

"id you believe him?" asked Odelia once we had put some distance between ourselves and the foreman's son.

"Nope," said Chase. "He was lying through his teeth. The question is: what was he lying about?"

"I think he's still in love with Steph," said Dooley. "And I think it's all very romantic."

"It's not so romantic if he killed Steph's husband," I pointed out.

"He must have been overwhelmed with grief when Steph left. And then when she came back with a new boyfriend, and announced they were getting married, that must have really hurt."

"He says that wasn't the case."

"Oh, but he was lying, Max. Even Chase says it."

"Mh," I said. "It's possible." I was hedging my bets. Though I had to admit Mr. Scunner hadn't exactly come across as truthful. And that we needed to add him to our list of suspects, that was obvious. Unless his dad irrevocably supported his alibi. In which case he was in the clear.

But try as we might, we couldn't locate Larry Scunner in the vastness of the vineyard. It was a lot of ground to cover to find one man, of course, and so Chase and Odelia decided to give it another shot tomorrow. He wasn't going anywhere.

"ad," said Robbie urgently. He'd found his dad in his office, where he spent a lot of his time. "When the police ask you where I was this afternoon, I was right here, all right?"

Larry Scunner's leathery face screwed up into a network

of tiny wrinkles. "What are you talking about? You weren't here. You weren't anywhere near the winery."

"I know, but that's none of their business. I told them I was here, and that you could vouch for me."

Larry eyed his son with interest. "This wouldn't by any chance have anything to do with Jeff Felfan being murdered, would it?" His frown deepened. "Son? You're not in any trouble, are you?"

"No, Dad. I was in town on some personal business. And it had absolutely nothing to do with Jeff. But you know what the cops are like. They'll keep digging and asking questions and before you know it they'll think I killed Jeff."

"Now why would you go and kill Jeff Felfan?" asked his dad quizzically.

"I wouldn't! I didn't, I just told you." His dad was being exasperating again. "Look, just tell them I was with you all afternoon, and then everything will be fine." But as he left, he could tell that his dad wasn't convinced. He was staring at him with that same worried expression on his face he often got.

He hated to do this, of course. He hated lying to his dad. But that couldn't be helped. If he told the old man what he'd really been up to that afternoon, all hell would break loose. And that was the last thing he needed right now.

CHAPTER 24

Steph would have preferred to spend the rest of the day in her room—possibly the rest of her life. But that wasn't how she was built. And besides, she had Zoe to think of. Her little girl needed her, and would need her more than ever in the future, now that she had lost her dad. Not that she would know until she was much older. Perhaps it was a good thing that she was still so young, and wouldn't remember her dad or what happened to him. But at the thought of Zoe not even remembering Jeff, she choked up, and that box of tissues came in handy.

She left the house for a stroll, hoping it would do her good, when she bumped into Robbie. Frankly she wasn't in the mood to see him right now, and hoped he wouldn't be his usual surly self. But he looked repentant about his outburst the day before and said, "I'm so sorry about Jeff. I just heard what happened."

"Thanks, Robbie," she said. She could sense he wanted to say more, or was expecting her to say more, but she wasn't ready to talk about it yet, and so she quickly moved on. The last thing she wanted right now was to talk about

Jeff. She knew she wouldn't be able to hold it together if she did.

She was crossing the driveway when a red Ferrari came roaring in her direction. It braked with a spray of gravel and she watched as Kevin got out.

"Where have you been?" she asked. "The police are looking for you."

"Let them look," said Kevin curtly, then must have realized he was being a jerk, for his expression softened. "I'm sorry. I should have been here for you. I'm so sorry about what happened to Jeff. Do they know yet who's responsible?"

Steph shook her head. "They think it might be the guy who busted our window last night. They've got him in custody. He says he didn't do it, though."

"They all say that," Kevin scoffed. He took off his aviator sunglasses and leaned against his flashy new car. "So why did he do it? Did Jeff know the guy or what?"

"I don't think so. He was applying for the same job I was, and launched a vile campaign against me, to try and make sure I didn't get the job, and succeeded."

"The world is full of dangerous people," said Kevin with an airiness that seemed hardly appropriate under the circumstances.

"Dad seems to think Beniamino had something to do with it, though," Steph continued. "Well, Ben and Dominic both. He figures they might want to get back at the family, but instead of targeting one of us, they went for Jeff instead —like a warning." She shook her head. "It sounds crazy, I know, but at this point I'm ready to believe anything." When she looked up, she noticed to her surprise that Kevin was staring back at her with eyes blazing with anger. He was actually shaking with rage, and his face was all twisted up. "Kevin? What's wrong?"

"Leave Ben and Dominic out of this," he growled. He'd

balled his fists and his face was working. "It's just like Dad to try and pin this on them. But they didn't do it. They would never do anything to hurt us. That's just Dad… being Dad."

"I know. I don't buy it either," she said. He looked away, then, and she wondered what was going on with him. These sudden mood swings, this unprovoked anger—this wasn't the Kevin she knew. "I was looking for you last night, and also this morning," she said. "You keep disappearing on me, Kev."

He seemed to have simmered down. "Like I said, I like to go for a drive. I don't know if you've noticed, but running a business is tough. I get stressed, so I jump in my car and take off. Feel the wind in my hair… It's the only way to unwind."

His explanation didn't ring true to her. As long as she remembered, Kevin had been famous for shirking his responsibilities. Even though nominally he was being trained to be Dad's successor, he wasn't pulling his weight. Not by a long shot. "Dad works you too hard, is that it?" she asked.

He didn't respond well to the slight note of sarcasm in her voice, and suddenly lashed out, "You have no idea, do you? While *you're* off gallivanting in Paris and Rome and New York, designing your fancy outfits, I have to put up with Dad's crap on a daily basis. This place is hell, Steph. I wish I could escape—just like you!"

And with these words, he escaped her company, stomping off like a recalcitrant teen. She stared after him, wondering what had gotten into him all of a sudden. Kevin had never been easy to get along with, but lately he was becoming truly insufferable. She wondered why. It definitely wasn't because Dad worked him to the bone. Quite the contrary. Dad still took on more work than was good for him, and had a hard time delegating, even though he should.

No, something else was going on, and if she wasn't feeling such a complete mess after what happened to Jeff, she would try and get to the bottom of it. Now, she simply didn't care. Compared to that personal tragedy, nothing mattered.

Maybe nothing ever would again.

※

Unseen by Steph or Kevin, their mother had been watching them from the second-story window. She saw Kevin storm off, like he seemed to do a lot these days, and Steph leave to go for a walk—again. Things weren't going well for her and Ian's offspring. She glanced in the direction of the office block, and saw that she wasn't the only one who was spying on Steph. Robbie, half concealed behind the entrance door, had been watching the girl intently. He now made to follow her from a safe distance. Christ, she thought. He looks like a stalker.

Raimunda shook her head. "Robbie is acting strange again," she said.

Behind her, Ian was checking something on his phone. "Mh?"

"Robbie is following Steph around like a little puppy."

"Maybe he thinks that with Jeff out of the way he'll get a second chance?"

"Maybe. Would that be a good idea, you think?"

"Mh?"

"God, Ian! Stop looking at that damn thing and listen to me for one second, will you?"

Ian looked up, a blank look on his face. "What's that?"

"I was asking your opinion about something."

"What?"

"Steph and Robbie."

"What about them?"

"Do you think we should encourage them becoming an item again, now that Jeff is gone?"

Ian thought about this for a moment, then shook his head. "I don't think that's a good idea. And I think you know perfectly well why it's not a good idea."

"Mh, I guess," she said. "Too bad, though. If Steph and Robbie got together again, she would probably take more of an interest in the winery, wouldn't she?"

"I doubt it. Steph never had any interest in the business. And neither does Kevin, by the way. Where is that boy, anyway? He keeps disappearing on me."

"He went for a drive. He just got back."

"He went for a drive in the middle of the day? Doesn't he have anything better to do? I swear to you, Rai, that kid will be the death of me one of these days."

"Don't let him get to you. You've got enough on your plate as it is."

"That, I do," said Ian, and was lost in his phone once more.

CHAPTER 25

Shanille had never gone to one of these so-called AA meetings before. Oh, she'd heard about them, of course, and her human had often advised his parishioners to attend meetings—especially those who showed up drunk in the confession box. But she never thought she'd see the day when Francis himself would attend a meeting. He still looked out of sorts, which was understandable since he'd only just sobered up, after going on a marathon bender.

At least he'd had the good sense to do it where no one would see him. He could have passed out drunk in the rectory, but he'd felt that wouldn't be the decent thing to do. And so instead he'd found that old shack, had grabbed several boxes of booze, and had started trying to drink away his misery.

Shanille could have told him that he was asking for trouble. He made a promise to Marigold, after all. That he would leave the priesthood for her. But after several months, he still had yet to make a move, and so finally Marigold's patience had run out, and she had—quite correctly, in Shanille's view

—assumed that Francis was never going to leave the church, and so instead she had left him.

And even though her human was still holding onto a sliver of hope that she would change her mind, Shanille didn't think she would. She had gathered all of her belongings, and had taken off with her daughter to yonder shores. Canada, of all places, where she had family. A new life for Marigold, and for Francis Reilly, of course. At least now he wouldn't be torn between his calling and his girlfriend.

She watched on as Francis settled in the last row, right next to Tex Poole, Vesta Muffin and Scarlett Canyon, who were also attending the meeting. Odd that she would know so many people here, Shanille reflected. She didn't see the appeal of alcohol herself. It tasted horrible, in her opinion. But then she was a feline, of course, and in that sense superior to her human contemporaries, who were weak and simple-minded creatures, easily seduced by all manner of temptation and vice. Francis said it often: the spirit is willing, but the flesh is weak. Though as far as she could tell from her extensive experience, both the human spirit *and* the flesh were equally weak.

At least Francis had her to keep an eye on him. Which is what she'd done out there in the woods, though she hadn't been able to stop him from succumbing to the temptation of the demon alcohol. She was going to have to up her game if she still wanted to have a human to cater to her needs in the future. Admittedly the experience had given her a great jolt. And made her realize how fragile her existence was. Francis could have died, and then where would she be? At the pound, probably, being pawed by snotty-nosed brats and their annoying parents.

No, if she was going to keep Frances as her keeper and carer, she needed to make sure he didn't fall off the wagon again. And as she listened to this woman Betsy Brogue drone on and on about the twelve steps, the first glimmer of an idea started to form in her mind. Step one: convince the others. But in light of recent events, she didn't think that would be hard. Step two... But before she could come up with a twelve-step program of her own, Betsy Brogue announced that Francis's sponsor would be none other than... Scarlett Canyon!

Oh, dear, Shanille thought as she closed her eyes for a moment. When she opened them again, Scarlett was covering the priest's face with kisses. Very inappropriate! Not to mention probably borderline blasphemous! Clearly Miss Canyon saw in Marigold's departure a chance to bag herself a man of the cloth!

And so for the next half hour, cat choir's conductor came up with a revised version of the twelve-step program. In her personal view, a superior version.

ಸ

You know that things are returning to normal when cat choir is being conducted by the one and only Shanille once more. After an absence of several nights, one of which had dissolved into turmoil and recrimination, Shanille was back! And she came filled with plans. Though those plans, oddly enough, had nothing to do with music, and everything to do with alcohol!

"I attended the AA meeting this evening," the iconic conductor revealed, "and things are looking bad, you guys."

"What do you mean?" I asked.

"Did you know that Vesta is attending these AA meetings, and Tex, too?"

"Yeah, I did know that," I said. "Marge made them. She found some empty bottles in the recycle bin and so assumed her husband and mother had become alcoholics." Though to be honest I thought she was probably exaggerating. Neither Tex nor Gran were exactly the epitome of the raging drunk. But then Marge tends to overreact sometimes. I had the impression she would make them go for a while, and then forgive and forget and things would return back to normal.

"It's not enough," said Shanille decidedly. "In fact it won't do!"

"What's not enough?" I asked.

"Yeah, what won't do, Shanille?" asked Dooley.

"Let's wait until the others are here," said Shanille, cleverly building up the suspense. "Where are Harriet and Brutus? And where is Kingman?"

We glanced around, and saw that Harriet was surrounded by a group of her admirers. She was regaling them with the tale of how she had personally saved not only Father Reilly, but also Shanille herself from a terrible fate. Shanille would surely have died, if Harriet hadn't gone into those woods, with considerable risk to her own personal safety, and had found Shanille, and had rescued her.

Brutus now wandered in our direction. He didn't look all that happy, I thought.

"Is everything all right, Brutus?" I asked.

"Fine, fine," he grumbled, indicating not everything was fine.

"It's Harriet, isn't it?" said Shanille. "She's telling everyone how she saved my life and she's not even mentioning you."

"No, she is not," said Brutus with a deep sigh.

"She didn't actually save me, you know," said Shanille "I was just so worried about Francis that I didn't want to leave him alone for even one second."

"Oh, let her tell the story," said Brutus. "If it makes her feel better."

"Okay, so maybe we'll start without her," said Shanille.

She must have realized that once Harriet gets going tooting her own horn, it can take all night.

"Wait, there's Kingman," I said. And true to form, Kingman came waddling up, greeting cats left and right, and waving to everyone like the Pope riding around in his popemobile. "Hiya, fellas," he said once he'd joined us. "Glad to see you looking so fit and healthy, Shanille. Good thing Harriet saved your life, isn't it? Who knows what would have happened if she hadn't. Probably eaten by wolves. Or a bear."

"I was fine!" Shanille cried. "Nobody saved me!"

"Sure, sure," said Kingman quickly. He turned to me. "What's this I hear about some wine merchant being gunned down by a Chicago hit squad? Or was it the Columbians?"

"He wasn't a wine merchant," I said. "And he wasn't gunned down. Well, he was shot, and so was the woman he was with."

"Not his wife, eh?" said Kingman, giving me a wink. "Found in the bed of some prostitute, mh? Saucy stuff. Your human writing a front-page article, no doubt?"

"It wasn't like that," I said with a touch of exasperation.

"What's this town coming to, huh?" said Kingman as he glanced in the direction of a pretty female. "Mobsters and hitmen, shootings and prostitutes. Pretty soon this place will be the crime capital of the country, if you ask me."

"Well, nobody is asking you, Kingman," said Shanille. "So let's discuss this idea of mine, shall we? So four of our humans have succumbed to the drink devil already, and if this keeps up, I'm sure many more will follow. And as I see it, it's our responsibility to keep them from straying from the path. Humans have a name for this. They call it a sponsor. A person you can call when you feel weak, and in need of a drink. The system is clearly flawed, though. Scarlett Canyon is supposed to be Francis's sponsor, and Vesta is Tex Poole's sponsor and vice versa. I mean, that must be some kind of joke, right? So I've come up with a plan."

"I like your plan, Shanille," said Dooley happily.

Shanille stared at him. "I haven't even told you yet."

"I know, but I can tell it's a good one. I like it already."

"Okay. So my plan is to launch our own sponsor system. Each of us will be assigned a human, and we're going to follow that human around and make sure they never touch a drop of alcohol again in their life!"

"Why am I here?" asked Kingman now. "Unless I'm mistaken, Wilbur isn't part of this AA business, is he?"

"No, he is not, but he should be. I hate to break it to you, Kingman, but your Wilbur is a drunk."

"No, he's not. I mean, he drinks, but he's not a drunk."

"Every person who drinks is by definition a drunk," Shanille insisted. "It's the nature of the beast. Humans are weak. They simply cannot control themselves. They drink one glass, then another, then another, and before you know it, they're lying passed out on the couch, snoring through another episode of The Simpsons."

"Homer Simpson!" Dooley cried. "He's so funny!"

"No, he's not," said Shanille sternly. "Homer Simpson is a drunk."

"But—"

"So here's what we're going to do. I'll keep an eye on Francis, obviously. You, Brutus, will keep an eye on Vesta."

"Me! Why me!"

"Okay, fine." She glanced in my direction, and immediately I shook my head.

"We're in the middle of a case, Shanille. I can't follow Gran around all day."

"No, we're following Odelia and Chase around all day instead," said Dooley. "They're not drunks, but they are spending a lot of time at a winery, so they might be turning into drunks very soon now. It's too soon to tell, though."

Harriet, who had finally managed to tear herself away from her group of admirers, said, "What did I miss?"

"FuSSy," said Shanille.

Harriet frowned. "What did you just call me?"

"FuSSy, or Feline Sponsor System, is the new project we're launching to get Hampton Cove to go dry," Shanille explained. "Yes, Dooley, what is it?"

Dooley, who had raised his paw, now piped up, "Shouldn't it be FeSSy? Only there's no U in feline, you see."

"I don't like FeSSy," said Shanille. "FuSSy is better."

"But—"

"Okay, so Harriet, I'm assigning you and Brutus to Vesta and Scarlett. You will keep an eye on them at all times, and make sure they don't touch a drop of alcohol."

"Who will keep an eye on Tex?" asked Harriet.

"Mh... I see what you're saying. Okay, so here's what we'll do. Brutus, you get Tex. And Harriet, you take Vesta and Scarlett both, seeing as they seem to spend practically all of their time together anyway."

"So just to be clear," said Harriet. "What do we do when we see one of our humans reaching for a drink? I want to get this exactly right," she explained.

"Good question. The moment your human reaches for a bottle, you use your own judgment to prevent them from imbibing that poisonous liquid."

"But what do we do, exactly?"

"Look, all of these people are in the AA, right? So they have taken a pledge to stop drinking. So as far as I'm concerned, the moment they touch a drop of alcohol, all bets are off. And I mean claws, teeth, ear-splitting caterwauling, the works. They get the full treatment. You make them stop, no matter how, okay?"

"Okay, Shanille," said Harriet, and I could tell from the sparkle in her eye she was looking forward to this new mission.

"So let's do this, folks," said Shanille, rubbing her paws together.

"You mean, no rehearsal tonight?" I asked, much disappointed.

"No rehearsal. Our humans need us, especially now. When they're alone in bed at night, yearning for a drop of that evil stuff, they need us more than ever. So let's get this show on the road, people. FuSSy to the rescue!"

CHAPTER 26

The Felfans, David and Pauline, were arriving at the airport at ten o'clock, and Steph had volunteered to pick them up. Her dad had suggested they send a car round, but she wanted to do it herself. She wanted the first face they saw to be hers, and not some unknown driver. And besides, she wanted to tell them what was going on face to face, and in the privacy of her own car, instead of being surrounded by the rest of her family.

She didn't know why, but her folks had never really warmed to the Felfans. Maybe it was the cultural difference, even though she thought at the time that being a vintner, her dad and David Felfan would have a lot in common. Even though he wasn't a vintner himself, the fondness the French have for wine in general and French wine in particular is well-known.

But the few times the two parent pairs had met, the atmosphere had been convivial but the firm friendship that Steph had envisioned and hoped would spring up hadn't blossomed. She herself adored her in-laws though. Both

David and Pauline were warm-hearted people, and from the moment Jeff introduced her, they had accepted her as their own daughter, and she'd felt as home in their Paris apartment as she did in Hampton Cove—or perhaps even more so.

She had told herself to stay strong, but the moment she saw their faces as they walked out of the airport terminal, she broke down in tears, and so did both David and Pauline. And for the next five minutes the three of them clung to each other like survivors of some terrible tragedy, which in effect they were.

"I can't believe he's gone," said Pauline finally. She was a fine-boned woman, dressed with impeccable taste, who was hiding her eyes behind large sunglasses, and the moment she removed them, Steph could see why: she had probably been crying from the moment she'd received the terrible news that her son was dead.

David, too, looked gaunt and pale, and clearly hadn't slept since the news had hit. "How are you holding up?" he asked, offering her a weak smile.

"As well as can be expected," she said. Which wasn't very well indeed.

"Have the police given you any more information about this man they arrested?" asked Pauline. "Is he the one who killed our boy, you think?"

"They haven't told me more than what I already knew," she said.

"And the man in charge of the investigation? Is he any good?"

"Yes, he is. My dad tells me he has a very good reputation." He was odd, though, to be investigating Jeff's murder accompanied by his wife and her two cats. Like some kind of weird quirk. But as long as he got results, that was all that mattered.

They walked to where she had parked her car, and for a moment they sat there, as Pauline glanced at the small rosary that dangled from the rearview mirror. It had been her present to Jeff and Steph. She said it would protect them. And it had, when that maniac had tried to drive them off the road. But it hadn't protected Jeff when he had been lured to his death. Maybe he should have worn a second one, though she doubted that would have stopped whoever was responsible.

She put the car in gear, and soon they had left New York's heavy traffic behind and were traveling East along the Long Island Expressway.

"We've talked about what happened, your father and I," said Pauline now. She always referred to themselves as her mom and dad, which she actually loved. "And we still want you to come to Paris and live in the apartment we've bought for you."

"Oh, I don't know, Pauline."

"Please think about it," said Pauline softly. "It's what Jeff would have wanted. It's the home for you and Zoe, and the place where your heart can heal. Surrounded by the beauty and the things you love the most—and the people who love you the most," she added quietly. "Not that your parents don't love you, of course," she hastened to add, feeling that perhaps she had stepped on some toes.

Steph assured her that she hadn't. But she felt it was too soon to think about the future. First she wanted to bury her husband, and get through these next couple of days. And then there was the investigation. She didn't think she'd be able to consider her future until the man who killed Jeff was brought to justice.

"Where's Zoe?" asked Pauline.

"At the house," said Steph. "You'll see her soon."

Pauline nodded, satisfied. "Maybe it's a good thing that she's too young to know what's going on," she said, echoing the exact thought Steph had had herself. "Though growing up without a father..." She placed a hand on Steph's shoulder. "At least she has her mother, and her family, who love her very much."

All through this, David had hardly said a word. Steph glanced over to him, but he was keeping himself to himself. Once again, she thought he looked very haggard. As if discovering that he'd lost his son had aged him overnight.

Later, when she was showing Pauline and David their room and explaining about meal times, Pauline took her aside and said quietly, "David isn't well."

"Are you worried?"

"I am," her mother-in-law confessed. "He says he's going to quit politics. Says he can't do it anymore. And he's going to retire from the law practice."

"So he won't run for mayor?"

"No, he's giving that all up." She darted a look of concern in the direction of her husband, who was lying on the bed with his eyes closed, clearly exhausted. "He says there's no point now that Jeff is gone. There's no point to any of it."

"Give it a couple of weeks," Steph suggested. "We are all going to have to process this in our own way, and so is David."

"I don't know. I've never seen him so sure of something before. As if Jeff's death has put things in perspective. Made him realize what's really important. And clearly being the next mayor of Paris isn't as important as he thought it was."

She could understand that. She was also re-evaluating her life now. Trying to figure out what she wanted to do. Fighting for that job at WelBeQ seemed so pointless now. Even though it had seemed so important a couple of days ago, she simply didn't care now. Or the job in Paris. Or any job, for that matter. All she wanted was to have Jeff back. But that wasn't going to happen.

A soft rap sounded at the door, and when she opened it, her mother said that the police had arrived, and could they have a quick word with David and Pauline, if they felt up to it?

CHAPTER 27

*D*avid and Pauline Felfan looked as shellshocked as any couple who had recently lost their son could look. As they sat in the downstairs salon, listening to Chase introducing himself and Odelia, they hardly seemed to be paying any attention at all. For a moment I wondered if they even spoke English. I knew that Chase didn't speak French, and Odelia must have wondered the same thing, for she suggested we bring in Steph so she could translate.

But then Pauline held up a slender and bejeweled hand and said, "That won't be necessary. Though are you sure you want my husband here? He isn't feeling well, you see."

"It's the jet lag," said David, clearing his throat.

He cut a tall, imposing figure, or he would have done, if he hadn't looked so pale and drawn. With his full head of gray hair and his fleshy face, he certainly looked like a man who made a deep impression on people. Even now, when he was clearly feeling under the weather.

"I'll be fine in a moment," he assured us, though he wasn't fooling anybody. "Steph told us you have a man in custody.

But she also told us you haven't given her a lot of information about him. Is he the man who killed my son, detective?"

"I'm afraid we had to release the person we had in custody. He's admitted to certain facts, but not the murder, and since we can't prove his involvement, for now he's a free man again. But he's still a suspect, and we're doing everything we can to build a case against him, though we're keeping our options open, and are also looking at other possibilities."

"I have a possibility for you," said David, sitting up a little straighter. "Perhaps Steph told you about this, but I was going to run for mayor of Paris. Now with Jeff gone, I no longer have plans in that direction. But when my son was still alive…" He broke down for a moment, with Pauline reaching out a concerned hand. But he quickly recovered, clearly eager to stay strong. "When Jeff was still alive, there was every chance that I was going to win that election and be the next mayor. My main opponent was a man named Bill Cymbal. Now, of course, with me out of the way, he's going to win. And so I've been thinking about this all through the flight to New York, and I'm convinced that Cymbal is behind the murder of my son."

"Oh, David," said Pauline, who seemed taken aback.

"You see, the man is ruthless. Absolutely ruthless."

"You don't possibly think…"

"No, but I do think, *chéri*. Steph told us that the gun used to murder my son is connected to an organized crime syndicate. Well, that proves it, doesn't it? Cymbal is a smooth operator, and he would never get his hands dirty, but he would know how to hire a professional killer and order a hit on my one and only son, knowing it would utterly destroy me. And that's what he wants. He wants to destroy me. And I'm afraid to admit, Detective Kingsley, that he has succeeded. I'm officially withdrawing my candidacy. I'll announce it the moment we land in Paris."

"Please reconsider, David," said Pauline. "You'd make such a great mayor. And you know how proud Jeff was of you."

"It was me who was proud of Jeff," said David quietly as a lone tear slid down his cheek. "And I just wish I would have told him before it was too late."

"He knew," said Pauline. "He knew how proud we were of him and Steph."

For a moment, no one spoke, unwilling to ruin the moment. But then David cleared his throat, "Well, there you have it. Your killer is the next mayor of Paris."

※

"I didn't know a mayor could be a killer, Max," said Dooley.

"I guess anyone can be a killer, Dooley," I said.

The interview was at an end, and the Felfans had left. I had the impression they were going straight to bed. This jet lag business clearly was a big pain.

"Yes, but a mayor has a responsibility to take care of people, not to murder them."

"One doesn't exclude the other. You can take care of some people and murder others." Though frankly this story about Mr. Cymbal reaching across the Atlantic to murder the son of his political opponent seemed a little far-fetched. If he wanted to hurt David Felfan's chances of becoming the next mayor wouldn't he resort to the usual stuff? Like spreading nasty rumors, perhaps, or hiring a private detective to dig up dirt on the man? Murder seemed a little risky. No matter how careful you were, sooner or later a connection might be made, and not only would Cymbal not be mayor of Paris, but he would find himself an inmate of its penal system. And I didn't think a man like that would take the risk.

Chase had gone in search of Steph, wanting to have another word with Jeff's widow, and in the meantime we were waiting in the nice salon. On the walls paintings had been placed depicting vineyards down the ages. It all looked very pleasant and very bucolic. Which reminded me of something.

"Did you know that Tex and Gran have joined the AA?" I asked.

"Yeah, Mom told me," said Odelia with a smile. "They're each other's sponsors, if you can believe it."

"Oh, I can," I said. "And Father Reilly and Scarlett are in the same boat. Though the pleasure is entirely Scarlett's, I imagine."

"Father Reilly's wife has left him," Dooley explained. "Though she wasn't actually his wife, because he's not allowed to get married. So his bishop told him to carry on with Marigold in secret, but she didn't like that, and now she's gone to Canada with her daughter, and Father Reilly has become a drunk."

"Poor Francis," said Odelia, shaking her head. "He really loved Marigold."

"And now he loves the bottle," said Dooley. "But Shanille is watching him. She's launched the FuSSy brigade, and they're going to stop their humans from drinking alcohol no matter what. 'All bets are off,' she said. Those were her exact words."

"What does that mean?" asked Odelia with a frown.

"Your guess is as good as mine," I said. "But it doesn't bode well for your dad and grandmother."

"I still can't believe Mom made Dad attend AA meetings," said Odelia. "I mean, does he drink more than he should sometimes? Yes, he does. But he's not an alcoholic, and neither is Gran."

"They're not alcoholics, but they can't stop drinking," said Dooley.

"Not being able to stop drinking is the definition of an alcoholic, Dooley," I said.

"No, it's not. An alcoholic is a member of the AA. As long as you don't join the club, you're fine. But of course Marge had to go and sign them up, so now they're card-carrying alcoholics and they've got the official AA badges to prove it."

Odelia's lips quirked up into a smile at Dooley's peculiar logic. And I had the impression she had more to say on the subject, but Chase walked in with Steph Stewart and so we were plunged back into our investigation of Jeff's murder.

CHAPTER 28

Chase gave Steph the same news he gave Jeff's parents: that they had to let Edmundo Crowley go, since they didn't have the evidence to bring charges against the man.

"So... you're simply going to let him walk?" asked Steph, who didn't take too well to the news.

"We investigated the man's computer and phone, and found no evidence that he hired someone to murder your husband, or obtained the gun to carry out the murder himself. And we showed Crowley's picture to a witness who saw a man enter Cipriana Cilke's flat yesterday afternoon shortly before she and Jeff were shot, and she didn't recognize him. Furthermore, the search of his phone and computer shows no evidence that he was behind the campaign that got you dismissed from consideration for the WelBeQ position. So unless he has a second computer, or is a very clever operator, he might not be the guy we're looking for."

Steph's eyes were wide and concerned. "Crowley wasn't behind that slander campaign?"

"At this moment we have no reason to assume that he was."

"I don't believe this. What about the NYPD investigation?"

"We're going to liaise with them on this. They're carrying out their own analysis of the man's phone and computer, as well as the results of the search of his apartment. And we're going to pay a visit to the officer who's in charge of that investigation. But unless they come up with something solid and conclusive…"

"But if Crowley didn't do it, then who did?"

"The investigation is still ongoing," Chase assured her. "We will get to the bottom of this, Steph."

"Crowley did confess to throwing those rocks through your window," Odelia said, "and also the reckless maneuver that had Jeff pull over. He says he did that after he found out that your complaint with the NYPD cost him the WelBeQ job."

"They didn't hire him?"

"No, they didn't," said Chase. "The NYPD contacted them and asked them about his candidacy, and afterward they decided to hire a different candidate."

"Oh, God. And now you're saying he wasn't even behind that campaign. So I cost an innocent man his job."

"Like I said, the investigation is ongoing, so it's too soon to draw any conclusions."

"This is all such a mess."

"Don't beat yourself up too much," said Odelia. "There will be other job opportunities for Mr. Crowley. And for you, as well."

"One other thing," said Chase. "Your father-in-law seems to think that his political opponent may be behind Jeff's murder. One Bill Cymbal?"

"I've heard about him from Jeff. He's a pretty shrewd politician. Though in spite of his maneuvering David was still leading in the polls, with Cymbal trailing far behind, so David would probably have won. But now he's saying he wants to retire from politics. Pauline says it's because of the shock of Jeff's death, and that he might reconsider. But I'm not so sure. David is the kind of person who doesn't make decisions lightly. And once he's decided something he doesn't backtrack."

"What do you think about his theory that Cymbal killed your husband?"

"Honestly, I don't know," said Steph, shaking her head. "I'm sorry."

"That's all right," said Odelia. "We just wanted to check with you. By the way, we've been trying to talk to your brother, but we seem to keep missing each other. You wouldn't by any chance know where we can find him, do you?"

"He's around," said Steph vaguely. "Though he keeps going for drives."

"We saw his car parked at the Kosinski place yesterday," said Chase. "Any idea what he was doing out there?"

Steph frowned. "Kevin at the Kosinski Winery? No, I don't know what he was doing there. My family and the Kosinski family aren't exactly on speaking terms."

"Clearly Kevin is."

"I'm sorry, but you'll have to ask Kevin about that."

And from the look of determination on Chase's face, he would.

"Okay, we're almost through," said Odelia kindly, when she noticed that Steph seemed tired and had started to become irritable. "We talked to Robbie Scunner yesterday. Now he claims he was at the winery at the time of Jeff's murder, but—"

"Robbie wouldn't harm Jeff," said Steph immediately. "You're barking up the wrong tree there."

"The thing is that Beniamino Kosinski told us that Robbie took the end of your relationship badly, and that he told people at your wedding that he was in mourning. So clearly he wasn't a big fan of your husband, Steph."

"It's all such a long time ago. I'm sure he got over it by now." But her words lacked the true ring of conviction. Clearly she knew something she wasn't telling us. And Chase, being the good copper that he was, pounced on it.

"We talked to Larry Scunner, and after a lot of hemming and hawing he came out and admitted that he couldn't positively swear one hundred percent that he'd seen his son at the winery yesterday afternoon around the time Jeff and Cipriana Cilke were killed. First he claimed that Robbie was here, but the man is such a terrible liar that it didn't take long before he broke down and admitted that he hadn't seen him when he first said he did. When I asked him why he lied, he mumbled something about being confused and getting his times mixed up. Though it wouldn't surprise me if Robbie had asked his dad to lie for him."

"There's also that dust-up between Robbie and Jeff on the morning of his murder," Odelia said. "Robbie seemed very angry with Jeff."

"I honestly can't believe Robbie would hurt Jeff," said Steph. "But it's true that sometimes I get the impression he's still hung up on me. That he never really got over me leaving. To me it never meant much. We dated, but it was all very sweet and innocent. We never made big plans for the future or anything. So when I left I didn't give Robbie a second thought. I know it sounds bad but that's how it was."

"But he felt different, didn't he?"

"I guess he did. He's been following me around, you know. He thinks I don't know, but I can see him spying on me. It creeps me out, to be honest. Not that I think he would do anything," she was quick to add. "But it's not very nice. I'll go for a walk, and suddenly I will bump into him—by accident, but not by accident. And then he'll get mad about something and stalk off. He's still very much like a boy. Immature, I mean. Throwing his weight around when he can't get what he wants." When Odelia and Chase shared a look, she hastened to say, "Don't get me wrong—he would never hurt me. Robbie is the sweetest, gentlest soul. And I feel terrible that he would think that he meant so little to me that I never even called or wrote after I left. But it's true. To me he was just a good friend, nothing more."

"But in his mind he was so much more," said Odelia, nodding.

"I guess so. Oh, it's all so very confusing, isn't it? Just one big mess."

"It's not your fault that Robbie is acting this way, Steph," said Odelia. "So please don't blame yourself."

"But what if he did... kill Jeff?" Her hands, which had been resting in her lap, had traveled to her face, which displayed her keen distress. "Then it's all my fault, isn't it? Somehow... I provoked him!"

"No, you did not," said Chase. "And besides, we don't know what happened. It could be Robbie, but it could be someone else entirely. Though, just to be on the safe side, maybe it's best if you don't go for long walks all by yourself for a while. At least until we've caught the man responsible for Jeff's murder, all right?"

Steph nodded forlornly. "Of course. You're absolutely right. I won't."

CHAPTER 29

"Robbie probably hopes to marry Steph now that Jeff is dead," said Dooley.

"That's entirely possible," I said. "Though I doubt whether she sees it that way."

Once more we were traipsing through the sprawling winery in search of a person. This time it was Robbie we wanted to talk to, though if we ran into Kevin that wouldn't be such a bad thing either. The place was so big that you could probably walk around for days and not bump into another living soul. Okay, so maybe I was exaggerating slightly, but still.

His dad had told us we would probably find Robbie in the garage, where he was busy fixing one of the trucks that had recently broken down. And so we had found the garage, but of Robbie there was no trace. But then I got an idea.

"Steph said that Robbie has been following her around," I told Odelia. "So maybe he's doing that right now?"

"Where did Steph say she was going?" asked Odelia.

"Look in on Zoe," said Chase.

And so we retraced our steps, and soon approached the

main residence, where the Stewart family lived. We circled the building, knowing that the nursery was at the back, and immediately Chase's sharp eyes located our quarry.

"Hey, you!" he yelled. Robbie was actually standing behind a tree, glancing up at one of the windows, most likely the nursery. The moment he caught sight of us, he blanched. "We want to talk to you!" Chase said, just in case the young man thought we were there simply to take in the scenery.

For a moment I thought he'd turn and run, but he seemed to have more sense than that. And so he stayed put until we'd joined him.

"Great view?" asked Chase grimly as he pointed to the nursery window, where we could now see Steph holding her baby in her arms, and feeding Zoe a bottle.

"I was just... checking... something," said Robbie lamely.

"Okay, so Steph tells us you've been stalking her," said Chase, not beating about the bush. "And your dad told us he didn't see you all afternoon yesterday. So what's going on, Robbie?"

"Nothing. I just—did Steph really say that?"

"She did."

"I'm not stalking her. I mean... I guess I've been looking out for her. What with her husband's murder and all, I just figured she could use someone to keep an eye on her."

"Where were you yesterday between two and three, Robbie?" Chase pressed. "And you better tell us the truth this time, cause sooner or later we're going to find out, and if we discover you were anywhere near the place where Jeff was killed, there will be hell to pay."

Robbie gulped once or twice, then stared at his feet. "I... I followed Jeff in my car. I just thought... Well, I don't know what I thought. I'd overheard him say he was meeting a colleague in town, and I just figured that couldn't be right. He works in New York—so how was he meeting a colleague in Hampton Cove? He's not even from around here. He's from Paris. It just struck me as odd, that's all."

"So you figured as Steph's self-appointed protector and hero you would see where her husband was going, thinking that he might be up to no good, is that it?"

Robbie nodded meekly. "I thought maybe he was having an affair or something. It happens, you know, when men become dads, that suddenly they... well, you know. Anyway, so I followed him from a safe distance, all the way to Hampton Cove, and then to that place where he was meeting his so-called colleague. Only it wasn't a bar but just a house, which struck me as pretty suspicious. And so I googled the place, and discovered it was a kind of private escort service. 'Cipriana and Hailey are two sexy ladies who will make your wildest dreams come true.' That's what it said on their website. So I snapped a couple of pictures of him going in, and thought I'd show them to Steph, to prove that her husband was cheating on her with a prostitute. Only before I had the chance I heard that he'd actually been murdered by this Cipriana person, so I didn't think it was a good idea to... well, you know..." Here his voice trailed off.

"To tell us you were there," said Chase. "Just in case we would think you had something to do with the killings." He rubbed his face. "Robbie, you do realize that lying to the police is a punishable offense? And so is withholding evidence?"

"I didn't see anything," he said defensively. "I didn't see what happened."

"Why don't you let us be the judge of that?"

"No, but I figured it didn't matter. This prostitute killed Jeff then killed herself. Only later I found out that it wasn't as simple as that, and there was another angle. But by then it was too late. If I told you what happened I'd be in trouble."

"You're still in big trouble, Robbie," said Chase.

"But we're also happy you finally told us the truth," said Odelia, giving her husband a look that said, 'Lay off the kid, will you? He made a mistake but he's not a killer.'

But Chase wasn't convinced. "Who's to say that you didn't go into that flat and killed them both? You were jealous of Jeff, weren't you? Figured he'd stolen your girlfriend—the woman you loved—still love to this day. So why not get hold of a gun and get rid of the guy? Without Jeff, maybe Steph will come back to you. Maybe you'll finally be reunited, and this time she'll stick around. No more Paris. No more New York. She'll move back here and be with you, just like she should."

"It's what I wanted," said Robbie. "It's my fondest wish. But I know it's never going to happen. She doesn't love me. She never loved me. Not the way that I love her. I knew that when I saw the way she looked at Jeff. At their wedding. She'd never looked at me like that. And I knew that she had never loved me. Not really." He seemed sullen, but his eyes had filled with tears, and I think we all realized he was telling the truth. "I didn't kill Jeff. Why would I? Steph loved him so much and he loved her. And when you love a person you want what's best for them, don't you? Well, I knew that Jeff was the best person for Steph. He made her happy. And I wanted him to keep on making her happy. Which is why I was so upset when I saw him go into that place to be with that woman. And before you say I killed him because he cheated on Steph—no, I didn't. I just didn't, all right? And I know I can't prove it, but I'm not that kind of person. I just… I just loved the wrong girl all my life. Which is stupid, I know, but there you have it." He swiped at his eyes.

"All right, settle down," said Chase, placing a hand on the man's shoulder. "It's all right, son. I'm glad you told us. But maybe you can stop following people around, all right?"

"You mean stop following Steph around."

"Yeah, it's not healthy. Not for you, and not for her."

"But someone has to protect her, detective," he said, and suddenly turned a couple of fierce eyes on Chase. "Whoever killed Jeff might come back to kill her, too. So someone should keep an eye on her."

"I don't think that's for you to decide, buddy," said Chase. "Now I can tell you're hurting. But you've got to let go of this obsession with Stephanie Stewart."

"It was better when she wasn't here," said Robbie, drying his eyes with the paper tissue Odelia had handed him. "When she'd moved to Paris." He stared off into the distance. "I've thought about leaving, you know. But my dad needs me. And anyway, I don't have any particular skills. I didn't go to college. All I've known all my life is the winery. It's all I know how to do. So where would I go?"

"You'll figure it out, son," said Chase, and I noticed how he had adopted a fatherly tone now. "You'll figure it out."

I saw him look up at the house, and just at that moment Steph glanced down at us, standing there chatting. "Yeah, I need to figure this out once and for all," said Robbie. "Cause one thing's for sure. I can't go on like this. I just can't."

When we were in the car and driving back to Hampton Cove, Dooley said, "Robbie Scunner is not a happy boy, Max. Not a happy boy at all."

"No, he certainly isn't," I agreed. But was he a murderer? Now that was a tough call to make, one for which we would need to gather more pertinent facts first.

Once more Kevin Stewart had eluded us. His car wasn't in the drive, and it wasn't in the garage either, and when Chase called the number his sister had given us, he got the man's voicemail, pleasantly inviting him to leave a message.

Sooner or later, though, we were going to catch up with

Mr. Stewart, and knowing Chase, that young man wasn't going to enjoy the experience of being on the receiving end of the cop's ire. Whether he did it on purpose or not, he was the only person we hadn't spoken to. And somehow I didn't think that was a coincidence.

CHAPTER 30

The police had only just left when Kevin came roaring up in his Ferrari. When he walked into the house Steph put her hands on her hips and decided to have it out with her brother once and for all. "Where have you been? The police are looking for you."

But he didn't seem inclined to respond. Like before, his face spelled storm, and instead of replying, he simply walked right past her without uttering a word.

"I'm talking to you, Kevin!"

But all she got was picture but no sound. And as she made to follow him, suddenly she thought better of it. Whatever Kevin was up to, it had nothing to do with what happened to Jeff, and so consequently nothing to do with her. If he wanted to act like a jerk, so be it. And if the police wanted to find him, sooner or later they would, and she got the impression from that big detective that when they did catch up with them, there would be hell to pay. And if he tried to pull a trick like this on Detective Kingsley, he had another thing coming.

Five minutes later she was rocking Zoe on her lap, and

sitting with her in-laws on the patio. The weather was glorious, and she should have felt happy on a day like this. But without Jeff, the sun could give of its best all it wanted, but it didn't make any difference.

"I just wish you'd come back to Paris with us," said Pauline. "You and Zoe could move in with David and me for the time being—while your apartment is being renovated. It's only around the corner, and you could pick your own furnishings, and select your kitchen, colors for the bathroom…" Pauline gave her a hopeful look. And Steph could understand where they were coming from. Of course she could. They'd just lost their only son, and now all they had were Steph and, more importantly, Zoe. The grandchild that would always remind them of their son. She would always carry a part of her father in her, and they wanted her close to them.

But she wasn't sure what she wanted to do. It was too soon anyway. She was still mourning Jeff, and had no idea what the future would hold for her and Zoe now. And besides, here in Hampton Cove at least she had her family. Even though Pauline and David were almost like family to her, it wasn't the same. And now, with Jeff gone, things were going to be different. A different dynamic, for one thing. No longer was she their son's wife. Now they had to build a new rapport.

"I don't know," she said truthfully. "I'm still trying to come to terms with what happened. And I'm not sure if I'll be ready to start making plans any time soon."

"Just leave her be, Pauline," said David, enveloping his wife's hand in his, and giving it a tender squeeze. "We're all in shock, and we're all mourning. Now is not the time to think about the future. Now is the time to honor the past. Honor Jeff."

"I know. But I'm worried," said Pauline. She didn't say

what she was worried about, nor did she have to. If Steph decided to stay in the States, they might never see their granddaughter again. Or only on rare occasions. Perhaps once a year or so. And that possibility seemed very hard for Pauline to bear. She'd lost her son, she didn't want to lose her granddaughter, too.

"It's just that... I hardly know anyone in Paris," said Steph, feathering a light kiss on top of Zoe's head. She knew a few people, of course, but they were all fellow students, and many of them had returned to their home countries after graduation. A few people were French, but not all of them lived in Paris. And after the Sofie Fashion job had fallen through, her excitement to move back there and build a life had taken a big hit. And now with Jeff gone... It just wasn't the same.

"You can easily find a job," said Pauline, not giving up so quickly. "David knows a lot of people, don't you, David? It won't take long to find a wonderful job with wonderful colleagues. And once you start living and working in Paris, you'll meet new people all the time, and you'll have plenty of friends. And you have us, of course." She gave Zoe such a longing look that Steph's heart almost broke.

"Let's just wait and see," she said, not wanting to pin herself down on anything right now. It was simply too soon. First they needed to arrange the funeral—and to do that the police had to release the body, which was another source of great sorrow for herself and Jeff's parents. They couldn't even say goodbye, for Jeff had been murdered. It was still hard for her to wrap her head around. It was surreal.

"That police detective was very kind," said David, who must have read her mind. "I told him all about Bill Cymbal and he's going to look into that man."

"Oh, please, David, you don't really think Cymbal had

anything to do with this, do you?" said Pauline. "You may not like his ideas, but he's not a murderer, surely."

"And I'm telling you he is," said David. "The man will stop at nothing to get what he wants. Right now it's the mayoralty, then cabinet minister, and after that the presidency. He's got it all worked out, and anything or anyone standing in his way will simply be mowed down." He slashed the air with a flat hand. "Chop chop. That's the way he's operated for as long as I've known him. He's like a machine that way. A relentless, remorseless, cold and calculating machine. Very ruthless."

"I find it hard to believe that he would be stupid enough to resort to murder. He's not a stupid man, David. And only a stupid man would think he can get away with murder."

"He's not stupid, but he's arrogant. Arrogant enough to think he's above the law. And very soon, if he's not stopped, he will be the law, and then woe betide *La France* and all its *citoyens*."

The discussion seemed endless, and frankly Steph wasn't in the mood. So while her in-laws continued to discuss the merits of David's theory, she took Zoe inside. It was time for her bath—and for Steph to have a lie-down.

CHAPTER 31

Dutifully we all filed into Uncle Alec's office. The Chief wanted an update on the state of the investigation, and so all the usual suspects were present again: Odelia and Chase, of course, and Dooley and myself. Our input was limited to not getting on the Chief's nerves too much—which meant we were sitting quietly and making ourselves invisible—while Chase was expected to deliver a full report.

"What I've been wondering," said the Chief, "is how the killer knew that Cipriana's flatmate would be out. Unless she was in on it, of course."

"I don't think he did know," said Chase. "If Hailey had stuck around, I'm sure he would have killed her, too."

"She had a narrow escape," said Odelia.

"You're sure she's not involved?" asked the Chief.

"Absolutely. Several witnesses saw her in the shop."

"And so you're satisfied that Jeff was the intended target, not Cipriana?"

"If we accept that Jeff was lured there, and wasn't there as a client, then yes, Jeff must have been the intended victim."

"He could have been a client, who happened to be in the wrong place at the wrong time," the Chief pointed out. "And then Cipriana is the one you should be looking at."

"Hailey had never seen Jeff before, so he wasn't a regular customer," said Chase. "And we checked his phone. He did indeed get a message from his colleague, asking to meet him in town that afternoon."

"But Clive Balcerak never sent that message," said Odelia. "Or at least he claims he didn't. He says he wasn't in Hampton Cove but in New York."

"Better talk to the guy, and check his alibi," said Uncle Alec. "He could be lying."

"We're meeting him tomorrow," said Chase. "It wasn't easy to pin him down. Said he had some big work thing and couldn't make himself available."

"Tell him to make himself available. This is a murder investigation, not a social call. Right." He splayed his fingers on his desk. "If this was a professional hit, and Jeff was the target, then who are we looking at? Who could be behind this thing?"

"David Felfan thinks his political opponent ordered the hit," said Odelia. "He's Jeff's dad, and he was running for mayor of Paris before this happened. He's decided to withdraw as a candidate, which means the next mayor will almost certainly be Bill Cymbal."

"Who ordered a hit on his opponent's son as an intimidation tactic," Chase completed this possible theory.

"I'm not sending you to Paris to talk to the guy," the Chief grumbled. "For now let's try to organize a Zoom call. And if you think he might be involved, let's liaise with Interpol." He frowned. "How likely do you think his involvement is?"

"At this point, we really have no way of knowing, boss," Chase admitted.

"The other possibility that's been suggested is that Beniamino Kosinski is behind the hit," said Odelia, moving on from the French connection. "He's—"

"Yes, I know who Beniamino Kosinski is," said the Chief. "But what does he have to do with this murder business?"

"Well, Ian Stewart suggested that Jeff's murder could be a warning. Both families have been at daggers drawn for years, and have been locked in a war of words. Beniamino could be trying to get the Stewarts to sell him their winery, giving him a virtual monopoly in this part of the South Fork."

"If you don't give me what I want, I'll start killing people," said the Chief. "It sounds good in theory, but frankly I don't think Ben is that kind of guy. I've met him a few times, and he doesn't strike me as the Don Corleone type of person."

"Yeah, we also met him, and he doesn't exactly look like a cold-blooded killer," said Chase. "In fact he gave us a crate of wine as a present."

"You didn't accept, did you?" asked the Chief, alarmed.

Chase smiled. "Of course not. Bribing the police—big no-no."

"He wasn't trying to bribe us," said Odelia. "Just being nice."

"Fine," said Uncle Alec. "So who else? Besides the wine guy and the French politician? Tell me you've got some other suspects lined up?"

"Well, there's Robbie Scunner," said Odelia.

"Who's he?"

"The Stewart Winery foreman's son. He's in love with Steph, and was deeply unhappy when she left for Paris, and returned with Jeff Felfan on her arm."

"Plain old-fashioned jealousy. I like him as a suspect. So where are we on alibi?"

"Well, he admits he followed Jeff into town, and even snapped a couple of pictures of the moment he entered

Cipriana's flat. But we showed his picture to our witness, and she didn't recognize him."

"She wouldn't, if he hired a hitman," the Chief pointed out. "Which is your overriding theory, if I'm not mistaken?" He gave his detective a scrutinizing look.

"You're correct, sir," said Chase. "But we've checked Robbie's phone records and also his bank statements, and didn't find anything that raises a red flag."

"At least tell me he saw the killer enter the flat after Jeff Felfan?"

But Odelia shook her head. "Says he left when he saw Jeff walk in. He googled the address, discovered it was an escort service, and was so excited to give Steph the news that her husband was a whoremonger he couldn't wait to get back to the winery. Only when he got there he couldn't find Steph, and by the time he did, Jeff's body had already been discovered so he figured he'd better keep his mouth shut about his little expedition, so as not to draw suspicion to himself."

The Chief sighed. "Dead end after dead end. Tell me some good news, please?"

"Kevin Stewart," said Odelia. "He's been eluding us. And according to Steph he's been acting really strange lately."

"Go on."

"We're still trying to get hold of him, but we saw his car parked in the Kosinski driveway, which is odd, since the Stewarts and the Kosinskis aren't on speaking terms."

"So what was he doing at the Kosinski place?" said the Chief, nodding. "If he keeps giving you the slip, have him picked up. Obstructing a police investigation. That should make him more cooperative. Right. Anything else I need to know?"

"No, that's it," said Odelia. "For now."

"Not much, but something at least," said her uncle. "So talk to Jeff's colleague. Check his alibi for the time of the murder. Talk to Kevin Stewart. Find out what he's up to. And keep digging, people. Get me some results—pronto!"

"Yes, Chief," said Chase dutifully.

"And now get lost," grunted Uncle Alec, and for some reason he looked at me when he spoke these words!

Once we'd left the office, Dooley said, "I get the impression that Uncle Alec doesn't like us very much, Max."

"I'm sure he loves us," I said. "It's just that he has a strange way of showing it." Though secretly I was starting to think that maybe Dooley was right. This would be odd, in a family of cat people like the man's mother, sister and niece. Then again, maybe that was exactly the reason he didn't like us— sometimes too much of a good thing can be a bad thing, and Uncle Alec had certainly been exposed to cats a lot in his lifetime.

"So now what?" asked Dooley.

"Now we go home," I said. Frankly I was starving. All this running around and talking to people left and right—and nobody had thought of giving us something to eat! I mentioned this to Dooley, who wholeheartedly agreed.

"Maybe we should ask Uncle Alec to officially deputize us," my friend suggested. "That way people can't ignore us, and have to feed us." It hadn't escaped his notice that wherever Odelia and Chase went, they got offered food and drink —even whole crates of wine in Beniamino Kosinski's case! But they never thought twice about giving two poor starving creatures like us the time of day.

"I don't think Uncle Alec would like the idea," I said, and that was putting it mildly.

"Or Odelia should keep a small plastic container of food in the car for emergencies," said Dooley.

"Now that's a good idea," I said. "Why didn't I think of that?"

And so we made up our mind to mention the idea to

Odelia on the first occasion. "We could even suggest several containers," Dooley went on, happy that I had taken to his idea with such fervor and enthusiasm. "Different types of kibble, you know, and also some wet food. She could create an entire picnic menu."

I wasn't sure she would go for it, but the idea definitely had merit, and my stomach, which was rumbling freely, felt exactly the same way!

Which gave me an idea. "Let's drop by Kingman," I suggested. Kingman always has some decent grub to share, since his human owns the General Store.

And while Chase got busy typing up yet another report, and Odelia another article, Dooley and I walked the short distance from the police office to Main Street, where we hoped to satisfy our appetite and tide us over until dinner.

CHAPTER 32

Only when we got there no food seemed to be forthcoming. Of the usual bowls located underneath the crates of fruits and veggies there was not a single trace—and neither, it turned out, of Kingman himself!

"Where is Kingman?" asked Dooley, who had noticed the same thing. Then his eyes went wide. "Oh, no. Maybe he's gone without a trace, just like Shanille!"

"Shanille wasn't actually gone, Dooley," I reminded him. "She simply followed her human into the woods, to keep an eye on him just in case he was off his rocker. Which, as it turns out, he was."

"So where is he?" asked Dooley, glancing left and right. "He's always here. Never leaves his post."

"I'm sure he does, if only to have a wee."

Dooley laughed at this. "I'm sorry. It's just that I was picturing Kingman in a litter box. I don't think they actually make litter boxes big enough for him."

I smiled. It was hard to imagine Kingman going in a litter box. "Maybe he does his business outside." The General Store does have a small patch of green behind the store. It even has a tree, something all cats like—at least one thing we have in common with dogs. Though dogs like trees for the purpose of raising their hind leg against. We like it to keep our claws in shipshape condition.

And that's when we heard it. Some kind of ruckus coming from inside the store. And since curiosity is our middle name—not really, but you get my drift—we quickly ventured inside to see what was going on.

"Maybe the store is being held up!" said Dooley. "And we'll have to call 911!"

"We can't call 911, Dooley," I reminded my friend. For one thing, cats don't own phones. And for another, say we manage to dial the required number, how are we going to make ourselves understood? Not many people speak our language, after all.

It took us a while to understand the scene that was playing out before us. Wilbur Vickery stood next to the big fridge that contains all manner of alcohol, in front of him on the floor sat Kingman, staring up at the man and growling—actually growling! And on the floor between them a can of cold beer lay on its side, like a fallen soldier, with the liquid spilling from the can.

"Are you crazy!" Wilbur was shouting. "What has gotten into you, Kingman!"

"I'm a member of FuSSy, you fool," said Kingman. "Touch that can of poison one more time—I dare you!"

But of course poor Wilbur had no idea what his cat was saying. So he bent over and picked up that can. He checked it closely—possibly for cooties—and was about to put it to his lips when Kingman performed a perfectly executed standing jump, raised his right paw high, and slapped that can out of his human's hand!

The can of brewski performed a nice arc through the air, and landed amid a selection of fine brown eggs, not exactly the kind of company eggs are in the habit of keeping, they being of the strict teetotaler persuasion.

"Kingman!" Wilbur yelled, as he clutched his head. "What did you just do!"

I could have told him, and so could Kingman himself, and actually he did, but it was no use, for Wilbur kept muttering to himself and complaining about weirdo cats, and going off to get a mop so he could clean up the beer from the floor.

"Why did Wilbur ask what Kingman did when he saw what he did?" asked Dooley.

"I guess he just couldn't believe his own eyes, Dooley," I said. "This not being the kind of behavior he's used to from Kingman."

Kingman now came waggling in our direction, but not before taking a disdainful sniff at the alcohol and wrinkling up his nose in abject disgust. "I never realized before how filthy this stuff is," he said. "There should be a law against it."

"There used to be," I said. "It was called Prohibition, and it had some very interesting side effects."

"It's frustrating, you know," said Kingman. "Having to keep an eye on him all the time. Last night when I got home from cat choir, he was on the couch, watching some late-night television, and I could smell the alcohol on his breath when he pulled me close for a cuddle. It's tough having to be my human's keeper all the time. He will try and sneak some liquor into his daily diet. Like now."

"The problem is temptation," said Dooley. "Your human has a shop full of alcohol, Kingman. All he has to do is reach out and take some of it. Other people have to go and buy it, but he doesn't even have to leave the house."

Dooley was right. Especially since Wilbur lives above his shop, and so whenever he runs out of something, all he has to do is walk down a flight of stairs and grab whatever he needs, whether it be bourbon or Scotch or a light beer.

"Maybe we should get rid of the stuff," said Kingman musingly. "The problem is how?"

"I think the problem is that if you get rid of the stuff, Wilbur will get rid of you!" I said.

But Kingman raised his head high and got a sort of defiant expression in his eyes. "I don't care. I'm willing to sacrifice my own comfort just to save my human from this self-inflicted destruction."

"Is he in the AA?" asked Dooley.

"No, he's not. But he should be."

"So does he drink a lot?"

"Any drink is a drink too many," said Kingman, quickly turning into a temperance evangelist, just like Shanille.

As far as I could tell, Wilbur wasn't exactly a raging drunk. If he was, people would have started avoiding the store, but that simply wasn't the case. The store always did great business, and Wilbur wasn't slurring his words or staggering about and losing his balance—all obvious signs of alcohol intoxication. Then again, many alcoholics are what they call functioning alcoholics, and you can't even see from their behavior that they have a problem. Was it possible that Wilbur was one of those? It hardly seemed likely. We would have smelled it.

"I think we need to expand our movement to include dogs," said Kingman now. "Cats can only do so much, but dogs can do some real damage, especially the bigger ones like Rufus."

Rufus belongs to Tex and Marge's next-door neighbors the Trappers, and is a sheepdog. Unlike some smaller breeds he's also very big and very fluffy.

"Now if Rufus were here, he could push over those shelves and crash all of those bottles to the floor," said Kingman wistfully. "And that would be the end of that." He was referring to the shelves containing the more expensive alcohol Wilbur had on offer. There was an assortment of wine, of course, with a nice offering of both the Stewart and the Kosinski wines, amicably standing side by side, unlike their vintners, but also the stronger ones, which are called the hard liquor.

"Why do they call these liquors hard, Max?" asked Dooley as we studied the shelves containing an eclectic variety of stock. "They don't look so hard to me."

"They're hard liquor because they're produced through distillation," I said. "Usually from grains, fruit or vegetables that have been fermented. Since the resulting beverage has a higher percentage of alcohol they are considered harder than the undistilled variety, like beer, wine and cider, which are fermented, but not distilled, giving them a lower alcohol percentage."

"And root beer? Is that also a hard liquor?"

"Root beer typically doesn't contain alcohol."

"So there you have it!" said Dooley. "Make Wilbur drink root beer from now on. He'll *think* it's beer, but in actual fact it's absolutely harmless. Problem solved!"

"I doubt whether Wilbur will be fooled so easily," Kingman muttered as he scanned the rows and rows of alcohol on offer in his store. "The man is clever."

We glanced over to Kingman's human, and saw that he was poking his nose, digging deep as if looking to extract a nugget of gold, before finally extracting a big green booger. For a moment he carefully studied the booger, an expression of mild curiosity and childlike wonder on his face, then proceeded to roll the specimen between thumb and forefinger, before flicking it into the candy container, where it found its final resting place between a Jolly Rancher and a Milk Dud.

Okay, so maybe Wilbur wasn't as clever as Kingman thought.

CHAPTER 33

Wilbur wasn't the only person in Hampton Cove that day who was finding it hard to enjoy their favorite pastime. Scarlett and Vesta, chatting pleasantly in the outside dining area of the Star Hotel, had ordered their usual drinks—a cappuccino for Scarlett and a hot chocolate for Vesta, when they found their beverages lacking that *je-ne-sais-quoi*. That hard to describe something that makes all the difference.

"We shouldn't," said Scarlett. "It would set us back to square one."

"I know," said Vesta. "But I wants it, Scarlett. I wants it so bad."

"Me too," said Scarlett. "In fact I never wanted anything so bad before the day you convinced me to go to that damn AA club of yours."

"It's not *my* damn AA club, Scarlett," said Vesta. "And it's not a club."

"I thought as much. It's not very social and they don't serve alcohol."

"That's because it's for people who want to stop drinking!"

"All right, all right. Don't flip your wig. I'm not dissing your club. They look like a fine bunch of people. I just wish they were a little more fun to be around."

Vesta sighed deeply. She loved her friend, she really did, but sometimes she could have sworn she did it on purpose. "Look, are we doing this or not?"

A big grin appeared on Scarlett's face. "We're doing it," she said.

"I like your thinking, sister. Let's do it!" They weren't actually member-members of the AA anyway. More like observers. Like at the United Nations.

So she glanced around, making sure Tex wasn't anywhere in the vicinity—it wouldn't do for him to see her swilling down booze after she'd knocked that flask out of his hands yesterday. He'd accuse her of being a hypocrite, and he'd have a point!

She gestured for the waiter, who promptly appeared, and they ordered two large martinis on the rocks. And as they waited impatiently, Scarlett was smacking her lips, which was probably a bad idea as she had just applied about a ton of lip gloss. "God, I wants it too," said Scarlett. "I mean, here I was all my life thinking I needed a man to make me happy, when all I needed was a stiff drink."

"Liquor sure is easier to digest than a man," Vesta agreed wholeheartedly. After her divorce she'd ventured out onto the market for singles, and had managed to snag the attention of a couple of male suitors. Most of them she'd been forced to throw back, though, and the ones she hadn't had quickly proven equally unpalatable. Unlike this big martini that nice waiter was now bringing up!

And she was just about to put her lips to the cool drink when out of the blue, suddenly something whizzed past her field of vision, and slapped that glass right out of her hands! The glass crashed to the flagged floor and broke into a thousand pieces, but what was worse: her martini was gone!

"Hey!" she said, looking around to see what was going on. Was it a plane, was it a bird, was it Superman? But before she could get her bearings, the same exact phenomenon happened again, only this time with Scarlett's equally tasty drink!

Zoom! Slam! Crash!

"What the…" Scarlett cried, greatly dismayed as only a person craving a cooling shot of the good stuff can get when seeing their glass snatched away.

And that's when Vesta saw it: it was Harriet, cool as dammit and licking her paw—presumably the same paw she'd used to slam those glasses out of Vesta and Scarlett's hands!

"What do you think you're doing!" Vesta cried. "That was my drink!"

"And mine!" Scarlett added.

"For your information, I'm your new sponsor," said Harriet, giving them both a cold look from beneath her lowered lashes. "And this sponsor means business. From now on I'm watching you two like a hawk. And if I see you touch so much as a single drop of alcohol, I'm going to do some serious damage." And to show them she wasn't fooling around, she held up that fateful paw and slash! Unsheathed a series of very sharp-looking lethal claws!

Yikes! thought Vesta.

Christ! thought Scarlett.

Both ladies gulped, then meekly nodded when Harriet asked if they were going to be good from now on. Because if not… And she drew her claw across her throat in a sign of what was to come if they didn't adhere to the rules of the club!

The moment Harriet had left—though Vesta was convinced she was keeping an eye on them from some hidden vantage point—Scarlett said, "I knew this club was bad news! I should never have joined up!"

"It's not a club but a…" But then she sighed. Oh, what was the point?

§

Francis Reilly wasn't feeling very well. The last few days were more or less a blur. He still remembered loading a couple of boxes of sacramental wine into the trunk of his car, and unloading them at that old shack in the woods a parishioner had once drawn his attention to, but from that point onward things became a little hazy. He seemed to remember standing in the shower with Tex Poole at some point, but that must have been a nightmare, for who in their right mind would want to take a shower with Tex Poole? Except for the man's wife, maybe.

And then of course Vesta had dragged him to one of those AA meetings. The indignation of the thing was what hurt him the most. Once upon a time *he'd* been the one sending people to those meetings! In fact he'd personally hosted many a meeting himself! And now there he sat, a sad drunk, having to listen to other sad drunks trying to get their lives back on track. And even though he'd tried to hide in the back, he just knew people had seen him and would whisper —and soon the story would go around Hampton Cove that Father Francis Reilly was an alcoholic!

Alcoholics Anonymous, my ass, he thought. There wasn't anything anonymous about being an alcoholic in a town as small as this one, that was for darn sure.

And so he sat in his vestry, trying to work out his Sunday sermon, and feeling very, very thirsty all of a sudden. If only he could have a nice stiff one, he'd feel much better. The words would simply flow onto the page, not like now when it felt as if he had to drag them kicking and screaming from the depths of his immortal soul. Someone—he suspected Vesta, to be honest—had disappeared the few bottles he'd tucked away in the vestry cupboard. The first thing he'd done upon his return was look, and they were no longer there. But what Vesta didn't know—what nobody knew—was that he kept another bottle hidden in a secret compartment underneath the altar—in case of emergencies.

So he now snuck out of his vestry and into the church proper, scanned the church pews to make sure none of his regulars were seated there, and when he had convinced himself that he was alone, quickly crossed the few steps to the altar, and lifted the cloth that covered the holy shrine. The bottle was still there, all right, exactly where he had left it.

A hot flush mantled his cheeks when he palmed it, and for some reason he discovered that he was hiding the bottle from sight. He glanced over his shoulder, and was startled to discover that Christ on the cross was staring straight at him.

"Please forgive me, Lord," he muttered. "But I need this more than you do right now." And before he could change his mind, he unscrewed the cap, and put the bottle to his lips, preparatory to allowing the divine nectar to flow into his mouth. And just as he was about to close his eyes, suddenly there was a sort of loud growling sound, and a whizzing motion that seemed to come out of nowhere, and before he knew what was happening, the bottle was slammed from his hands!

And there, at his feet, looking none too pleased, sat Shanille!

"Shanille!" he cried. "What has gotten into you, all of a sudden!"

Of course Shanille couldn't respond, since she was only an animal. All she did was stare at him with a sort of angry expression in her eyes, as if he'd personally insulted her, or had forgotten to feed her. On the floor, next to the feisty cat, lay his precious bottle, leaking wine onto the smoothly polished granite steps that led down from the altar. And when he picked it up, he was dismayed to find that the bottle was devoid of that precious nectar he was so much in need of right now.

"It's a sign," he whispered as he held up the empty bottle. "A sign from God!"

And as if she understood what he was saying, Shanille uttered a long lament!

"No more," he said decidedly. "*Vade retro satana!*" And it was with a newfound resolve that he decided that perhaps a better way to deal with Marigold and Angel's departure was not to drink away his sorrows, but to face them head on.

Shanille must have liked his resolution, for instead of uttering a series of blood-curdling yowls, she purred happily, and started rubbing against his leg.

"There, there," he said kindly as he picked up the feline. "All is well now."

※

In his office, seated behind his desk, Tex was feeling the strain. It had been a long day, filled with patients who had demanded a lot from this conscientious doctor. And now that his last patient had left, he felt the tension drain from his body, and thought the quickest road to true and meaningful relaxation lay in that small metal flask that he always kept in the bottom drawer of his desk. Too bad Vesta had confiscated it as a symbol of their dedication to go dry from now on.

Going dry was all fine and dandy, and he was all for it, but from time to time a little pick-me-up wouldn't hurt, now would it? Just a sip. Or maybe even two. No one would know. And it wasn't as if he was actually an alcoholic. He didn't need alcohol. He was in complete control of his habit of imbibing the odd glass of wine, or even a nice brewski from time to time when he was shooting the breeze with his brother-in-law Alec and his son-in-law Chase. Especially when there was a game on. So was he going to have to give all of that up? Just because Marge had gotten it into her head that he was an alcoholic? It just seemed very silly.

Now Francis Reilly, there was a true drunk. But him? Not a chance.

And then he remembered that he still had half a bottle of rosé in the fridge, a gift from a patient he'd helped on the road to recovery from a bad fall last month.

A smile spread across his features as the taste of that nice rosé came back to him. Very crisp and sweet, but with such a delicate and fruity aftertaste. In fact, he decided as he quickly got up, it was exactly what the doctor ordered!

He hurried into the kitchen, his tastebuds doing a happy dance in his mouth in anticipation, and yanked open the fridge. And there it was: exactly where he had left it! It was hidden behind a big piece of watermelon Vesta had put there, which was probably why she hadn't seen it on her mission to rid the place of alcohol.

So he grabbed the bottle, and decided to dispense with the formalities of using a glass. He was going to drink this baby straight from the bottle!

And he was just about to put the bottle to his lips when a scream rent the air. It seemed to come from somewhere nearby, and almost sounded like, "Tex, no!" He whirled around, fully expecting either his mother-in-law, his wife or his daughter to be standing there. But he was still all alone in the kitchen, not a soul in sight. So he shrugged, figuring he was hearing things, and was lifting the bottle to his lips when it was unceremoniously slammed from his hands and landed in the sink, where it proceeded to leak its precious contents into the drain!

"Nooooooo!" he cried, but too late. As he reached the sink, the last remnants of the delicious liquid were glug-glugging away and then were gone forevermore!

And it was then that he became aware of some kind of low growling sound, as if he was in the presence of a vicious predator. And that's when he saw it: on top of the fridge, Brutus was sitting, baring two sharp rows of teeth, and growling away for all he was worth. Almost as if he'd turned into a puma overnight!

He gulped. "That's a n-n-nice k-k-kitty," he said, quickly taking a step back, even though he'd always heard that when a puma is about to attack, you shouldn't move a muscle. "T-t-there's a good boy."

And somehow, as he stared into the big black cat's eye, sweat beading on his brow, he saw a distinct hint of menace, but also a barely veiled threat: do that again, mister, and I'll have your guts for garters!

CHAPTER 34

The next morning, bright-ish and early-ish, we drove into New York for a chat with Clive Balcerak. Jeff's colleague had agreed to meet us in his favorite coffee shop, which was just around the corner from Capital First, the bank where the two men had shared duties and responsibilities but also locked horns.

"Cat choir was fun last night, wasn't it, Max?" said Dooley.

"It was, yeah," I said. "One of the better ones."

Though ever since Shanille's return, every cat choir we were having and were ever going to have was going to be stellar. "Doesn't it strike you as odd that it took Shanille to go missing for us to appreciate her for who she is?" said Dooley.

I had come to the same conclusion myself. "It's true," I said. "Everybody seems to shower so much attention on Shanille it's becoming a little embarrassing."

"She seems to love it, though."

"She does. She's clearly loving every minute of it."

Shanille had told us the story of how she had prevented Father Reilly from making a grave mistake, and how grateful the priest had been for her intervention. Clearly the FuSSy mission was going strong. And then Harriet had told us a similar story about Gran and Scarlett, and Brutus had clinched it by entertaining us with the story of how Tex had almost wet his pants when Brutus caught him sneaking a drink from a bottle containing some pink alcoholic liquid!

"Maybe we should get in on Shanille's mission," said Dooley.

"We can't. We're on this murder investigation," I said. Though I wouldn't have minded becoming a FuSSy pussy myself, to be honest. Since this murder inquiry didn't seem to be going anywhere, and being a feline AA sponsor was about saving lives, perhaps our energies would be better spent keeping an eye on our alcohol-inclined humans. Then again, we couldn't abandon Odelia and Chase, now that they were facing what was without a doubt a pretty tough investigation.

"I think we should get the dogs in on Shanille's FuSSy project," said Dooley now. "We all know that unlike cats dogs like to stick to their humans like glue, and if they see that they're about to take a drink, they can make them stop by putting their paws on their shoulders and bringing their faces very close to theirs."

I grinned. "I like your thinking, Dooley. Let's suggest it to Shanille."

"I think it's the breath. Dogs have bad breath. And humans can't stand bad breath. So when a dog breathes into their face, they will always associate the terrible smell of the dog with the taste of alcohol, and it will cure them."

"It's not a bad theory," I said. "Reminds me of Pavlov's dogs."

"Do they have smelly breath, too?"

"It wouldn't surprise me if they had. We should tell

Odelia. Maybe she can write an article about it, and maybe even get it accepted as a new AA step."

"Step thirteen: every time you want to have a drink, smell your dog's breath." He became animated. "It's going to revolutionize the treatment of alcohol addiction, Max, I just know it will."

"They'll call this thirteenth step the Dooley Step," I said with a smile.

"Ooh, I'd like that. My contribution to the world. Maybe I'll win a Nobel Prize!"

"I'll bet you will. For outstanding work in physics. Or chemistry. Or physiology or medicine. Maybe you'll even win all of them!" After all, alcoholism touches on all of those disciplines.

"And peace, Max. Without drunks the world would be a much more peaceful place. No more noisy people waking you up in the middle of the night." But then his face fell. "There's only one problem. Where am I going to put five Nobel Prizes? I don't have a nightstand."

"I'm sure Odelia will make room on hers."

"What are you guys talking about?" asked Odelia.

"The Nobel Prizes Dooley is going to win," I said. "For coming up with a revolutionary new way to treat alcohol addiction."

Odelia turned to us. "Dad told me about his close encounter with Brutus yesterday. How he made his hair turn white."

"Wasn't Tex's hair white already?" said Dooley.

"I mean, even whiter than it already was. Who came up with this idea to use cats as AA sponsors?"

"Shanille," I said.

"Understandable," Odelia nodded. "After what happened to Father Reilly. That must have really shaken her." She suddenly turned serious. "If I ever start showing signs of addiction, promise me you'll be as tough on me as Shanille is on Francis?"

"You'll never become an addict," I said. "You're not the type."

"I wouldn't be too sure about that," said our human. "We all have our weaknesses. Mine, as it happens, is chocolate," she added with a wink.

Dooley blinked at this, then nodded thoughtfully. "Understood," he said.

Contrary to what we'd been led to believe, Clive Balcerak wasn't an ogre or a monster. He was a very polite young man, cleanly shaven, perfectly coiffed and dressed, and wearing glasses. He looked more like a choirboy than most choirboys, and didn't strike me as the office or schoolyard bully at all, more like the kid who gets bullied by the bigger kids, his glasses trampled, his hair mussed and his nice clothes muddied. But then of course looks can be deceiving.

The coffee shop where we had arranged to meet was one of those small eateries that are all the rage in Manhattan, and are very popular with the office crowd. This particular place was teeming with men and women in suits, talking or texting on their phones, and generally looking very busy, efficient and competent.

We took a seat at the long table that stretched along the window, and offered us a great view of the street, where more people were walking to and fro, also talking on their phones or checking their email. Many of them had AirPods in their ears, which made them look as if they were actually talking to themselves.

"It's so funny, isn't it, Max?" said Dooley as we watched

this sea of humanity pass along in front of us. "So many people and they're all talking to themselves!"

"They're speaking into their phones," I said.

"But... they're not holding it to their ears. How can they hear what the other person is saying?"

"Those little white things that are stuck in their ears? Those are actually wireless earphones. All part of the cordless revolution. And pretty soon they'll have something implanted in their brains and won't even need those anymore."

"It's a funny world out there, Max," said my friend.

"You can say that again, buddy."

We both shivered. The whole concept brought back memories of a subcutaneous chip Vena Aleman, Hampton Cove's venerable cat butcheress, had once implanted in us. Not our finest moment!

But we weren't in Manhattan to comment on the state of the world or the well-known viciousness of veterinarians, of course. And so we tuned back in.

"Terrible what happened to Jeff," said Clive, shaking his head sadly. He sat nursing a large latte and daintily nibbling from a blueberry muffin. "Management called a meeting yesterday and told us. Is it true that there's a mafia connection?"

"You will understand that we're not at liberty to discuss the details of an ongoing investigation, won't you, Mr. Balcerak?" said Chase.

"Oh, no, of course. Just a persistent rumor that's been doing the rounds."

"The thing is, Mr. Balcerak, that Jeff supposedly received a message from you to meet him at two o'clock that afternoon. But when we checked Jeff's phone we found the message but it wasn't sent from your phone but from a pay-as-you-go."

"Oh, my God," said Clive. "Someone used my phone to send Jeff a message?"

"They didn't actually use your phone," said Chase. "Without getting too technical, they made it look as if you were sending the message, while in actual fact they were using a different SIM than yours. It's called caller ID spoofing."

"Is that actually a thing? I thought it was just a myth," said Clive.

"Oh, no, it's real. Criminals can spoof your number by using this technique. Which is why Jeff actually thought you were the one sending him a message. But instead they lured him to the place where they were planning to kill him."

Clive's face showed his distress. "Poor Jeff. He must have been so happy. We haven't always seen eye to eye, you know, me and Jeff. I don't know how it started, but we just didn't get along for some reason. Minor incidents led to friction and before long it almost seemed as if we were sworn enemies." He barked an incredulous, humorless laugh. "And the worst part is that I was effectively thinking about meeting him outside work. To talk things through, see if we couldn't patch things up between us. If only I'd done it sooner…" He stared off into space for a moment, even going so far as to return his half-eaten muffin to his plate.

"When a man doesn't finish his muffin, it means he's hurting," Dooley said.

"He's probably feeling bad because Jeff died before they could reconcile," I said. "And also, they used Clive's number to lure the man to his death."

"Okay, so we know you didn't actually send that message," said Chase. "But you will understand we have to cross our T's and dot our I's. Where were you two days ago between two and three, Mr. Balcerak?"

"Well, as I told you on the phone, I was helping a friend

move into his new apartment. I gave you his phone number. You can check, he will confirm this."

"I did call your friend, and he confirmed you helped him move, but this was in the morning. He has no idea where you were in the afternoon, Mr. Balcerak."

Clive gulped a little. "Well…" He gulped some more, and inserted a finger between his shirt collar and his neck. "The thing is, detective…"

"Yes?"

"Is this… This is a confidential conversation, isn't it? I mean, if I tell you something in confidence, it doesn't have to go any further?"

"That depends."

"Depends?"

"Whether it has a bearing on the investigation."

"I see…" His eyes had turned a little shifty, and I wondered if he was going to make a break for the door, like you see in the movies. But instead he seemed to resign himself to the inevitability of his fate. "I'm having an affair with my boss," he said finally. "My manager. And the thing is, she's married—and not to me."

"No, I gathered as much," said Chase, though not unkindly so.

"So you see, it's all very delicate. I mean, I love her, I do, and I've told her as much. And she says she loves me. But she's got three kids, and she also loves her husband. So we've been meeting in secret, at a small, discreet hotel in Brooklyn, which is where we were two days ago. I'd much rather you didn't ask her to confirm what I've just told you, but if you talk to the guy behind the reception at the hotel, he'll tell you. And if I'm not mistaken he has a camera, so you'll be able to see me and Melissa acting very furtive and not a little guilty."

"Thank you, sir," said Chase. "I know that wasn't easy for you."

But now that he got that off his chest, he seemed to buck up considerably. "I wanted to tell you from the beginning, but it's not just about me. I've got Melissa to think about. Anything I tell you might implicate her, and her family, of course."

"We won't contact Melissa unless we have to," said Odelia. "And even then we'll try to be as discreet as possible. But you understand that in a murder inquiry we have to check every possible lead, even the ones that end up being dead ends."

Clive winced at the mention of the words 'dead end,' but said he understood.

CHAPTER 35

Our next stop was the NYPD. And if you think that this well-known police department comprises a single building, like in Hampton Cove, you're well mistaken. Since New York is a large city, it requires a lot of officers to police it, over thirty thousand of them, along with almost twenty thousand civilians, spread across dozens of precincts. The one we wanted was in Brooklyn, where Steph had filed a complaint against the unknown person who had cost her the WelBeQ job.

"Are we going to meet your colleague now, Chase?" asked Dooley. The question, when duly translated by Odelia, was answered in the negative. And so Chase reiterated, for our edification, the impressive structure of his old force.

"Sounds like the NYPD is a lot bigger than the Hampton Cove PD," Dooley said finally. This made Odelia laugh, which in turn made Chase laugh, too.

"Yeah, I guess so," said the burly copper. But then it was time to have a chat with the person in charge of the WelBeQ investigation. This proved to be a very warmhearted and garrulous lady, who was also very big and very round. She had her hair in braids, which dangled pleasantly about her face as she talked.

"I think she likes her donuts," Dooley whispered, even though there was no chance for her to overhear us. "She likes them, like, a lot."

The female police officer's name was Shelley, and if she liked donuts, I liked her, for she proved a real hoot.

"I heard you're an old colleague," she said. "So what made you up stakes and move out to the sticks?" She held up a hand. "Not that I've got anything against the Hamptons, mind you. If I had the money, I'd be out there in a heartbeat!"

"The opportunity was there," said Chase with a shrug. "So I took it."

"Now that's the kind of guy I like! Sees an opportunity and grabs it! Not like my Dennis. He wouldn't even know how to spell the word opportunity, let alone take it when it hits him in the face." She shook her head. "He's not a bad sort, my husband, but lazy! Put him in front of the TV and he won't move all evening! And to think he was such a live wire when we first met. A regular spark plug! And now you should see him. He's all sparked out!" And she laughed the most uproarious laugh I'd heard in quite a while.

"What does he do for a living, your Dennis?" asked Odelia.

"Works for the Department of Sanitation. Sanitation worker, or sanman as he likes to call himself. Hauls garbage all day long, tons and tons of the stuff!"

"I can imagine he's tired when he comes home at night," said Chase. "Hauling trash is hard work."

"Oh, honey, I know! And I mean no disrespect. But his colleagues all coach Little League after hours, or shoot hoops with their kids, or take their wives out for dinner at some fancy restaurant on their wedding anniversary. But not Dennis. Oh, no. Do you know he managed to forget our wedding anniversary? We were married twenty years last Friday, but no present, no dinner, not a single peep!"

And as Shelley prattled on, I could tell that Odelia and Chase were starting to wonder if she would ever arrive at their investigation. Before long we knew everything there was to know about Dennis, including his sleeping habits (flat on his back and snoring all night) his bathroom habits (never took a bath, only showers, even though she had often told him to take a bath when he got home from work), his smoking habits (Marlboro Light) and his drinking habits (Bud Light). But finally she seemed to have exhausted her favorite topic of conversation, and opened her laptop.

We were in a small conference room, since she didn't have her own office, but worked in an open-plan office along with dozens of her colleagues. On the wall of the office a poster reminded us to 'Stay alert. Be aware. Speak up,' and we listened intently as she told us about the steps she'd taken following Steph's complaint.

"Obviously we looked into this guy she mentioned, this Crowley character. Called WelBeQ, who were very cooperative, checked the guy's phone records, bank statements, his phone and computer, but like I told you on the phone we struck out. I hate to disappoint you, but Crowley is not your guy. Unless of course he hired some other guy. I had our IT people take a closer look at those emails and they're convinced they were sent by a professional, definitely not Crowley."

"A professional?" asked Odelia. "You mean like a hacker or an IT specialist?"

Shelley nodded. "Criminal organization, most likely. Some gun for hire."

Odelia and Chase shared a look. "The thing is that Steph Felfan's husband was shot," Chase explained, "in a setup that has all the hallmarks of a professional hit."

"So it's entirely possible," Odelia added, "that the slander campaign and Jeff Felfan's murder are connected, and were both carried out by the same outfit."

"Do you have any idea who's behind the WelBeQ campaign?" asked Chase.

"None," said Shelley without hesitation. "Whoever set it up, they've managed to cover their tracks very, very well. Impossible to trace is the message I got."

"Too bad," said Dooley. "Now we'll never know who's behind this thing!"

"Don't despair, Dooley," I said. "There are other ways of finding out."

"Like what? You heard the nice lady, Max. Even the specialists struck out."

"All we have to do is to figure out who wanted to harm Steph and Jeff Felfan," I said. "And wanted it enough to hire this criminal gang to do their dirty work for them. It's all about motive, Dooley. The moment we know why, we know who."

But my friend didn't look convinced. And frankly at that moment neither was I. It's one thing to spout great theories about crime, but another to figure out who was behind this thing! Whoever it was, they wanted to hurt the Felfans something bad.

We said our goodbyes to Shelley before she launched into another diatribe about Dennis, and soon were on our way back to Hampton Cove. In the car the atmosphere was a little subdued, I must say, and our humans weren't entirely convinced that the trip had been worth it. After all, they didn't know a lot more now than they had before. Except maybe the part about the professional gang.

And of course about Shelley's husband Dennis. But there, I think, the expression TMI applied: Too Much Information!

CHAPTER 36

Steph hadn't heard from the police since the day before, and frankly she was getting a little antsy. They had talked to Robbie, and they were going to talk to Kevin, and so far she had no idea what the result of these conversations was. It seemed to her that the police were simply twiddling their thumbs, instead of being out there looking for her husband's killer.

So today she decided to take a more active role. She simply couldn't sit around doing nothing while whoever killed Jeff was out there, doing God knows what—maybe even getting ready to kill her! Or Zoe. The thought made her blood run cold. What if her dad was right and this was connected to Ben Kosinski? And what about Kevin's car parked in the drive of the Kosinski place? Where did that fit in? She would have asked her brother, but as usual he couldn't be found. And when she asked her mom, she said she had no idea, and didn't seem to care either.

So she took her car and went for a drive, just like Kevin liked to do, and drove straight to the Kosinski Winery, just like her brother seemed to enjoy doing! When she got there, the gates swung open even before she had a chance to announce her arrival. Clearly whoever was operating that big metal gate had recognized her, which wasn't hard, since she was their neighbor, after all.

When she arrived at the end of the long drive, she wasn't surprised to see a gleaming red Ferrari already parked there. So she swung her own car right next to Kevin's, and went in search of Beniamino—most of all, she wanted answers.

And so without taking the usual route and knocking on the front door, instead she decided to go round the back and see if she couldn't find Ben or Dominic out there, or maybe even Kevin, if he deigned to speak to his sister. If she rang the front door, they would probably foist her off with some lowly servant or butler, and she would never get to see the man in charge. Better surprise them!

But when she reached the back of the house, which looked out across a very impressive garden, complete with fountains and gurgling brooks, of Ben or Dominic there was no trace, and neither was her brother anywhere in evidence.

The frustration of being kept out of the loop had made her reckless, and she kept up her investigative streak by going in search of the garage, where she knew Ben kept his impressive collection of cars. The man was a well-known petrolhead, and had even been featured on television showing off his latest acquisition, a gleaming Lamborghini Reventón. Price tag: one million dollars.

She didn't find Ben in the garage, and when she asked Ben's chauffeur, who doubled as his mechanic, he said he had no idea where his employer was, but had she tried the house?

She obviously had not. She left the garage and as she did, saw that the space above it had been turned into a loft, with curtains in front of the windows and boxes of geraniums. She frowned, wondering if this was where the chauffeur lived. One of the curtains moved, and suddenly she saw Kevin appear!

He was clearly as shocked to see her as she was to see him, for the moment their eyes met, his jaw dropped and he moved back as if stung.

Oddly enough, he wasn't wearing any clothes!

So that's where he'd been. Having an affair with someone! Could it be Ben's wife? Or the chauffeur's wife? Ben didn't have a daughter, so it couldn't be her.

Then, eager to get to the bottom of this mystery of her disappearing brother once and for all, she mounted the metal staircase bolted into the side of the garage, and pushed into the loft, the metal door opening when she applied pressure to the door handle. Clearly Kevin and his lady love hadn't expected visitors, for they hadn't even bothered to lock the door!

She stormed into the room, her eyes quickly scanning her surroundings—a messy but cozy living area, lots of framed pictures of sports cars on the walls, television blaring away, tuned to a NASCAR race, and the smell of coffee in the air. Her keen gaze spotted movement, and the sound of nervously exchanged words, and the next moment she was stomping in that direction, locked on her target like a homing pigeon. Fully expecting to find Kevin in bed with some woman, what she saw instead was her brother, standing next to an equally half-naked... Dominic Kosinski, both looking a little startled and also a little scared.

Her eyes flicked from Kevin to Dominic, at first not understanding what she was actually seeing. "Kevin?" she said finally. "What the hell is going on?"

Kevin didn't speak. Instead he just stood there, clearly struck dumb.

"Hi, Steph," said Dominic, breaking the awkward silence. A handsome young man with an abundance of black curls and a chiseled torso that wouldn't have looked out of place in GQ or Men's Health, she was reminded of how much he looked like his dad, even though Ben had let himself go a little in recent years.

"I don't understand," said Steph. "What are you doing here, Kevin?"

But her brother remained silent. So Dominic did the talking. "Kevin and I have been seeing each other," he said, "on and off for the past ten years. And more seriously for the past six. We haven't told anyone, for obvious reasons, but lately we've been thinking about breaking the news to Kevin's family."

Kevin's spine suddenly seemed to collapse under the strain, for he sank down on the bed, whose sheets were tangled and had clearly seen a lot of activity lately, and sort of slumped where he sat. "Please don't tell anyone," he said in a hoarse voice. "You might be ready, but I'm not," he told Dominic when the latter gave him a look of surprise. "Especially Dad," he added. "He's going to be furious."

"He needs to know, Kev," said Dominic. "We can't go on like this forever."

"Don't you think I know that?!" suddenly Kevin burst out. "I want to tell him, but you know what he's like. He'll think it's some kind of plot hatched by your dad to take possession of the Stewart Winery." He raised his hands in frustration. "All the man can think of is his stupid winery and his stupid feud with your dad. It's crazy."

"I know it is," said Dominic, taking a seat next to him and putting an arm around his shoulders. "But at some point we'll have to tell him, Kev. We have to."

"Do your mom and dad know about this?" asked Steph.

Dominic nodded. "They do."

"And they're okay with this?"

"Of course. They're not as obsessed with this competition

thing as your dad, Steph." He eyed her with a touch of reproach, as if she was responsible for the way her dad liked to carry on. "But I asked them not to tell anyone, and they agreed it's too soon. But they want me to be happy—want us to be happy, and so Dad suggested that he talk to Ian and break the news to him."

"That's the worst idea ever," said Kevin. "The moment your dad sets foot on my dad's land he's going to get out the big gun and shoot him on sight."

"He won't do that," said Dominic. He eyed Steph. "Would he?"

"Of course not," said Steph. "Dad isn't crazy. Though maybe you should start by talking to Mom. Then she can talk to Dad." It was the way they'd always broken bad news to their parents, from bad grades to that time when Kevin had wrapped Dad's expensive new Mercedes around a lamppost. They told Mom, who told Dad.

"Steph has a point," said Dominic.

"But what about the winery?" she asked.

"What about it?" said Kevin, raking a hand through his blond hair.

"If you and Dominic... get married—if that's what you want."

"It is," said Dominic, even though Kevin didn't look convinced.

"Then the two wineries are going to be joined together? Is that the plan?"

"I don't give a hoot about the winery," said Kevin, much to Steph's surprise. "All I want is to go far away from here and start a new life with Dominic. No more winery, no more fighting. I'm sick to death of this stupid competition. If I hear Dad say the words 'Kosinski is a crook and a Polish mobster and yadda yadda yadda' one more time I'm going to be sick, I swear. God, talk about a broken record."

Steph smiled. "I also hate it when he begins."

"Ben and Catherine have been more of a mother and father to me than my own parents," said Kevin. "They've accepted me from the start, and I've never heard them say a single cross word about Dad. They don't think in those terms. Live and let live, that's Ben's motto, and it's not just words—he actually means what he says. He really does. And furthermore he's the kindest, wisest, funniest man I've ever met. Unlike Dad, who is just so angry all the time."

"Sour grapes," said Dominic with a smile.

"Exactly," said Kevin, grinning.

"So that's why you were going for drives all the time," said Steph. "And why you wouldn't tell me where you went."

"I didn't want anyone to know."

"Not even me? I'm your sister, Kev."

"You've always been closer to Dad than me. I just figured…"

"That I would tell? Well, I wouldn't. And I won't. Just so you know."

She felt a little offended that her brother would think she'd tell about Dominic to their parents. Maybe it was true that she had a better bond with them than Kevin, but that didn't mean she was going to blurt out his big secret to them.

"I'm sorry," he said softly. "I just thought—well, I wasn't thinking, I guess."

"Though I agree with Dominic that they should know. You can't keep this a secret forever, Kevin. At some point you're going to have to come clean."

"I know. I just…" He looked up at her, a miserable expression on his face. "It's going to change everything, isn't it? Once people know? Everybody will have something to say, and will start interfering." He took Dominic's hand. "I guess I'm afraid it's going to ruin things between us. Just when everything is going so well."

"Nobody is going to come between us, Kev," said Dominic. "We won't let them."

"Dad is going to blow a fuse."

"He'll get over it. He has to."

"Fine. I'll tell them. But not right now. I want to wait for the right moment, and now with Jeff's murder and everything I don't think we should add to their distress."

"Fair enough," said Dominic.

They both looked up at her, and she held up her hands. "Your secret is safe with me, boys."

"Thanks, sis," said Kevin, and she could tell that a huge weight had been lifted from his mind. Clearly he'd been nervous about her reaction as well. She could have told him he had nothing to be afraid of. She loved her brother, and if he thought Dominic was the right person for him and made him happy, that was all that mattered to her.

CHAPTER 37

It was a thoughtful Steph who returned home one hour later. Even though she had promised Kevin she wouldn't say anything, she still felt her parents should know. If her dad's attitude toward the Kosinskis was alienating his son, the person he was depending on to follow in his footsteps and one day take over the business, he needed to be told, so he could do something about it. Dad probably had no clue that Kevin was thinking of leaving, and if he found out, he'd be devastated.

And as she thought about these things, she almost bumped into Robbie, who was lurking about as usual. But it wasn't her habit to be nasty to people, so instead she smiled and said, "Hey, Robbie. Everything all right?"

"Sure," said Robbie, returning her smile. "Where have you been?"

"Just driving around, you know. Clear my head, as if that's even possible."

"You must be going through a hard time now, with Jeff gone," said Robbie.

"Yeah, it's not been an easy couple of days. But we'll get through, it, won't we?"

And then suddenly, before she could stop him, he leaned in and kissed her!

Immediately she pulled back. "Don't do that!" she blurted out.

"I-I'm sorry," he said, his cheeks coloring brightly. "It's just that… with Jeff gone, I just figured…"

"That you and I would get back together? If you really thought that, you're delusional, Robbie. We're never getting back together, all right? Never."

And she walked off, feeling both annoyed and upset. But as she entered the house, she felt that maybe she had been too harsh on him. Then again, he needed to get the message that they were never going to be a couple. And if he kept trying, things were going to get really uncomfortable for the both of them.

❧

Larry had witnessed the scene from his office window, and his heart sank. He watched as his son kicked a rock so hard it almost hit Steph's car, then shoved his hands deep into his pockets, and walked off in the direction of the vineyard. Clearly Robbie wasn't okay. This hang-up about Steph was in his system, and was poisoning him inside. It was affecting his work and everyone around him. This couldn't go on. And so he vowed to have a long talk with his son that night. If Robbie didn't change his ways and drop this obsession with Steph Stewart, measures would have to be taken. A solution reached—a permanent one.

And frankly he already dreaded the kind of solution he had in mind.

Steph had entered the house and when she heard voices in the living room, found her parents and Jeff's parents sitting together, looking through old photo albums of Steph and Kevin. They looked up when she entered, and both parent pairs seemed relieved to see her, as if letting her out of their sight for even half an hour caused them to worry, which she was sure they did.

"Did you find Kevin?" asked her mother.

"No, I didn't," she lied, though not very convincingly, she felt. Kevin had always been the liar in the family, not she.

"We were talking about the memorial service," Pauline explained, "and so we started thinking about pictures to put on the invitations, but then looking at these I guess we got distracted. You never told us you were such a cute baby, Steph."

"It's not something you casually drop into the conversation," she said as she glanced at a picture of her and Kevin playing with a toy car. Kevin looked infinitely more fascinated by the thing than she did. Possibly she had been hoping for a Barbie doll instead of a stupid car. "I have some nice pictures of Jeff," she said. "They're on my phone, but I can send them to the printer."

"I also have many, many pictures of Jeff," said Pauline. "Not on my phone, but at home. I told you we should have brought them," she told her husband.

"I didn't think we'd need them," said David. "And anyway, I think we should pick a picture of Jeff how we want to remember him—which is how he looked now." His face crumpled up like a used tissue, and Pauline placed her hand on his arm. "I'm fine," he assured his wife, though they could all see that he wasn't.

"I think you should do a speech," said Pauline now.

"I can't," said her husband. "Please don't ask me because I just can't."

Steph was concerned about her father-in-law. For a man who'd been giving speeches all his life, and who was a shoo-in for the job of mayor of Paris, and perhaps even higher office down the line, he was only a shadow of the man he used to be. Grief had hit him hard—even harder than Pauline, though maybe she was simply not allowing it to overwhelm her, the way it overwhelmed David.

"It's fine, David," said Dad gently. "You don't have to do a speech if you don't want to."

"I just want to take my boy home," said David brokenly. "Bury him in the family plot."

"And you will," Dad assured him. "We just have to get through these next couple of days, that's all. I promise you that it will get easier."

David gratefully accepted a tissue from Mom, and wiped his nose. Just then, Mom's phone dinged, and for a few moments she was frowning at the device, then got busy responding to whoever was messaging her. Probably something to do with the business, Steph thought.

But then Mom looked up, and glanced at her in a searching way for a moment, before getting back to the message she was typing.

For the next hour or so the two parents pairs and Steph got busy planning the memorial service. David said it wasn't the right time, but Pauline told him there would never be a right time. And she was right, of course. When was the right time to bury your son? But David managed to pull himself together long enough to participate in the conversation, and soon they had the bare bones of what they wanted to do. The funeral director would then take what they had, and create a beautiful service to commemorate Jeff. Once his body had been flown back to France, David and Pauline planned to organize a funeral in the church where Jeff had been christened, and where his parents had been married. They would even get the same priest who'd christened Jeff, acting as a poignant coda to his life.

Having finished this impromptu meeting, David and Pauline retired upstairs. David needed to lie down, and Pauline didn't want to leave his side, since he had developed a very unhealthy pallor, and she worried about his heart.

For a moment Steph sat with her parents, but then the door opened and Kevin entered. And he wasn't alone, for he had brought Dominic along with him.

The two men were holding hands, and Kevin had a sort of determined look on his face. He looked briefly at his mother, then cleared his throat.

So that's what Mom's frantic messaging had been about. Kevin must have asked her if it was a good idea to introduce his boyfriend to his dad.

"What's this?" asked Dad, his mood immediately turning frosty when he caught sight of Dominic. "What is a Kosinski doing in my house?!"

"Dad, there's something I have to tell you. Something important."

"Something *we* have to tell you, Mr. Stewart," Dominic added.

"No," said Dad in a low voice as his eyes went wide. And as Kevin and Dominic launched into their announcement, his face actually took on the same ashen pallor as David's had a few moments before.

CHAPTER 38

It was already late in the afternoon when we arrived at the house to talk to Steph. Odelia and Chase wanted to give her an update on the investigation, even though quite frankly there wasn't a whole lot to discuss. But they felt they owed it to her to keep her in the loop. Especially Odelia had developed a fondness for the young fashion designer, and wanted her to know that they weren't giving up hope of finding the person who was responsible for her husband's murder.

When we got to the house, we saw Kevin step from the front door, hand in hand with a young man we'd never seen before. Though he shared a strong resemblance to Beniamino Kosinski. Could it be…

This time Kevin didn't race off in his fancy Ferrari, but waited patiently for us to join him and his friend.

"I would like you to meet Dominic Kosinski," said Kevin. "My fiancé." He smiled at the surprise on all of our faces—even Dooley and me. "I've just told my parents. I think they're a little surprised. But all in all it didn't go as badly as I'd expected."

"I think your dad was simply too shocked to react," said Dominic with a grin.

"Yeah, he's going to need time to recover," said Kevin with an equally big grin.

"So is this where you kept sneaking off to?" asked Chase.

"Yes, sir," said the young man. "I couldn't very well tell you, since I hadn't told my parents. But we've been in a relationship for six years, and have dated on and off for ten, and I figured it was finally time to come out and tell my folks." He glanced over to his fiancé, and they both looked pleased as punch. "My sister caught us this afternoon, you see, and some of the things she said made me think. So I finally got up my courage and decided to face my parents—especially my dad."

"You were with Dominic when your brother-in-law was killed?"

"I was, yes."

"And I can confirm that with a resounding yes," said Dominic.

"And now we're off to celebrate," said Kevin. "I'm getting married!"

"Yoo-hoo!" his partner caroled.

And so they stepped into Kevin's Ferrari and were off at a fast clip.

"Another suspect less," said Chase with a sigh. "Pretty soon we won't have any left!"

"He seemed happy," said Odelia. "In fact they both did."

"If they've been in the closet for ten years, I'll bet they're glad."

"Why have they been in the closet, Max?" asked Dooley. "Were they punished?"

"They haven't literally been in a closet all this time, Dooley," I said. "It's just an expression. They haven't told anyone that they were in love, and now they finally have. So they're feeling happy and relieved, cause now they don't have to hide—"

"In the closet."

I smiled. "For instance."

"They could have hidden anywhere. They both have very nice houses, with plenty of very nice rooms," he said as we entered the house in search of Steph. "They could have been hiding in the bathroom, or in the bedroom, or even in the attic. Closets are fine, but not for ten years. That's way too long. I'll bet they got very clusterphobic in there."

"I think you mean claustrophobic."

"That's what I said. Clusterphobic."

We found Steph in the kitchen, where she was assisting the cook in getting dinner ready. "We bumped into your brother just now," said Odelia. "With Dominic Stewart."

"I know!" said Steph, who looked better than she did last time we spoke. She had a blush on her cheeks, and flour in her hair, which she had pinned up in a messy bun on top of her head. She was kneading dough, that was going to be used to create something called dumplings. "Dad was totally shocked. For a moment there I thought we'd better call an ambulance, but then he pulled through."

"Did you know?" asked Odelia as she sampled a tasty-looking dish.

"I found out by accident this afternoon when I went looking for Ben. It's why Kevin's been running off all the time. He and Dominic sort of live together in a loft above Ben's garage. They all knew about it—Ben and Catherine and their staff. But they respected Dominic's privacy too much to blab. Which is admirable. The staff here can't keep a secret if they tried." She gave Odelia a keen look. "So have you found my husband's killer yet?"

And as Odelia and Chase informed her about the state of the investigation, Dooley and I decided to wander off in search of something to eat. I mean, we were in the kitchen, so there had to be something! But even though we could smell food, we didn't find it—they had it all tucked away someplace we couldn't see! Talk about sneaky! Of course they would tell everyone who would listen that they did it to keep out mice and rats. But in actual fact they did it to keep us out!

At some point the cook must have taken pity on us—though it could be that she simply couldn't take us looking unwaveringly piteously in her direction—for she placed some nice pieces of chicken on a dish and we ate them with relish.

And so our stomachs filled, we decided to go for a tour of the house. On the second floor we heard loud voices, and moved closer to have a listen. The voices belonged to Steph's parents Ian and Raimunda, and the topic of conversation was, as one would have expected, their son Kevin. And since the door was ajar, we simply slipped into the room, and eagerly listened in on their back-and-forth.

"I always knew he was gay," Raimunda was saying. "Didn't I tell you? Never came home with a girlfriend, and he skipped senior prom, even though Mallery Cooper later told us her daughter Becky had wanted him to go with her. That should have told us everything we needed to know, cause Becky was a looker."

"I don't care that he's gay," said Ian. "But why a Kosinski! There are so many nice boys around, why pick the Kosinski kid of all people, that's what I don't understand!"

"They've been together ten years," said Raimunda with a frown. "That means they started dating when they were eighteen. No wonder he gave Becky Cooper the slip. He and Dominic were already an item. Wait till Mallery hears about this."

"Oh, who cares about Mallery Cooper, or her stupid

daughter!" Ian cried as he grabbed his hair with his hands. "Our boy is getting married to the Kosinski kid! This is the worst day of my life. Do you know what this means? We'll be the talk of the whole town!" He paced the room frantically. "He did it on purpose, didn't he?"

"Who did?"

"Ben, of course, who else! He set this up—I'm sure of it. He set this up to humiliate us—to humiliate me!"

"Oh, get over yourself, Ian. Ben had nothing to do with this. Or do you really think our son is such a pushover that he would be forced into a relationship against his own will?"

"No, I guess not," Ian had to admit. Then he suddenly looked up in alarm. "Does he know? Ben, I mean. Does he know about this?"

"According to Kevin Ben has known all along. Right from the start."

"He's known for ten years and never said a word? What's wrong with that man!"

"What's wrong with you! Can't you stop obsessing about Ben Kosinski for one second and be happy for our boy! He's getting married, Ian. Our boy is getting married. And if you don't stop with this Kosinski nonsense we just might lose him. I can tell you right now that if you keep this up, he and Dominic could very well decide to move away from here, and we'll never see either one of them again!"

"But—"

"Not one more word, Ian! I mean it!"

Ian gave his wife a pleading look. "But it's Kosinski, Rai. *Kosinski.*"

"So? Better get used to it, honey. Cause in just a few months Ben Kosinski will be part of this family."

"Oh, God!"

CHAPTER 39

Robbie could have kicked himself. Now why did he have to go and make a total fool of himself by trying to kiss Steph? Wasn't it bad enough that he'd been mooning over her for the past couple of days? Not to mention the fact she had just lost her husband and was in no state of mind to even contemplate reciprocating his heartfelt sentiments of devotion? Why couldn't he just play it cool?

He was checking the gauges on the tanks again, though his heart wasn't in it. All he wanted was to find Steph and apologize. Profusely. Make her look at him again the way she used to. It was only a fraction of the affection he'd seen on her face when she used to look at her husband, but it would do. He'd settle for that.

He looked up when he saw his dad walk past the door. At least he hadn't witnessed the embarrassing scene, otherwise he'd have given him hell. Moments later he saw another person pass by. It was Raimunda, and she was going in the same direction as his dad. Probably something to do with the winery, as usual. Those two seemed to spend an awful lot of time together. He had often wondered why the woman in charge of PR needed the advice of the winery foreman, but then he figured they probably knew best. There was stuff that his dad hadn't yet taught him, even though he was training him to step into the job one day.

He finally gave up. His mind was a raging whirlwind of conflicting thoughts crashing and colliding, and all of them centered on one person: Steph Stewart.

So he decided to finish up later and get a cup of coffee first.

Heading out of the warehouse he set foot in the direction of the administrative compound, where both his dad and the Stewarts had their offices. He walked into the small canteen and was glad to find it empty. He couldn't be bothered with small talk right now. And he was pouring himself a cup from the machine when he heard a strange sound. Heavy breathing and some occasional grunts and moans.

He frowned. If he didn't know any better he would have thought that a couple were making love nearby. Taking a sip from the hot brew, he went in search of the source of the strange sounds. Walking into the corridor, he quickly determined they seemed to be coming from his dad's office. And as he stood in front of the door, he saw that the blinds were pulled, and that whoever was in there was really going for broke. On an impulse, he shoved down on the door handle, and found the door unlocked. And as his eyes took in the scene, his heart sank.

For in front of him, on his dad's desk, were his dad and… Raimunda Stewart!

He stood there for what felt like minutes but must have been seconds, for suddenly his dad became aware they were being watched, and jerked his head up.

"Robbie!" he cried, the veins in his neck standing out like ropes.

The word jerked him out of his stupor, and his coffee cup crashed to the floor.

He took a step back and slammed the door.

"Robbie, wait!" he heard his dad yell.

But he was already running down the corridor, the terrible images playing in his mind. He knew he'd never be able to get rid of them as long as he lived!

He had to tell someone, and the only person he could think of was Steph. He entered the house to look for her, but she was nowhere to be found. Hurrying up the stairs, he went straight to her room, but the door was open and the room was empty. In desperation, he went door to door, quickly checking inside, and in the last room he entered, he did indeed find someone, but it wasn't Steph.

Instead it was Ian Stewart. The curtains had been pulled, and the room was covered in darkness, but he could still make out the man's profile as he was sitting on the bed. He cleared his throat to speak, wanting to ask her dad where he could find Steph, and that's when he saw it: Ian wasn't alone on the bed. There was a woman with him, who couldn't possibly be his wife, since she was otherwise engaged with Robbie's dad. And as his eyes adjusted to the darkness, he saw that this woman was none other than Hazel Smolski—the Stewarts' housekeeper!

"God, no..." he muttered, his eyes widening in shock. What was happening!

"Robbie?" said Ian, who had become aware of his presence. "Robbie!"

But Robbie had already left, slamming the door on his way out.

The company had retired to the patio, and Odelia and Chase had accepted a glass of Stewart Winery's best, taking appreciative sips as they sampled this fine wine. In the absence of her parents, Steph was acting as the hostess, and reminiscing about her husband with her in-laws, David and Pauline. Jeff's dad looked a little less close to the grave than he had been when we last saw him. Some color had returned to his features, but this could have been the effect of the wine, of course, which seems to stimulate as well as relax.

The wine itself was being served by a youth answering to the name Joe Smolski, who was the housekeeper's son. He was a strapping young man, and clearly had done this before, for he poured a mean glass and didn't spill a single drop of the precious liquid. He reminded me of someone, though for the life of me I couldn't have told you who it was. It would come to me, though. It always did.

"Do you think we should say something, Max?" asked Dooley as he directed a worried glance at Odelia sipping from her wine glass.

"Say what?" I asked. We were both relaxing on the edge of the patio, which was shaded from the sun by a large outdoor cantilever umbrella. The atmosphere was mellow, the air was warm but mitigated by a light pleasant breeze, and as far as I was concerned, all was well with the world and I felt a nice nap coming on.

"The alcohol!" Dooley cried. Clearly he wasn't as relaxed as I was. "They're drinking alcohol, Max, both of them. We have to stop them before they turn into full-blown alcoholics!"

"There's a difference between a person who drinks the occasional glass of wine and the professional boozer, Dooley," I said. "And neither Odelia nor Chase fall into that last category, so there's really nothing to worry about—nothing at all."

But in spite of these words, I could tell that he simply kept on worrying. With every sip that Odelia drank, he was getting more and more worked up.

"Just ignore them," I suggested therefore. "Look the other way."

"But how can I look the other way? They're our humans, Max."

"Exactly. They're both responsible people, and they're fine."

Who wasn't fine was Ian Stewart, who came breezing by five minutes later. He looked as if he'd just taken a shower, but it hadn't refreshed him the way it should have. He had a sort of hunted look on his face, and his eyes were darting all over the place, looking for a danger that wasn't anywhere in sight as far as I could tell.

"Excellent wine, Mr. Stewart," said Chase as he lifted his glass.

"Thank you, Detective Kingsley," said Ian, but his heart wasn't in it.

"And one other thing," said Dooley. "They shouldn't drink, because they're both on duty! And we all know what happens when cops drink when they're on duty—they neglect their duties."

I grinned. "Drink when you're on duty and neglect your duties. Good one, Dooley. Nice wordplay."

But Dooley wasn't in the mood for levity. "It's not right, Max, and you know it."

"I know that I want to take a nap," I said.

"And besides, you should be thinking about catching Jeff's killer, not being lazy and enjoying yourself!"

I groaned. "I am trying to catch Jeff's killer."

"By taking a nap?" he said reproachfully.

"I'll have you know that naps are known to stimulate cognitive performance, Dooley. You will often find that the solution to a problem that has been vexing you for days, will suddenly pop into your head after an exceptionally fine nap."

"Sherlock Holmes never took naps," Dooley countered. "When he was dealing with a particularly difficult case he could go days without sleep or even food."

"I guess our methods are different," I said stiffly. Imagine having to go days without sleep or food. I'd go bananas.

I looked up when Raimunda Stewart joined us. She, too, looked a little distracted, I thought. Though the correct word would probably be frazzled. She had that same nervous way about her that I had seen in her husband. Something wrong with the winery's PR campaign, no doubt, or perhaps they were only now experiencing the full impact of the death of their beloved son-in-law. Grief hits different people at different times, and clearly it was only hitting home now.

Joe Smolski was back again, topping up glasses left and right, and to Dooley's satisfaction both Chase and Odelia declined a refill at this juncture. My friend relaxed—insofar as he could relax while alcohol was being consumed in our presence. Clearly he considered himself a founding father of the FuSSy project, even though we weren't really involved.

"They're not drinking anymore, Max," he said with a sigh of great relief. "I think we're out of the danger zone."

"There never was any danger zone, Dooley," I said. But my words fell on deaf ears, for he kept darting nervous glances at Joe Smolski, this official purveyor of the vice of alcohol. In his mind, no doubt, that young man was nothing less than a drug pusher, and should be arrested on the spot, hung, drawn and quartered.

"Alcohol should be illegal," he said now, supporting this view.

"Yes, Dooley, whatever you say." When was I finally going to get my nap!

As if in answer to my silent prayer, suddenly Robbie materialized, followed by his dad, whose red face was something to behold. Both father and son seemed extremely worked up about something. Okay, so maybe no nap time for me!

"Steph, I have something to say to you."

"Oh, not again, Robbie," said Steph, turning to her persistent admirer.

"It's your dad—and your mom," said Robbie.

"Robbie, not here!" his dad hissed. "Not now!"

"Yes, here and now, Dad!" Robbie cried, turning on his old man. He then held out an accusing finger that was pointing directly at Raimunda. "Your mother has been having an affair with my dad!" he cried, much to the consternation of those present. Except perhaps David and Pauline Felfan, who didn't bat an eyelid.

On Raimunda, though, the effect of this statement was profound. She brought a distraught hand to her face and cried, "Oh, God!"

"Mom?" asked Steph. "Is this true?"

But Raimunda was already nodding her head in confirmation.

"Mom!" Steph said. "You and Larry?"

Once again there was a wordless nod. Steph's mom had squeezed her eyes tightly shut, and her distress was palpable in her nonverbal communication.

"I'm sorry," the woman squeaked now. "I'm so, so sorry, honey."

"And your dad," Robbie said, not having finished his speech, "is having an affair with Hazel. I just caught them going at it in the bedroom!"

Now all eyes turned to Ian, whose face had turned a nice shade of purple.

"Dad, you're not serious," said Steph. "How long has this been going on?"

Joe Smolski chose that exact moment to reappear with a bottle of the finest in hand, a pleasing smile on his visage and a willingness to serve and pour.

And that's when I got it: young Joe was the spitting image of Ian Stewart!

I wasn't the only one who noticed this remarkable likeness, for all eyes now turned to Joe, then to Ian, and once again, though slower this time, back to Joe.

The wine server became a little flustered by all this attention, for his eager-to-please smile faltered. Perhaps he thought that he'd brought along the wrong bottle, for he glanced at the object, and even checked how much was left in it.

"Dad—don't tell me that Joe…" Steph's unfinished sentence hung in the air, but I think we all knew that Joe was Ian's son—conceived from his illicit extramarital affair with Mrs. Smolski.

The fact that Ian was staring intently at his shoes—nice Italian leather ones, but that's neither here nor there—could be construed as an admission of guilt. And Steph interpreted it that way, for she threw up her hands. "So I have a brother. Nice. Wonderful, Dad. Way to go." She now narrowed her eyes at Robbie. "Mom, is Robbie another addition to the family, like Joe is?"

But this was a bridge too far, as Raimunda and Larry both shook their heads in unison, then Larry said in a low voice, "Robbie is Wendy's son, Steph, I swear."

"Well, good for him," said Steph, who wasn't taking too well to this news.

Suddenly Robbie went down on one knee, and held up

what looked like a ring from a gumball machine. "Stephanie Stewart," he said. "Will you marry me?"

In response, Steph's jaw dropped, then she screamed, "Have you completely lost your mind!"

"No, but I've lost my heart," he said lamely. Then he seemed to realize his mistake. When it comes to wedding proposals, timing is everything, and this eager young man had got his timing catastrophically wrong. Though of course the cheap bauble didn't help. "I just thought—I mean I figured... Steph, I didn't think—"

"Well, that's your problem, isn't it, Robbie! You never think!"

I had kept my eye on David and Pauline, who hadn't reacted in any meaningful way to this cavalcade of admittedly shocking news. Now Pauline leaned in to her husband and murmured, "It's all very French, isn't it?"

"It is," David agreed. "Perhaps one of the Stewart ancestors was French?"

They shared a look of bemusement at the hullaballoo reaching a fever pitch. Ian was shouting something at Larry, who was giving his son a tongue-lashing for his lack of sensitivity, while the latter was accusing his dad of not giving a damn about his dearly departed wife. And in the midst of all this, Odelia and Chase quietly rose to their feet, dabbed their lips with a napkin, and excused themselves to their hostess Steph, who was yelling something at her mom about her utter selfishness to bring this up at a time when they should all be mourning Jeff.

Odelia directed a pointed look in our direction, and as one cat Dooley and I sprang up and toddled after them. And as we left the scene, the noise of quarreling family members followed us all the way to the driveway.

We actually met Kevin on our way out, like cars passing in the night—or in the daytime as was the case. He gave us a jolly wave—clearly in a good mood. And why not? He was getting married soon. And he didn't know yet that he had an illegitimate half-brother named Joe and that his mom had been enjoying carnal relations with the foreman.

"Poor guy," said Chase, shaking his head. "He won't know what hit him."

"It's the alcohol," said Dooley. "This is what alcohol does to people."

CHAPTER 40

That night, Steph sat in her room, unable to sleep. Zoe had long since fallen into a peaceful slumber, and she watched the baby as she lay in bed, a smile on her face. "At least I still have you," said Steph softly. After the spirited discussion that afternoon, she had the feeling that deep wounds had been cut, and that her family might never be healed again. The whole business had made her feel betrayed. Though ever since Jeff's death she was probably more vulnerable.

A knock sounded at the door, and she went to open it. It was Kevin.

"Can I come in?" he asked quietly.

She stepped back and gently closed the door. She didn't think the others were sleeping—too much had happened, and she imagined they were all lying awake, just like her, probably talking about the things that had been revealed.

"I just wanted you to know that I've decided to leave," said Kevin. He was sitting cross-legged on the bed, and she felt just like old times, when her brother and she had been chatting sometimes deep into the night like this. She hadn't realized how much she had missed those times. "I'm going to give my share of the winery to Joe and I'm going to leave and never come back."

"You want to give the winery to Joe?" asked Steph.

Kevin shrugged. "He is our brother. So he has a right to his share."

"That's not for you to decide, Kev. That's something Mom and Dad have to figure out, along with Hazel, of course."

Kevin grinned. "Hard to imagine Dad and Hazel. How old is Joe?"

"Nineteen."

"So this affair has been going on for twenty years at least."

"And Mom knew about it—and Dad knew about her. It's crazy."

"It is," said Kevin. "Though I shouldn't speak. I've been having an affair with Dominic for ten years that nobody knew about."

"At least you weren't married to a different person."

"Yeah, I guess that's true."

He reached out a hand to tickle Zoe's belly and Steph said, "Let her sleep."

"She's going to have a lot of uncles now. Uncle Kevin and Uncle Dom, and now also Uncle Joe. She'll get lots and lots of presents and will be spoiled rotten."

"I'm also leaving, by the way," said Steph. "I'm going back to Paris. I remembered this afternoon how much I miss being in charge of my own life. And somehow, out here, it's all about Mom and Dad and about the winery, isn't it?"

"I know. If we want to make something of ourselves, we have to get away. Which is what I told Dom. But he doesn't agree. He wants to stick around and take over the Kosinski Winery one day."

"I guess he's made of the right stuff—whatever that means."

"It means he's the son his dad wanted him to be," said Kev. "Whereas we didn't turn out the way our parents wanted. We don't fit into their dream since we have dreams of our own."

"I still think you should stick around, though," said Steph. "I mean, Mom and Dad aren't going to be running this place forever. And once they step down, you and Dom will take over, and you can join both wineries into one big super-successful business. And frankly speaking—what else can you do, bro?"

This had Kevin burst out laughing, before quickly controlling himself when Zoe stirred. "Nice one, sis. Don't hold back. Tell me what you really think."

"No, what I mean is—this is what you trained for. This is what you love."

"I love the work. Not so much the people that are in charge."

"Like I said, Dad won't be in charge forever. So don't be an idiot and throw away your birthright on a whim. Use your head for once, knucklehead." And she rapped his head with her knuckles for good measure before he slapped her hand away.

After some joshing and gentle ribbing he smiled at her.

"God, I'm going to miss you when you go back to Paris."

"Not as much as I'm going to miss you. But I'll be back."

"I know. You're like a bad penny. You keep turning up."

"Fart face."

"Buttface."

They both dissolved into giggles.

☙

Jan wasn't sure about this. He hadn't told Rai, for one thing. And he'd noticed that whenever he didn't tell his wife what he was up to, it usually meant it was a pretty bad idea. Rai was smart, and whatever she said was mostly right. But whether it was a good idea or not, it had to be done. Especially after what happened today.

His family was falling apart, he could tell. Steph would go back to Paris and take their grandchild with her, and Kevin would marry Dominic and go and live on the Kosinski farm. Or maybe they'd both move away altogether. And then what? He'd have to train Joe to run the Stewart Winery one day? The kid was great, and he loved him to pieces, but he simply didn't have what it took, and Hazel knew this. Which is why she never told him that Ian was his dad. So the kid wouldn't get any ideas. Now the cat was out of the bag, of course, and he'd have to give him something.

If only he'd locked that door. He always locked the door. Had locked it for the twenty-five years Hazel and he had been together. For the first fifteen Rai hadn't known, and even when she found out, she hadn't been as thrown as she could have been. But then she had recently started her affair with Larry, soon after Larry's wife Wendy died, so she couldn't really say anything, now could she?

And so they made a deal: they'd stay together for the kids, and for the winery, and each go about their own business, on the condition they be discreet about it. And now, on the same day, that idiot Robbie had to go and catch them both at it, and of course blurt it out to anyone who would listen, the blithering fool.

Oddly enough Rai and he had never been better together. Somehow their bond had never been stronger and more united. They were a couple in every sense of the word, except in the bedroom, of course, where they had soon discovered they weren't fully compatible. And so this arrangement had worked out well for the both of them. And for Larry and Hazel, of course. Though maybe less so for Joe.

He walked along the path that led to the edge of his property, until he reached the fence. He leaned on it, and glanced in the direction of the Kosinski place. He thought he could see it, even from this distance, but he could be mistaken. It was dark out, and the moon was concealed behind a thick pack of clouds.

A twig snapped, and he jerked his head up. On the other side of the fence a thickset figure materialized.

"Are you alone?" he asked.

"Yep. You?"

He nodded, and stared into the face of Ben Kosinski.

"Remember how we used to meet like this?" asked Ben.

"Long time ago," said Ian.

Their dads had feuded, the same way they had. Only they were boys back then, and hadn't understood any of the silliness their dads got up to, so they used to meet here at the fence that divided their farms, to play in the shade of the old willow tree nearby. Until someone must have seen them and told their dads, and gave them a good thrashing, and that was the end of that. Later on, Ian understood why the Kosinskis were the enemy: they wanted to lay their hands on Stewart land, and so had to be fought every inch of the way.

He didn't know when exactly the feud had become personal for him. Maybe when Ben asked Raimunda out on a date, even though everyone in town knew that Ian and Raimunda were meant to be together. It had cemented the idea in his mind that Ben was trying to take what was his, the way all Kosinskis did.

"Tough day?" asked Ben now.

"You can say that." He eyed the man closely. "Did you know about Kevin and Dom?"

Ben nodded. "Have known all along. But the boys swore us to secrecy."

"They should have told us," said Ian, still feeling annoyed. He hated things being sprung on him, or his relatives keeping secrets. Though he knew he was being hypocritical, of course, since he had also kept secrets from his kids.

"They were afraid of how you'd react," said Ben. "And with good reason, wouldn't you say?" He had quirked an ironic eyebrow in his direction, which annoyed Ian.

"Okay, so looks like there's gonna be some changes," he said, deciding to get down to business. "Our families are going to be united by this marriage between our two boys, and so we need to decide how to handle things from now on."

Ben barked an incredulous laugh. "You're a real romantic, aren't you? How to 'handle' our sons' marriage? Nice way of putting it. I'd say we organize a big party to celebrate that our sons have found each other, and invite the whole town."

Ian pursed his lips into an expression of disapproval. He hated spending money on strangers, and if they invited 'the whole town,' as Ben put it, that would mean spending a small fortune on a bunch of hangers-on and other loafers.

"I was thinking more along the lines of a small gathering. You know, friends and family only."

"Of course you are, you cheapskate," said Ben with a grin. He clapped him on the shoulder, a gesture the fastidious Ian did not appreciate in the least. "Why don't you and Rai come over to my place for dinner tomorrow? We can discuss this in more convivial circumstances. I pour a mean wine," he added archly.

Ian's lips moved into a reluctant smile. "Fine. Dinner it is. And then we can talk about the future of our farms as well." Loath though he was to admit it, this marriage between their sons was going to change things for their respective businesses as well, since both Dom and Kevin were the designated future heads of their family wineries. And if Kevin was to be believed, there was even talk of joining the two wineries into one, something that would have Ian's dad turn in his grave. But Kevin had presented them with a *fait accompli*, apparently.

The two men said their goodbyes, and soon Ben was swallowed up by the darkness. And as Ian started heading back to the house, he wondered what the future would hold for the Stewart Winery. Nothing good, he thought somberly.

CHAPTER 41

Chase had finally been able to get Bill Cymbal in front of him. Not face to face, since we were in Hampton Cove and Mr. Cymbal was in Paris. But they were talking on Zoom, with the future mayor of Paris taking up a lot of screen real estate. Either he was sitting too close to the camera, or he had a very large face. Frankly I thought the former was the more likely explanation.

"Detective Kingsley!" said the politician. "So nice to see you, sir!"

"Likewise," said Chase.

The cop was sitting at the kitchen table, talking to his laptop, and if Mr. Cymbal could have seen him, he would have been surprised to see that even though he was wearing a shirt, he was also wearing boxers. But then nobody cares about the lack of vestimentary refinement when talking on Zoom. Until a person gets up and shows his lack of pants, of course, something I hoped Odelia had warned her husband about.

"So I understand you have questions for me about Jeff Felfan?"

"That's right. Did you personally know Mr. Felfan, sir?"

"No, I did not. Never met the man. I know his father, of course, Felfan Senior. He's an esteemed colleague of mine, and I was saddened to hear he won't be running for mayor in the upcoming election." He flashed a smug grin at us, and I had the impression his sadness wasn't all that profound. "Is that a cat I see behind you, Detective Kingsley?"

"Yeah, that's my wife's cat," said Chase.

"He's a big fella, isn't he? I like the hefty ones, and the color, of course. Did you know that orange is the color of my campaign, detective? Color of the future!"

"I'm blorange," I muttered, "not orange."

"Okay, so about Jeff Felfan," said Chase, getting back on track, "I don't know if you're aware of this, sir, but Jeff's dad has leveled certain allegations against you."

"I know. He accuses me of murdering his son so he would withdraw from the race. Nonsense, of course. I may play hardball, but I'm not a murderer. And besides, I believe in winning the race on election day, not by getting rid of the opposition by murdering their kids. Is it true that he thinks I hired a hitman?"

"There has been talk of a professional hit, yes," Chase said carefully.

"Crazy talk! Where would I find a hitman! On your Craigslist, perhaps? And besides, David knows as well as I do that politicians are under a microscope in this country—and maybe in yours, as well. Anything we say or do is scrutinized in great detail. If I put even as much as a foot wrong it's going to be plastered all across social media. I frowned at a kid during a visit to the zoo last week, and half an hour later the video had gone viral! Said I hated kids. They even turned it into a meme. So you can imagine what they would do if I hired a hitman to kill Jeff Felfan. It would be the scandal of the century, and I'd be thrown in the deepest, darkest dungeon for all eternity."

"In the Bastille," Dooley said knowingly. "Or even the guillotine!"

"I don't think they still have the death penalty in France," I said.

"Oh, will you look at that? Another fine pussy," said the politician.

Dooley waved at the camera.

"See?" said Mr. Cymbal. "That's what I'm all about. Smiling at kiddies and petting pussies. Murdering people? Not so much. And I'm prepared to prove it to you, sir. I'm prepared to have my phone and computer examined by the French police. I have nothing to hide, and that's exactly the way it should be for the future mayor of the greatest city in the world."

"Is he going to be mayor of New York, Max?" asked Dooley.

"I think he's referring to Paris, Dooley," I said.

"I like Paris," said Dooley dreamily. "Remember Marion?"

Of course I did. The feisty cat owned by the manager of the hotel where we'd been staying not all that long ago. We would sit on the roof together, the three of us, and Dooley would moon at her, while Marion and I would look at the real moon. A nice time was had by all, and we had even caught a killer that time.

Somehow I didn't think the man sitting before us now was a killer. Not because he sounded so convincing—all politicians sound convincing, it's one of the first things they learn in politician school—but because he had a point. If he hired a professional assassin, it would be very hard to keep it a secret. Even if he wanted to, he simply wouldn't do it. Not if he was smart. And Bill Cymbal struck me as a very smart man. Except that he didn't know orange from blorange.

. . .

*A*nd there was more bad news—or perhaps even the worst news of all: cat choir was canceled. The news reached us through Harriet and Brutus, who had been out and about all day, following their assigned humans around and making sure that not a drop of alcohol passed their lips.

"I think we managed," said Harriet as she gave us an extensive overview of the events as they transpired that day. "Gran tried to create a diversion at some point by shouting, 'Mouse! Mouse!' but of course I didn't fall for that. And then when they split up, with Gran going in one direction and Scarlett in another, I panicked for a moment, but lucky for me Scarlett went into the hair salon, so I simply told Buster to keep an eye on her for the time being, while I went after Gran."

"I caught Tex on three different occasions," said Brutus, shaking his head. "Yesterday he tried to sneak a drink from the fridge, and this morning he actually dropped by the liquor store when he thought I wasn't looking. And finally he called Wilbur and asked him to deliver a six-pack to the office. But from what I could gather Wilbur has instituted an alcohol ban on all AA members."

"But I thought AA members were supposed to be anonymous?" asked Dooley.

"Not in this town, they're not," said Brutus with a grin. "You know what Hampton Cove is like. If it's news, it will travel—and fast!"

"Being an alcoholic is hardly news," I said.

"Depends who it is," said Brutus. "Ever since Father Reilly joined up, there's been a lot more scrutiny."

"He should have gone to an AA meeting in Happy Bays," said Harriet. "That way he could have stayed anonymous. Now the whole town knows about him."

"Poor Father Reilly," said Dooley. "He's a Famous Alcoholic now. An FA."

"Oh, and just so you know," said Harriet, "Shanille wanted to let you know that cat choir has been canceled until further notice. FuSSy takes precedence."

"What?!" I cried. "But I like cat choir. It's my way to unwind!"

"I guess you'll have to unwind some other way," said Harriet. "Or don't you agree that helping our poor humans stay sober and healthy is more important?"

"I guess so," I said, but I think she could tell that I didn't. Not really.

"Oh, and also," said Brutus, "dog choir has decided to join the fight. So Rufus and Fifi and all of their friends have also started their own FuSSy team."

"It won't be called FuSSy, though," I said. "Will it?"

"They're calling it CaSSy," said Harriet proudly. "Which stands for—"

"Let me guess," I said. "Canine Sponsor System."

"Exactly! FuSSy and CaSSy to the rescue, you guys!"

"But no more cat choir," I said morosely.

"Oh, will you stop fussing already!"

"Very funny," I muttered.

CHAPTER 42

*D*ooley and I decided to head into town anyway. Maybe there were still some cats who were going to get together—just for old time's sake. Not all cats' pet parents are alcoholics, you see. Some of them drink coffee or soda.

I felt a little downcast not only because cat choir had been canceled, but also because of the state of our investigation. Clearly we weren't getting anywhere fast, and it was affecting my mood.

We passed into the backyard, and from somewhere nearby sounds of cussing came. When we took a peek through the hedge, we saw that it was Kurt Mayfield, our next-door neighbor, and his shirtfront was awash with an effervescent substance that our powerful noses ascertained could only be beer. On the grass an empty can of Heineken lay, the final remnants of the fermented brew leaking into the ground and no doubt soon giving an earthworm delirium tremens.

"What did you have to go and do that for!" Kurt cried in dismay.

But Fifi merely winked at us, then whispered, "CaSSy to the rescue!"

We passed through the hole in the hedge and into Marge and Tex's backyard, wanting to take a gander at the food bowls in Marge's kitchen. Before one sets out on a long walk, it's important to strengthen the inner cat with plenty of grub, you see. But when we got there, loud sounds of a quarrel reached our ears. It sounded like Ted and Marcie Trapper, and when we hurried in that direction, we saw that two wine glasses had been smashed on the patio floor, a red liquid spreading out. On Ted's shirt, the same red liquid was creating a big stain that bloomed out across the man's chest.

"Salt!" Marcie cried. "Or that will never come out!"

"My good shirt!" Ted bleated. "My very best shirt!"

Rufus, apparently the instigator of the incident, sat on the floor looking as cool as Clint. He was actually licking his butt, not a care in the world. Then he must have spotted us, for he gave us a grin. "The alcohol ban is in effect, you guys."

"I can see that," I said, as Marcie came hurrying out of the house carrying a plastic container of salt. She then started dumping it on her husband's chest and rubbing it into the red spot, with Ted whining all the while about his nice clean shirt that was now for sure ruined—and it was all Rufus's fault!

We decided not to stick around for the sequel. Somehow it didn't interest me all that much to know if Marcie would be able to get Ted's shirt spotlessly clean again. Some mysteries simply aren't deep enough to plumb.

So we moved along, and made the trek into town.

"Maybe we should have joined FuSSy, Max," said Dooley. "It looks like a lot of fun."

"It looks like a lot of trouble," I said. "Not to mention those humans are going to strike back at some point. You can't separate man from his drink, Dooley. Somehow they will always find a way."

"But we're clever, Max. Cleverer than our humans."

"That may be so, but they have something we don't have."

"What is that?"

"They control the purse strings, and so they control our food supply. What if they get fed up and decide to put all of those FuSSy and CaSSy members on a diet? There will be wailing and gnashing of teeth, Dooley, mark my words. And a lot of it."

And we didn't even have to go far to see my observation borne out. We passed by the General Store, hoping to catch Kingman and convince him to head to the park with us, or maybe just shoot the breeze. But when we got to the back, there he was, looking forlorn. And when we asked him what was going on, he said that the pet flap was locked.

"Wilbur locked me out!" he lamented. "He had just poured a beer into a glass and was going to drink it in front of the television. So naturally I jumped up onto the couch and swiped the glass from his hand. And then when he grabbed another beer, and this time didn't even bother with a glass, I swiped that one from his hand as well. He looked at me for a moment, sort of stunned. But finally he got himself a third can, popped the top, and so I did it again. And that's when he got mad and kicked me out of the house." He gave us an intensely sad look. "He kicked me out of my own house, you guys! And then he locked the pet flap. Locked it! With my food still inside! And my nice warm blanket. Now what am I going to do!"

"Now you're going to wait until Wilbur has a change of heart," I said.

"I'm not touching that man's beer again, that much I can tell you. If he wants to get drunk, that's fine with me. Locking the pet flap? It's a disgrace, that's what it is!"

"Maybe you can call the Secretary-General of the United Nations," Dooley suggested. "And tell him that a crime has been committed against humanity."

"Not exactly against humanity, though," I said. "Against catdom, maybe."

"I'm sure you have a case, Kingman," said Dooley.

"I don't care!" the big cat wailed. "I want my home back!" And at this point he lost all pretense of dignity and independence by pounding on the pet flap. "Wilbur, let me in!!!" He actually reminded me of a character in the Flintstones.

I patted his shoulder consolingly, and we watched him jump up onto the windowsill, looking into the kitchen, which was on the ground floor.

"I don't see him, but I know he's there," he said. "He's ignoring me, isn't he? Wilbuuuuuuur!" he yelled as he started patting the glass. "I won't do it again!"

It was a sad scene to see one as strong and independent as Kingman being reduced to this. And a harbinger of things to come if these dry advocates kept this up.

"He's going to hurt his paws," said Dooley as we watched the spectacle. Unfortunately for Kingman Wilbur wasn't ready to forgive and forget, for the pet flap remained closed for business. So finally he came back down from his perch.

"If you want you can walk home with us," I said. "There's plenty of food in our bowls, and you can have my favorite spot if you want. You can even sleep at the foot of the bed. We'll sleep on the couch."

"Thanks, Max. That's very kind of you. But it's not the same, is it?"

I knew what he meant. If I had to spend the night at the foot of Wilbur's bed I probably wouldn't like it either. There's simply no place like home, is there?

"If only Wilbur had kids," Kingman lamented. "Then he wouldn't have such a hard heart."

"I don't think Wilbur is hard-hearted," I said. "I think he wants to have a drink in peace, without having to clean beer stains out of his carpet or his clothes."

But Kingman wasn't listening. "If he had kids, he would have grandkids by now, and his heart wouldn't have turned to stone. He would be a grandpa, and would spoil those kids rotten. He'd do anything for them, the way grandparents do. And then he wouldn't lock me out, same way he wouldn't lock those kids out."

And as he kept yammering on about Wilbur and the man's heart of stone, something seemed to click inside my big noggin. It had been a long slog, this investigation, but for the first time I was starting to see the light at the end of the tunnel. Or did I?

CHAPTER 43

"Are you sure about this, Max?" asked Odelia for the hundredth time.

"Let's say I'm almost sure," I said, hedging my bets.

"If we do this and you're wrong..."

The implication was obvious: if we accused the wrong person, there would be hell to pay, and perhaps even Uncle Alec wouldn't be able to protect Chase from certain disgrace and perhaps even dismissal.

"These are some pretty important people," Odelia continued.

"Okay, look," I said. "If I'm right, you're going to save lives. If I'm wrong, you simply tell them that you're members of the AA and have fallen off the wagon."

"Very funny, Max," said Odelia.

We were in the car, sitting outside the main gate of the Stewart Winery, with Odelia and Chase arguing amongst themselves as to the best way to proceed. It was a miracle I'd managed to get them both out of bed. It had taken me a long time to convince Odelia, and had taken her an even longer time to convince her husband. But there we were, and if we didn't get a move on, it could be too late.

"We can't just ring the bell and ask them to let us in," said Odelia.

"So we scale the fence," said Chase, as if it was the kind of thing he did every day. "It's not that far to the house, and it's like Max says: if we don't do this, and someone dies, we're going to feel horrible knowing we could have stopped it."

That seemed to decide Odelia, for she opened the car door and got out.

Further down the road another car was parked, but as far as I could tell there was no one in it. It was a dark sedan, and I wondered if whoever had parked it also had business with the Stewarts.

We watched as Chase expertly scaled the fence, after ascertaining that it wasn't charged with electricity, which wouldn't have been a good experience. Odelia helped me and Dooley up, then was helped herself by Chase. Moments later we were in the vineyard, and our adventure had started for real!

"We should have told someone we were coming," said Dooley. "Now they will think we're intruders, and Ian will get out his big gun, or maybe Larry, and they'll shoot holes in us!"

"Not if they don't know we're here," I pointed out.

"But I'll bet they have alarm systems, and cameras!"

I had to admit I wasn't entirely convinced I was right either. But I was willing to take a chance. Though as we snuck along the dirt road that led through the vineyard and up to the house, I was starting to get a little uneasy in my mind. What had I got us into this time!

Soon we reached destination's end, and found ourselves looking up at that great house. All the windows were dark, with not a soul in sight. Chase pointed to the window in question, and Odelia nodded. And so we snuck around the house, and onto the patio. If I was correct about this, the back door would be unlocked, and the alarm switched off.

Chase took a deep breath, then put his hand on the door handle. He locked eyes with Odelia, who gave him a curt nod, and he pushed down on the handle.

The door easily swung open, and as we stood there, no alarm sounded.

Phew!

And now for the hard part: sneaking through a house filled with people without getting caught!

For Dooley and me this was a piece of cake, of course. Cats are built for sneaking. But for Odelia and Chase this was a lot harder. But they managed admirably. First we passed through the kitchen, then into the hallway, and up the sweeping marble staircase to reach the second-floor landing. Odelia counted the doors as we snuck along the corridor, until finally we had reached journey's end.

"This is it!" Chase mounted. "No turning back now."

We all took a deep breath, and Chase opened the door and we entered the room.

And there, on the bed, I could see a dark figure straddling another figure. Chase must have seen it, too, for instantly he flicked the switch and the room was bathed in a bright light. The figure on the bed was a man dressed in black from head to toe, and he was straddling David Felfan, strangling the man with what looked like a piece of wire! Next to David, Pauline lay motionless, eyes closed. She looked dead—as dead as David would have been if we had arrived a minute later!

The man immediately jumped from the bed, and made for the window. But Chase cut off that avenue of escape, and since Odelia was between him and the door, there was simply no way out. He must have realized this, for he held out his hands at this point, as a sign of surrender. "You cops?" he asked.

"Detective Kingsley," said Chase in response. "Hampton Cove PD."

"Shush!" I said suddenly, for I'd heard a sound in the corridor.

Immediately Odelia turned off the light again, and moments later the door opened and a man entered. "How is it going?" asked the man. "They dead yet?"

Odelia turned on the light, and we all found ourselves looking into the surprised face of… Ian Stewart.

CHAPTER 44

"I don't get it," said Harriet. "Ian Stewart killed his own son-in-law?"

"He didn't kill him with his own hands," I said. "But he did hire a professional assassin to have Jeff killed. And then he hired that same assassin to kill Jeff's parents." Though lucky for them we had arrived just in time to save both David and Pauline Felfan's lives. Ian had knocked them both out by putting GBH in their wine glass before retiring to bed. And then let this friendly neighborhood hitman into the house by unlocking the door and switching off the alarm.

"His name is Novio Bosiaki," said Dooley, rolling the words on his tongue. "It has a nice ring to it, don't you think? He's Serbian, or so Chase was told."

"It doesn't have a nice ring to it for Jeff," I pointed out. "Cause if Novio Bosiaki hadn't plied his favorite trade, that young man would still be alive today."

"Where did he find this hitman?" asked Brutus.

"The internet, where else?" I said.

"Craigslist?" Harriet ventured.

"Not exactly. Some obscure website on the darknet."

"Why is it called the darknet, Max?" asked Dooley. "Is it because Mr. Bosiaki likes to work in the dark?"

"Something like that," I said with a smile.

We were on the porch swing in Marge and Tex's backyard, while our humans were whiling away the time by enjoying a wonderful feast. Tex was behind the grill, as per usual, and for once the barbecue was fully dry: no alcohol was being served. Not at our request, mind you, but at Gran's. She felt that if she and Scarlett and Tex were going to stand a chance of breaking their record number of days without imbibing their favorite alcoholic beverage, they needed a little support from their family and friends. For it's hard to stay sober when everyone around you is swigging the good stuff by the gallon.

"Okay, so why did Ian Stewart kill Jeff?" asked Harriet. "I thought he loved his son-in-law?"

"Maybe he did, maybe he didn't, but what he didn't like about Jeff was that he was French. Not in the sense that he was a Frenchman, but that he was taking Steph and their little girl to go and live in France—permanently. Ian and Raimunda wanted Steph in Hampton Cove, but even more than Steph, they wanted Zoe to live nearby, so they could see her all the time. You see, from the moment Zoe was born, Ian and Raimunda simply couldn't bear the thought of not having access to her all the time. They suspected that Kevin was gay, and very likely wouldn't be able to give them a grandchild. And Steph already told them that she and Jeff had decided to have just the one kid. So Zoe was all they had."

"Surely no grandparent is crazy enough to kill their son-in-law just to make sure they have access to their grandchild," said Harriet.

"In Ian and Raimunda's case, they were that crazy about Zoe. From the moment that little girl was born they loved her with all their hearts, and decided that nothing and no one would come between them—not even Steph or Jeff."

"That's just nuts."

"Sometimes the love of a grandparent for their grandchild is nuts."

After Ian's arrest, a forensic investigation of his phone and computer revealed deleted email and text message exchanges between Ian and Novio Bosiaki. Detailed instructions on how to reach Jeff and the best way of disposing of him. And ways to make it look like a murder-suicide, though that hadn't worked out so well in the end. When Jeff had arrived at Cipriana's flat, she'd already been knocked out by the GBH the hired killer had administered—having forced her to swallow it down in a cup of coffee. Then when Jeff arrived he'd forced him to lie down on the bed and shot him, staging the scenario he and Ian had dreamed up.

Novio Bosiaki's picture had been shown to the witness, and this time the old lady had confirmed that this was the tall man she'd seen entering the building.

"But why murder Jeff's parents?" asked Harriet. "That makes no sense."

"Oh, but it does, from Ian's warped point of view," I said. "You see, earlier that evening Steph had told her parents that she was planning to move to France with Zoe. That she wanted to pursue a career in fashion design and live in the apartment that Jeff's parents had bought for them. And so Ian decided that David and Pauline had to die. He contacted Novio and made sure that the couple was drugged and would put up no resistance when the killer strangled them in their bed. He was going to string David up against the door, making it look as if he'd strangled Pauline first, then committed suicide by hanging."

"We got there just in time," said Dooley, who had been greatly impressed by the whole thing. "If not for Max, they would both have been dead as a doornail." When he realized his *faux pas* he quickly put a paw in front of his mouth. "Oops."

"Was Ian also involved in this slander business that cost Steph two jobs and Jeff the inheritance from his godmother?" asked Harriet.

"Yes, he was," I said. "When he heard about the WelBeQ job offer, he asked Novio to send those emails, which wasn't hard, since Ian had plenty of pictures of his daughter to choose from. Novio then contacted a computer hacker associate, who set up the campaign. Same thing with the Paris job, and the Paris apartment."

"Anything not to have Steph leave the country," said Harriet, nodding.

"Steph, but even more than Steph his granddaughter Zoe," I said.

"So… how involved was Raimunda in Ian's plans?" asked Brutus.

"Now that," I said, "is a tough one to answer. Personally I think she must have known. Maybe even helped set up that smear campaign. But unfortunately we have no way of proving it, and Ian isn't talking, and neither is Raimunda."

"So she's going to get away with it?" asked Harriet. "That's not okay."

"She won't have to stand trial, and she's not going to prison," I said. "But she will have to watch Steph and Zoe move to Paris—the exact thing she feared the most." Steph's decision had only been validated by her dad's betrayal. When she had learned that Ian ordered Jeff's murder, the shock had been so great she nearly fainted. Luckily she had David and Pauline to support her. Funnily enough the bond between them had only become stronger after Jeff passed away, and now Steph viewed her in-laws almost more like her parents than her real parents.

She was going to wait for the memorial service, and leave straight after. And return only for the trial of her dad, which was going to be tough on everyone.

"What's going to happen to the Stewart Winery now that Ian is in jail?" asked Brutus.

"Raimunda has announced she's taking a step back, and Kevin is going to be in charge from now on, with the valued assistance of long-time foreman Larry Scunner, and of course Dominic and Kevin's future father-in-law. Looks like the plan to join both wineries is going to be fast-tracked now that Ian is gone."

"What an amazing story," said Harriet. "Almost beats the story of FuSSy's success in turning Hampton Cove dry. We're not there yet, but we're working on it. In fact we're thinking about taking our campaign to other towns, and maybe even the rest of the country. If all pets did what we do for our humans, we just might succeed where Prohibition failed. Score one for Team FuSSy—one of my better ideas!" She looked proud as she said it, even though it had actually been Shanille's idea, something she seemed to have conveniently forgotten.

I glanced at our humans, and saw a sorry sight: Uncle Alec was pushing his food around on his plate, Gran sat nursing a soda and looking sad, and even Scarlett, who's usually always so happy and peppy, looked as if she was attending a funeral. In fact Tex was the only one who seemed to have come through this whole AA episode with his good mood intact. He actually seemed to thrive.

"Look what I brought," said Odelia as she dug into a plastic bag she'd conveniently hid under the table. Two bottles of wine popped up. "One is from the Stewart Winery, and the other from the Kosinski Winery. I promised Kevin Stewart we were going to help him settle once and for all which one of these is the best. They're both whites and are supposed to be crisp, dry and aromatic, whatever that means." She gave her grandmother a radiant look. "What do you say, Gran?"

But Gran darted a quick glance at Harriet, then shook her head sadly, while seeming to shrink even more into herself. "Thank you, sweetie, but I'll pass."

"Me, too," said Scarlett, first having checked with Harriet.

The Persian was shaking her head in abject disapproval. "What is she up to?" she said. "Max, you have to stop her. She's pushing dope to drug addicts!"

"It's not as bad as all that, is it?" I said. "It's just one glass of wine, Harriet."

Harriet gawked at me. "Not you, too!"

"Not everyone who drinks is an alcoholic. So stop making such a big fuss. Our humans aren't alcoholics, and neither are most of the people in this town."

"What about Father Reilly?" she demanded. "Or are you going to sit there and tell me he doesn't have a problem?"

"Marigold left, and he was going through a rough time. A personal crisis that led to him making a bad choice. But he's all right now," I said soothingly.

"I don't believe this," said Harriet. "Brutus—tell him!"

"Tell him what?" asked Brutus.

"Tell him he's wrong! And recite the thirteen steps!"

"Oh, God, not again," said Brutus. "I don't even know them by heart."

"Step one," she began, and started droning off the steps.

"Sometimes I wish I had earplugs," Dooley whispered to me at some point. "So I could drown out the sound of Harriet's yapping."

We shared a grin, which hadn't escaped Harriet's notice, for she raised the volume of her incantation.

"How about you, Dad?" said Odelia, holding up her two bottles.

But Tex hesitated, darting a questioning glance at his wife. When Marge nodded, his face lit up like a Christmas tree. "Why not?" he said. "Just a small glass for me."

"Two small glasses, buddy," said Chase, who was doing the honors. "We have to decide which one of these is the best. A responsibility we don't take lightly."

"Fine, two small glasses," said Tex with a jolly expression on his face.

Gran and Scarlett looked on like two kids watching a third kid eat a gigantic piece of delicious cake while not being allowed to eat a piece themselves. They were both licking their lips as Tex poured the cooling liquid down the hatch.

"Pretty good," the doctor determined. "Now let's try the other one."

"I want one, too," said Gran timidly.

"So do I," said Scarlett, just as quietly.

They both stared at Harriet, who was still going through her declamation.

Marge must have sensed that harmony was far off at the dinner table, for she suddenly came over to where we were sitting, and asked Dooley and me to scoot over and make some space. She sat down next to Harriet, and for the next few minutes a murmured conversation was carried out that, try as I might, I couldn't overhear.

"What is she saying?" asked Dooley.

"I don't know," I said, not hiding my frustration.

"I think she's offering her a drink," said Dooley, straining his ears. "At least I think I heard the word 'wine' and also the words 'cut them some slack.'"

"Sounds to me as if she's trying to convince Harriet to stop being so fussy," I said with a slight grin.

"She is very fussy, isn't she?" said Dooley. "A fussy pussy. Not good for Gran."

"Or Scarlett."

"Or anyone."

The conversation finally came to an end, and Marge got up and walked over to the table, took a pair of glasses, filled them with wine from Odelia's bottles and handed Gran and Scarlett a glass each.

Both looked at her as if manna had finally descended from heaven, and they couldn't quite believe their luck. "Is this for me?" asked Gran.

"Can we drink this?" asked Scarlett. "Are you sure?"

"Absolutely," said Marge. "Now drink up, both of you."

And as both ladies sipped from their drink, Charlene poured Uncle Alec a glass, and soon the humans were all having a nice drink from the wines produced by the finest wineries in Hampton Cove, and judging them to be equally delicious.

And Harriet? She just sat there looking stunned.

"What did Marge say to you, Harriet?" I finally asked when I couldn't curb my curiosity any longer.

"None of your business!" she snapped, and jumped down from the swing and walked off. "Brutus! Are you coming!" she said over her shoulder.

"What did she say?" I whispered to Brutus.

"I don't know," he said, "but I got the impression FuSSy is finally finished."

He flashed us a quick grin, then quickly traipsed off after his lady love.

"Good riddance," said Dooley, who seemed to have had a change of heart about the whole temperance thing. "Too much of a good thing is a bad thing, Max. And that goes for the good things you do to stop the bad things from happening, too."

I wasn't sure if what Dooley said was good or bad, but I heartily concurred.

A loud shout sounded from Kurt Mayfield's backyard. "Fifi! Stop that!"

And from the Trappers a sudden howl of fury told us that Rufus was also staying the course. "Rufus!" Marcie yelled. "Bad boy! Bad!" And Ted: "My nice shirt!"

FuSSy might be dead and buried, but CaSSy was still going strong.

Which just goes to show that cats really are smarter than dogs.

But then I guess we already knew that, didn't we?

Just then, Odelia unwrapped a piece of chocolate for dessert. Dooley's eyes instantly went wide. And before I could stop him, he had jumped down from the swing, hopped up onto the table, and was swiping that piece of chocolate out of Odelia's hands!

"Hey!" Odelia cried. "What do you think you're doing!"

"I'm saving you from this terrible addiction!" Dooley said, panting a little from the exertion.

Okay, so I'm going to make a slight emendation here: maybe not *all* cats are smarter than dogs.

EPILOGUE

The Poole household had already retired to bed, and since the cats had gone out for the night, a peaceful quiet had descended on the house. Tex was fast asleep, snoring softly, but Marge wasn't. Just that day the latest book from her favorite author had been delivered at the library, and she'd reserved a copy for herself, which she was now reading. She'd vowed to read one chapter and then put the book aside, but she was four chapters in and simply couldn't stop reading! Her cheeks flushed, her eyes gritty, she finally decided that enough was enough, and that the adventures of the unfortunate heroine Sally, who met the perfect man on the train only to lose sight of him again, would have to wait until the morrow.

She was a little thirsty, though, and so she reluctantly slipped from between the covers, and tripped downstairs and into the kitchen to drink some water from the tap. And it was as she stood there that she heard the sound. The clinking sound of glass against glass. It could only come from the garage. Figuring it could be the cats, or some other animal that had managed to get in, she went in search of the source of the noise. The moment she flicked on the light, it became clear that it wasn't the cats, or some other animal. Unless she classified Ted Trapper in this latter category, of course. For it was indeed her next-door neighbor who stood there, looking very much caught in the act of doing something he shouldn't!

"Marge!" he cried, his voice a little quaky and his very wide and surprised.

"What have you got there, Ted?" she asked, though it was obvious what he got there: an empty wine bottle which he'd been in the process of depositing not in its appropriate receptacle, namely his own, but in the Poole glass recycle bin.

"Um..." said Ted, clearly flustered. "The thing is, Marge..."

"Yes, Ted?" she asked, having trouble suppressing a smile.

He noisily cleared his throat. "Well, see, the thing is, Marge..."

"The thing is that you've been putting your empties in my recycle bin instead of your own," she said, starting to feel sorry for the guy. "As to the reason, I can only guess." Though it probably had something to do with the fact that he was trying to hide his drinking habit from his wife, which his next words confirmed.

"Please don't tell Marcie," he said. "I've been meaning to stop, but this stuff is just so good—too good to be believed. I got it from this wine merchant on Frampton Street. He told me it's the goods, and he wasn't lying. I keep them in the garden house, under the bags of manure, so Rufus won't root them out. And rat me out." He was perking up as he began to expound on the quality of his hidden stash. "I'll pay you, if you want," he offered. "As long as this can stay between us, please?" He gave her a pleading that would have melted anyone's heart.

"You do realize that because of you I sent my husband

and my mother to the AA meetings?" she said, feeling a little bad now about that particular decision.

"I know. Tex told me all about it," said Ted. "And frankly I've been thinking about doing the same thing. But first I need to finish these last couple of bottles."

"How many have you got left?"

"Only three," he said with a touch of regret. "And then they're gone. And I'll be gone, I promise. No more midnight sneaking around in your garage, I swear."

"Hand over one bottle and we won't mention it again," she said, figuring both Tex and her mother deserved a little treat after what she put them through.

"Deal!" said Ted, looking much relieved.

He took his leave, then, and Marge went to bed.

"Were you talking to someone just now?" asked Tex sleepily.

"Ted was in the garage, putting his empty bottles in our recycle bin."

"Oh," said Tex. Then, moments later, "Did you just say that Ted puts his empties in our recycle bin?"

"Yep. But don't tell Marcie, or she'll be upset and send him to the AA."

Silence. Then: "Of course I won't tell Marcie." Though somehow Marge had the impression that he just might. At least if that big grin on his face was anything to go by.

THE END

Thanks for reading! If you want to know when a new Nic Saint book comes out, sign up for Nic's mailing list: nicsaint.com/news

DOOLEY'S INTRODUCTION
(CONTAINS SPOILERS)

Dooley wrote his own introduction for Purrfect Bouquet. Only it contains spoilers, so I decided not to use it. But now that you've read the book, here's Dooley's take on the story:

> "Max and I had another amazing adventure. It all revolved around wine. Well, wine and babies, actually. You see, there was this couple who had a baby, but they also had parents, like most of us do, and so his parents and her parents both wanted as much access to the baby as possible, only her parents wanted it just that little bit more. And so instead of being nice to their son-in-law and buying their granddaughter gifts, like most grandparents, they had their son-in-law murdered. And then they tried to have his parents murdered, too. Just because their daughter was going to live in Paris, and take their granddaughter along with her. I guess they didn't like Paris, or maybe they didn't like their in-laws.
>
> But Max figured it out in the end, like he always does. He's very clever. And he's my best friend, which

makes me very proud. He says I help him a lot in his investigations, but I'm not sure if that's true. I think he figures it out all by himself, with no help from me. He says I give him moral support. I have no idea what that means. Maybe it means I'm a moral cat, which is probably a good thing, since I wouldn't want to be an immoral cat. Immoral cats do bad things, and I'd never want to do a bad thing in my life. How that helps Max I don't know, but I'm sure glad it does.

So if you want to read about our latest adventure, go right ahead. It's available from all good bookstores, and possibly from some of the not-so-good ones, too. It doesn't cost much. Max says it's about the cost of a cup of coffee, which is something most humans love. So instead of a cup of coffee you can read our book. Or maybe you can read our book and buy a cup of coffee. And maybe even a piece of cake. Max says this is called splurging. I'm not sure if it's moral or immoral, but it has a nice ring to it. So go buy our new book and splurge!"

EXCERPT FROM PURRFECT HOME (MAX 57)

Chapter One

I was gently dozing on the patio, as one does, when the sound of strange mutterings reached my sensitive ears. The mutterings seemed to come from somewhere nearby, and were accompanied by the occasional grinding of teeth. And since humans are the first species that comes to mind when the topic of teeth grinding is broached, I immediately assumed that one of our own humans was expressing a beef with something or someone.

As it happens, this human was Gran, and she was reading the newspaper.

Now I could have told her that no good ever came from reading a newspaper, since they're mostly filled with bad news that is designed to frustrate and annoy—except perhaps the comics section—but since our human Odelia works for a newspaper, I wisely kept my tongue.

After all, if Odelia were to stop writing for the Hampton Cove Gazette, and getting paid for the privilege, she wouldn't be in a position to buy us sustenance on a daily

EXCERPT FROM PURRFECT HOME (MAX 57)

basis in the form of kibble and wet food, or provide a nice roof over our heads.

And so I decided to take a wait-and-see approach to these mutterings.

"Why is Gran acting so strange, Max?" asked Dooley, who'd noticed the same phenomenon and only too rightly asked himself questions about Gran's mental health. "And why is she making those funny sounds with her teeth?"

"She's reading the newspaper," I explained. "And when humans read the newspaper, this is how they often react."

"Oh," said Dooley, and lapsed into thought. He came out of this after a couple of moments, to ask a follow-up question. "So why is she looking so angry?"

"She must have read something in the paper that made her angry," I said with a shrug.

Dooley cleared his throat. He was determined to get to the bottom of this mystery. "Gran? Why are you muttering and looking as if you want to strangle someone?"

He was right. Gran did look as if she was ready to strangle whoever had written the article she was reading. You could see it from the way she was holding the paper: in a tight grip, her knuckles white, and about to strangle the paper in lieu of the person she really wanted to strangle, even though the poor paper wasn't to blame.

"It's these darn retirement homes," Gran said darkly. "They're death traps, every single one of them. Once they get you, you never get out of them alive!"

"What's a retirement home?" asked Dooley, always keen to improve his general knowledge.

"It's a place where retired people go," I said. "But only when they feel they're too old to live alone and need some assistance in their day-to-day existence."

"Listen to this," said Gran, "Justine Scott died at the ripe old age of ninety-seven. She had been a resident at Happy

Home for the Elderly for the past twenty-five years.'" She shook her head in a clear expression of disgust. "I used to know Justine. And if they think ninety-seven is a 'ripe old age' they're very much mistaken. That woman had more energy than a spark plug. Whenever they organized a Friday night get-together at the community center she could dance everyone's socks off!"

"Was she a good friend of yours, this Justine?" I asked.

But Gran was looking sad now, and judging from the faraway look on her face was thinking of her friend Justine, and all the adventures they'd lived through together.

"It's always sad when someone dies, isn't it, Max?" said Dooley. "Especially a good friend like Justine."

"She wasn't a friend," said Gran, coming out of her reverie to set the record straight. "But she was far too young to die is the point I'm trying to make here. And it's all the fault of this so-called Happy Home for the Elderly!" This time she was actually balling up the newspaper and depositing it next to her lounge chair. She had been taking in some sun, and for the occasion was dressed in a purple bathing suit with sequined silver letters emblazoned across her chest that spelled out, 'World's Greatest Gran.' "I told her not to go, but she wouldn't listen, would she?"

"You told her not to go to this place?" asked Dooley.

"Of course! I told her retirement homes are deathtraps. But off she went, and now she's dead." She shook her head in dismay at the terrible fate that had befallen her not-friend.

Dooley gasped in shock and horror. "Do you mean... they killed her?!"

"Of course they did," said Gran. "And I can tell you right now that you'll never see me going to one of these places. I'd rather jump off that there roof!"

Dooley glanced up at that there roof and gasped again. "Gran, you shouldn't say such things!"

"I know, and it's all because of that horrible Happy Home," she grumbled.

I had closed my eyes for a moment, and when I opened them again, I saw that Dooley was staring at me intently.

"What?" I said, once more getting the impression that he desired speech with me.

"Max, we have to do something! This Happy Home has killed Gran's friend Justine Scott! We have to start an investigation! Find the killer! Get justice for Justine!"

"They didn't actually kill her," I said.

"But Gran just said they did!"

"I know that's what she said, but she didn't mean it literally," I said, yawning a bit and wondering if I shouldn't go and lie in the shade of those rose bushes at the bottom of the garden, where it's always so nice and cool.

"I don't understand," said Dooley, and looked more puzzled than ever. That's what you get when humans start giving you these mixed messages. It's tough on a literal-minded cat like Dooley.

"What she means is that when you go into a retirement home, chances are that you will never get out of it alive," I said, then realized this didn't sound exactly right.

"See! They kill people over there!"

"Not really," I said, starting to tire a little of this conversation. "Look, a retirement home is a place where people go who are incapable of living alone, so as a rule these people are not quite as young as they used to be. In other words: they're pretty old. And since as a rule people don't get any younger as they age, it's only to be expected that at some point they'll pass on to that great big retirement home in the sky."

Dooley glanced up at the sky, fully expecting to see this fabled home.

"Heaven is what I mean," I said, just to make my meaning

EXCERPT FROM PURRFECT HOME (MAX 57)

perfectly clear. "They go to heaven. Just like this Justine Scott."

"But... so they don't actually kill them?"

"No, they don't. Well, most of them anyway." From time to time you hear about nurses murdering residents, but I like to think this is an exception, not standard practice.

And as Dooley pondered this, I closed my eyes once more, grateful for this interlude. The peace and quiet didn't last long, though. Gran might have grabbed her phone and was now texting furiously, presumably updating her friend Scarlett on her decision never to become a resident of Happy Home, but Dooley had once again marshaled his thoughts and was ready to give me the benefit of his latest brainwave.

"Do you think there are also retirement homes for cats, Max?"

"No, I don't," I said. "Though it's possible that as our humans get older and move into a retirement home themselves, they decide to take us along with them."

"Oh," said Dooley. "So when Odelia is old, we'll go and live at one of these places with her?"

"Odelia isn't quite old enough to go to a retirement home yet. And in fact many people don't go to a retirement home at all. They stay with their families, like Gran."

Gran had gone from living by herself in her own little apartment to living with her daughter and son-in-law, much to that son-in-law's occasional chagrin. But all in all it was a good arrangement, especially now that Odelia had recently given birth to a new human being in the form of Grace, who was Gran's great-granddaughter and was eyeing me from a corner of the patio, where she was keeping herself busy in the plastic shell-shaped sandbox Chase had bought for her. Apart from creating cakes and cookies from sand, and subsequently trying to eat them, she seemed more interested in Dooley and me than in her latest toy, though. And I could

EXCERPT FROM PURRFECT HOME (MAX 57)

already foresee that soon we were going to have to find a safer spot to enjoy some peace and quiet.

Gran's phone rang out its merry tune—Taylor Swift if I wasn't mistaken—and she immediately picked up. And as she chatted with Scarlett, vociferously reiterating her opinion on retirement homes in general and Happy Home for the Elderly in particular, I suddenly experienced a powerful pulling sensation in the vicinity of my tail. When I glanced over, I saw that Grace had grabbed hold of this sensitive appendage and was depositing a scoop of sand on top of it. When I tried to move my tail, she squealed with joy, then scooped some more, all the while applying a surprisingly powerful grip!

"What is she doing, Max?" asked Dooley.

"Seasoning my tail with sand," I grumbled.

Of course Gran was too busy talking to Scarlett, so it looked as if I was on my own!

"Leave the tail, Grace," I said gently, giving the thing a tug.

But she wasn't giving up quite so easily. Instead, she doubled down, and actually went and sat on it!

"She's funny, isn't she?" asked Dooley.

"Funny isn't the word I would use," I said as the little tyke now started pouring sand on top of my head!

"Grace, no," I said. "Sand should stay in the sandbox, not on top of the cat."

But of course the little girl wasn't interested in my point of view on the correct usage of sand. In fact she was enjoying the game so much she was squealing with joy, and patting my head with what can only be termed an intense caress.

"Does it hurt?" asked Dooley, interested.

"Yes, it does!" I cried as a bit of sand got into my eye. "Ouch!"

At this point Gran finally remembered her duties as a

babysitter, and came over to direct Grace back to her designated play area and away from yours truly.

She didn't like it, and wrestled within Gran's grip, darting anxious glances over her shoulder in my direction, clearly feeling that her great work wasn't done yet.

But I was done, and I took advantage of this sudden lull in the proceedings to remove myself from the scene and seek urgent refuge elsewhere. If those rose bushes had looked enticing before, they looked like an actual sanctuary now! And so I headed over there, only to be confronted with Brutus and Harriet in a state of intimacy I won't describe to you but which no cat should be forced to experience on an empty stomach.

Excusing myself profusely, I staggered away from the sordid scene, and headed into the next-door backyard, where hopefully no little girls would hound me!

Dooley, who had followed my progress with marked interest, said, "What were Harriet and Brutus doing, Max?"

"Um... kissing," I said.

"Doesn't kissing usually involve a person's lips?" he asked.

"They were probably working their way up to that," I said, not really feeling in the mood for the birds and bees talk at that particular instance. I had the impression I had swallowed some of Grace's sand, and it didn't exactly taste moreish.

Lucky for us we soon bumped into Marge, and when she saw the state I was in, that wonderful lady took pity on my predicament, and proceeded to rid me of the last remnants of the sandstorm I'd just been in. She even took a gander at my eye, and when finally she gave me the all-clear, I expressed my relief and gratitude not only in word but also in deed, by giving her a gentle headbutt against the leg. She responded by giving us each a tasty treat from the fridge, and since the pet flap is too small for Grace to pass through, I gradually started to feel safe again from the baby menace.

Retirement homes may be deathtraps, but homes where newborn babies are allowed to roam free are probably even worse!

And as Dooley and I settled down on the couch in the living room, I said, "Don't get me wrong. I love Grace. But she can be quite a handful sometimes, can't she?"

"We have to be nice to her, though, Max," said Dooley. "Cause one day when Odelia is old and gray and so are we, it's going to be up to Grace to take care of us all. And if we don't indulge her occasional whims now, she might decide to put us all in the Happy Home for the Elderly instead!"

I gulped a little at this piece of fine reasoning, and could only agree wholeheartedly.

"You're right, Dooley," I said. All things considered, a little bit of sand in my eye and a toddler stomping on my tail was a small price to pay for her future hospitality!

Chapter Two

We were in Odelia's office dozing and catching up on some much-needed rest when a knock sounded at the door and a woman strode in. She was older than Odelia but not old enough to be eligible for room and board at a retirement home. She also looked a little nervous, but then most people who visit Odelia in her office are a little trepidatious at first. Mostly these people are struggling with some personal issue and unless you are used to enlisting the assistance of a reporter of Odelia's repute, it's only natural to feel ill at ease at the prospect of revealing your secret to a complete stranger.

But Odelia has this way about her that puts people at ease

straight away, and I could tell that she was having this effect on this person right now.

The woman introduced herself as Annette Williams, and she wasn't actually there because she was faced with a baffling problem herself, but because her daughter was.

"You see, Kirsten has only been working there for six months," Annette said once the introductions were out of the way and she was comfortably seated in front of our human. "And she likes the job, she really does. And most of the residents are perfectly nice. It's this one man, see, Mrs. Kingsley. He's the one who's keeping me up at night."

"Sorry, but where did you say your daughter works, Mrs. Williams?" asked Odelia.

"She works as a CNA, a certified nursing assistant, at Happy Home for the Elderly," said Annette.

Dooley and I shared a look of intense surprise.

"Of all the retirement homes in all the towns in all the world," Dooley murmured, and I nodded emphatically. What were the odds?

"Go on," said Odelia kindly. "This man has been keeping you up at night?"

"Well, his name is Henry Kaur," said Annette. "And at first I thought nothing of it, but he's been giving her gifts, you see. Expensive ones. He gave her a watch that must have cost a small fortune, and a pair of earrings, and he's been making her promises."

"What kind of promises?"

"He seems to suggest that when he dies, he's going to leave her something in his will."

"I see," said Odelia, a worried frown on her face.

"Now Kirsten isn't worried. She says he's a very kind man, and so if he wants to give her a token of his appreciation from time to time, that's fine with her. But then she's young, of course, and inexperienced when it comes to men. She's never even had a boyfriend."

"How old is your daughter?"

"Nineteen. She took her CNA training right after she graduated from high school. And I told her that it's not normal for a man to give her all these expensive gifts, you know. He's going to expect something in return, and once he does, it's going to put her in an awfully difficult position. Because she loves her job, she really does, and so I'm afraid that one day soon he's going to try something with her, and she won't be able to say no, because if she does, and complains to the manager, it's going to be her word against his, and it's going to create this whole impossible situation."

"Has he tried something with her, you think?"

"I'm not sure, but I don't think so. Kirsten and I have a great relationship, and I raised her not to keep any secrets from me. So if he did try something, I'd like to think she would have told me." She gave a helpless shrug. "I really don't know what to do."

"Has Kirsten talked about this with her manager?"

"No, because as far as she's concerned, there is no problem. I've told her over and over again it's not okay for this man to shower her with gifts. But she simply doesn't see it."

"Or maybe she doesn't want to see it," said Odelia. "Because if she did, it might jeopardize this job that she loves so much."

Annette nodded helplessly. "It's hard for me to have to sit back and wait for this man to make his move, which I'm absolutely convinced he will."

"Okay, so have you talked to Kirsten's manager?"

"I want to, but Kirsten told me not to. And let's face it, she's not a child anymore, and this is not school, where a parent can go in and talk to a teacher. This is a professional setting, and frankly I have no business there. Which is what makes it all the more galling." She balled her fists. "I want to do something, but I feel so totally helpless, you know."

"No, of course," said Odelia. "I understand completely. If I were in your shoes I'd feel the same way. So what do you suggest? That I have a discreet word with these people?"

"I want you to find out what's going on with this guy," said Annette. "I want you to go there and take a look around, and check this person out."

"I don't think they allow reporters to snoop around," said Odelia with a smile.

"No, but surely you have someone who can do that kind of job for you? I've heard such great things about you, and about the people you work with. There was this one case you worked on, where some of your operatives went undercover at Glimmer Magazine and even solved the murder of the CEO of Advantage Publishing."

Odelia laughed. "I think you're confusing me with a private detective, Mrs. Williams."

"Annette, please. But you did solve that case, and many others like it. So please, can't you keep an eye on my little girl? Make sure nothing bad happens to her?"

"Sounds to me she's not so little anymore," said Dooley.

"No, but to our parents we'll always be their little girls and boys," I said, "no matter how old we are."

"Gran could go," said Dooley. "She could go undercover and find out what's going on with this strange and dangerous man."

"She could, if she hadn't just told us this morning she'd rather jump off a roof than move into a retirement home."

Dooley shivered. "She really shouldn't say things like that. She might jinx things."

"Too true," I agreed.

"Okay, I'll see what I can do," said Odelia finally, when Annette repeated her urgent plea. "I do have one person who might be able to go undercover, since she's about the right age. It's the same person who worked that Advantage Publishing case so successfully."

Dooley grinned at me. "Looks like Gran is going to Happy Home after all."

I nodded. "Kicking and screaming, I imagine."

Chapter Three

"The problem is that these places aren't all that easy to get into," said Odelia once Annette had left and she was pondering the ramifications of the promise she just made. "So even if I can convince Gran to go undercover, they won't take her."

"Because she's a high-maintenance person?" asked Dooley, causing both Odelia and me to burst out laughing.

"No, because they're full!" said Odelia. "There's probably a waiting list as long as my arm, and even then, Gran is probably too young. She's only seventy-five, after all."

"How old do you have to be before you can go to a retirement home?" I asked.

"It's not so much age-related but more depending on your personal situation," said Odelia musingly. "And Gran is healthy. Both mentally and physically. Too healthy."

"Maybe Dan can pull some strings?" I suggested, referring to her editor Dan Goory.

"Yeah, maybe," she said, but I could tell it wasn't going to be easy to get Gran into this place. And even then, if this man was indeed as dangerous as Annette seemed to think, the mission was fraught with a certain measure of danger, and sending Gran in there might not be such a good idea. She wasn't exactly Jane Bond.

But before Odelia could consult Dan, another person walked into her office, this one a woman of about the same age as Annette Williams, only looking more sophisticated. Her chestnut-colored hair was as glossy as the hair you see in those shampoo commercials, and she was dressed in fine threads that must have cost a pretty penny. She placed a Louis Vuitton handbag on Odelia's desk and took a seat.

But even though she was probably more well-off than Odelia's previous client, once she started talking it turned out she was just as anxious and troubled as Annette.

"It's my husband," she said after introducing herself as Sara Brooks. "I think he's cheating on me with his personal assistant."

"What does your husband do, Mrs. Brooks?" asked Odelia.

"He runs a retirement home," said Mrs. Brooks, much to our surprise. "I don't know if you've heard of it. Happy Home for the Elderly. He's the general manager and has been for the past fifteen years. And for just as long I've had reason to suspect that he's been having an affair with a woman named Dee Phillips, his PA."

"Okay," said Odelia, taken aback a little by this startling coincidence.

"The thing is, I want a divorce, but I want full custody of the kids. And my lawyer told me that I need evidence of my husband's infidelity. Pictures, or video, anything to prove in court that he's being unfaithful to our wedding vows."

"And you want me to..."

Mrs. Brooks nodded emphatically. "Yes, I want you to get me this evidence, so I can finally get out of this marriage and move on with my life. I don't want to have anything more to do with that man, you see, and this evidence will get me that."

"You do realize I'm only a reporter, don't you?" said Odelia, wavering.

"I know, but you get results. Everybody says so. And since

we don't have a decent PI in this town, and I don't want to go to one of the big New York agencies, who won't know the area or the local sensitivities, I decided to come to you."

"Well, I'm honored, of course," said Odelia. "But I'm not sure if I'm the right person for the job."

"Oh, please say yes," said Mrs. Brooks, scooting forward in her chair and placing her hands on the desk in a beseeching manner. "I don't know what else to do. The lawyer says if I can't prove Brian's infidelity I don't have a case. We'll get joint custody and I'll probably have to deal with that man for the rest of my life. I just want to be free and clear of him. Never have to see or hear from him again for as long as I live."

"You have strong feelings about your husband," said Odelia.

"I loathe him. I detest him," she said in a low voice. "He's a lying, cheating louse."

"I didn't know humans could be married to a louse," said Dooley, surprised.

"I don't think she's actually married to a louse," I said. "It's a figure of speech."

"He's a rat," Mrs. Brooks went on, squeezing her eyes tightly shut. "He's vermin."

"Still a figure of speech?" asked Dooley, and I nodded. He sighed. "It's all very confusing. Why don't humans ever say what they actually mean?"

"He's horse manure," Mrs. Brooks said, and I got the impression she would have gone on for quite some time if Odelia hadn't stemmed the flow of words.

"Are you in a position to get a person into the retirement home your husband runs, Mrs. Brooks?" she asked now.

"Oh, absolutely," said the woman. "Were you thinking of going in yourself?"

"No, I was actually thinking about getting my grandmother in there, and then she could try and get this evidence you need."

"No problem," said Mrs. Brooks decidedly. "I'll get her in there, all right."

"One question," said Odelia, glancing in our direction. "Are pets allowed?"

And this was the moment Dooley and I shared a look of extreme horror. Yikes!

ABOUT NIC

Nic has a background in political science and before being struck by the writing bug worked odd jobs around the world (including but not limited to massage therapist in Mexico, gardener in Italy, restaurant manager in India, and Berlitz teacher in Belgium).

When he's not writing he enjoys curling up with a good (comic) book, watching British crime dramas, French comedies or Nancy Meyers movies, sampling pastry (apple cake!), pasta and chocolate (preferably the dark variety), twisting himself into a pretzel doing morning yoga, going for a run, and spoiling his big red tomcat Tommy.

He lives with his wife (and aforementioned cat) in a small village smack dab in the middle of absolutely nowhere and is probably writing his next 'Mysteries of Max' book right now.

www.nicsaint.com

ALSO BY NIC SAINT

The Mysteries of Max
Purrfect Murder
Purrfectly Deadly
Purrfect Revenge
Purrfect Heat
Purrfect Crime
Purrfect Rivalry
Purrfect Peril
Purrfect Secret
Purrfect Alibi
Purrfect Obsession
Purrfect Betrayal
Purrfectly Clueless
Purrfectly Royal
Purrfect Cut
Purrfect Trap
Purrfectly Hidden
Purrfect Kill
Purrfect Boy Toy
Purrfectly Dogged
Purrfectly Dead
Purrfect Saint
Purrfect Advice
Purrfect Passion

A Purrfect Gnomeful

Purrfect Cover

Purrfect Patsy

Purrfect Son

Purrfect Fool

Purrfect Fitness

Purrfect Setup

Purrfect Sidekick

Purrfect Deceit

Purrfect Ruse

Purrfect Swing

Purrfect Cruise

Purrfect Harmony

Purrfect Sparkle

Purrfect Cure

Purrfect Cheat

Purrfect Catch

Purrfect Design

Purrfect Life

Purrfect Thief

Purrfect Crust

Purrfect Bachelor

Purrfect Double

Purrfect Date

Purrfect Hit

Purrfect Baby

Purrfect Mess

Purrfect Paris

Purrfect Model
Purrfect Slug
Purrfect Match
Purrfect Game
Purrfect Bouquet
Purrfect Home

The Mysteries of Max Box Sets

Box Set 1 (Books 1-3)
Box Set 2 (Books 4-6)
Box Set 3 (Books 7-9)
Box Set 4 (Books 10-12)
Box Set 5 (Books 13-15)
Box Set 6 (Books 16-18)
Box Set 7 (Books 19-21)
Box Set 8 (Books 22-24)
Box Set 9 (Books 25-27)
Box Set 10 (Books 28-30)
Box Set 11 (Books 31-33)
Box Set 12 (Books 34-36)
Box Set 13 (Books 37-39)
Box Set 14 (Books 40-42)
Box Set 15 (Books 43-45)
Box Set 16 (Books 46-48)
Box Set 17 (Books 49-51)
Box Set 18 (Books 52-54)

The Mysteries of Max Big Box Sets

Big Box Set 1 (Books 1-10)

Big Box Set 2 (Books 11-20)

The Mysteries of Max Short Stories

Collection 1 (Stories 1-3)

Collection 2 (Stories 4-7)

Nora Steel

Murder Retreat

The Kellys

Murder Motel

Death in Suburbia

Emily Stone

Murder at the Art Class

Washington & Jefferson

First Shot

Alice Whitehouse

Spooky Times

Spooky Trills

Spooky End

Spooky Spells

Ghosts of London

Between a Ghost and a Spooky Place

Public Ghost Number One

Ghost Save the Queen

Box Set 1 (Books 1-3)

A Tale of Two Harrys

Ghost of Girlband Past

Ghostlier Things

Charleneland

Deadly Ride

Final Ride

Neighborhood Witch Committee

Witchy Start

Witchy Worries

Witchy Wishes

Saffron Diffley

Crime and Retribution

Vice and Verdict

Felonies and Penalties (Saffron Diffley Short 1)

The B-Team

Once Upon a Spy

Tate-à-Tate

Enemy of the Tates

Ghosts vs. Spies

The Ghost Who Came in from the Cold

Witchy Fingers

Witchy Trouble

Witchy Hexations

Witchy Possessions

Witchy Riches

Box Set 1 (Books 1-4)

The Mysteries of Bell & Whitehouse

One Spoonful of Trouble

Two Scoops of Murder

Three Shots of Disaster

Box Set 1 (Books 1-3)

A Twist of Wraith

A Touch of Ghost

A Clash of Spooks

Box Set 2 (Books 4-6)

The Stuffing of Nightmares

A Breath of Dead Air

An Act of Hodd

Box Set 3 (Books 7-9)

A Game of Dons

Standalone Novels

When in Bruges

The Whiskered Spy

ThrillFix

Homejacking

The Eighth Billionaire

The Wrong Woman